A Nixon Man

A Nixon Man

Michael Cahill

St. Martin's Press
New York

Design by Claire Vaccaro

Library of Congress Cataloging-in-Publication Data

Cahill, Michael.
 A Nixon man / Michael Cahill.
  p. cm.
 ISBN 0-312-18749-1
 1. Nixon, Richard M. (Richard Milhous), 1913–1994 —Influence—Fiction.
I. Title.
PS3554.A363N59 1998
813'.54—dc21   98-13706
                                                   CIP

First Edition: August 1998

10 9 8 7 6 5 4 3 2 1

A Nixon Man

One
The Monkey

My father was a Nixon man. Before that he'd been a Goldwater man. On most nights he could be found roaming the house like a ghost, wearing a tattered robe, reading about Ike. But on November 7, 1972, he wore his suit and tie well past midnight.

The fog cradled our house that night, dimming the streetlights, making soft halos like flashlights hidden under bed sheets. Traveling silently through the fog was a signal, bounced repeatedly from somewhere back East, arriving at the KCBS relay tower at Fifth and Howard where it was released to the San Francisco Bay Area, and to our yellow house.

"Four more years! Four more years!"

Downstairs, twenty or so men and women ate snacks, sipped cocktails and watched the returns on TV. Not me, though. I was eleven and it was too late for me, so I sat propped up in bed. For as long as I could remember, I had been afraid to go to sleep.

"Four more years! Four more years!"

I pictured my father gazing at the TV, where those famous fingers fanned the smoky, floodlit air.

"Four more years," shouted the crowd.

"Four more years!" shouted my father, and I imagined his large hands flapping in the air too, then swooping down and alighting on my mother's freckled shoulders and moving her to dance with him.

She was a Nixon woman, though her enthusiasm did not burn as brightly as his.

"Four more years!"

My father had a rule for watching any sporting event: Always root for the underdog. He didn't care who was playing, really, he'd just ask who was trailing, who had the injured quarterback or the worst record going in. The owner of these credentials inevitably earned his support, and no one had ever earned it more than Richard Nixon, a man who of late had succeeded in making the office of the leader of the free world look like the battered plywood clubhouse of the beloved underdog. Tonight, though, that underdog had won re-election with 60.8 percent of the popular vote and 97 percent of the electoral vote, the largest margin ever.

"*Chee chee chee chee!*" From the basement came a chattering, carried up to my room by the galvanized furnace register.

"*Chee chee!*"

They could hear him downstairs, too. "I'll go see what's wrong," said my mother. I could hear her quick steps as she fled the living room.

"*Chee chee chee!*"

"Would you like to buy a monkey?" I said to the dark.

Downstairs, my father asked a friend, "Say, would you like to buy a monkey?" His favorite joke. "I'll sell him to you cheap, cage included." A new twist.

"Aw, William, you know you couldn't live without him," said the friend, laughing.

Every wall in our yellow house had the high, four-inch-wide decorative moldings characteristic of turn-of-the-century construction. Above them the thick white paint was marred by a green haze that ran all the way around every room. Ours was probably the only house in the neighborhood to sport this green detail because it alone sheltered a New World monkey. That green beast always tried to take the higher ground, searching for the heights of the humid jungle from which he had been kidnapped, and the moldings served as both his highway and sanctuary. Their narrowness forced him to lean against the walls, and wherever he passed, he left behind his tropical pigment.

From these perches the monkey watched us come and go, studying the tops of our heads, often without us realizing that his black eyes were on us. Ebony-tipped tail wrapped around his body protectively, he would wait. His eyes glazed over. He blinked slowly. I used to think he was trying to erase the furniture and deep pile carpet, laying over them the contours of his lost hot forest. I imagined sometimes that he was able to transform a room so completely that he was transported back to his homeland. On more than one occasion he suddenly launched himself onto my head and sank his teeth into my ear, which to him must have looked like a tasty grub out stealing a ray of sun beneath jungle branches. There were also moments when he was not simply a monkey, but undeniably a male monkey. His frustration would throb up poignantly and he'd swing a favorite stuffed animal of mine up and out of my reach, ravish it quickly and efficiently, then toss it earthward in disgust. My mother came home with a different animal every time she and my father had a fight. The one that inspired her to buy the monkey must have been a big one.

"*Chee chee chee chee!*" he cried from the basement. I imagined my mother going to him in her evening dress, armed with grapes and monkey chow.

"I once shook hands with Richard Nixon," said my father to his friend, and I winced, wondering how many times we would have to hear this story.

"It was during the Senate campaign," he said.

I knew the story well and used my Walter Cronkite voice to mimic him as I lay there in the dark. "He looked me right in the eyes," I said along with him. "He said, 'Beautiful day,' and I agreed that it was." My father paused for a moment, possibly to take a sip of his

3

drink, and I waited for him to catch up. "I could tell right then that he'd be President," we said together.

The phone rang, and I heard my father rumble into the kitchen to answer it. I couldn't tell what he was saying and had no idea to whom he spoke. From my bed, his voice sounded deep and cautious, like he was telling a secret, or a lie.

I was eleven, and though I might have lied a little, I only lied to others and wouldn't have known where to begin if I'd wanted to put one over on myself. There was just not that much to me yet. One part of me always knew what the other parts were up to, and in the way that children do, I figured this was the case with those around me, those with whom I shared meals and prayers.

"Four more years! Four more years!"

"Chee chee chee chee!"

Through the furnace register, I heard the softness of my mother singing a lullaby to the monkey. She had stopped singing them to me. Down the hall my sister's radio played "A Horse with No Name," a song that made me mad, and in the kitchen, my father hung up the phone. It was a long time before I heard his footsteps again as he returned to the party.

None of us knew why my father couldn't sleep at night. He tried everything, from hot milk and pills to vigorous exercise after dinner, but it was no use. While he yearned for sleep, I did my best to fight it off. I didn't know why, but sometimes I was scared of what might happen when I closed my eyes. Many nights I propped myself up and listened to the radio, read a comic, anything to avoid sleep. It was clear that the President was going to last another four years, but I wasn't so sure about my family.

I listened to the foghorns, and to the party. I heard a crashing sound outside on the street. Gradually the monkey settled down and his screeches trailed off. The foghorns pushed against my pale cold window and I couldn't help it, I fell asleep as the President began to speak.

The sound of pans clanging over the *Today* show woke me. I got dressed and made my way down to the kitchen where my mother held a piece of toast out of the monkey's reach and gave it to me. I got down on all fours and shoved my way in close to the furnace register. The dogs shoved back. They felt entitled to all of the heat since they waited by the cold register all night for the furnace to come on. If I shared my toast with them I didn't feel so bad about being pushy. Their fur and breath were soft in the warm furnace wind, and when my mother turned away to peek into the oven, I held one of their paws to my nose and stole a sniff. Peanut butter. Dog paws smell the sweetest when they're warm.

My favorite of the four dogs was black and white with a tail like the Road Runner. My mother had found him under her station wagon at the Cala food mart. She named him Pie, because that's what she was carrying. He had a bad temper and owed no one his allegiance. Once Pie bit the circuit judge down the street and the judge told my mother that if it happened again, he could legally have the dog put down and the brain autopsied to determine if rabies were present. This she relayed to me.

Confusion arose because she neglected to mention that Pie would be killed before his brain was cut out. The specter of my arrogant sleek dog wandering the house, his skull a pink-scooped empty bowl, bumping into furniture and barking at the wind, haunted me as I lay with him in the heater blast, pressing my ear to his shoulder, listening to his heart. Slowly, I increased the pressure until he emitted a low growl. It sounded like a bear in a cave. It tickled my earlobe. I increased the pressure. Pie turned up the volume, making the monkey nervous. We continued until my mother shouted for us to quit it. She never quite trusted that dog.

Orange juice. The stove door squeaked shut at the top of the hour and the *Today* show team analyzed the President's staggering victory. Suddenly the monkey clutched my mother's sweater and his ears pricked up at the rumbling of my father's huge nonskid feet. They swept past me, mashing the linoleum, creaking the joists as sixteen-penny nails momentarily lost their grip. Toenails skittered on the linoleum as the dogs cleared a path for him.

I pressed close to the furnace grate, and as he passed, he clapped enormous hands together, trapping pints of air, singing, "Oh what a beautiful morning, oh what a beautiful day, I've got a beautiful feeling, everything's—" He stopped, saying, "Shhh, Shhh! Listen," as Barbara Walters recounted the massive win. He stood in the middle of the kitchen, hands frozen in mid-clap, his grin unearthly wide.

"Your mush is ready." My mother.

"Amazing. Just amazing." His morale was so high that morning he forgot himself and said, "That Barbara Walters is certainly a handsome woman."

"Why don't you sit down." My mother slapped two bowls onto the table. He was not supposed to notice other women. "Who called us so late last night?" she asked, her head in the refrigerator.

"I knew it!" He shook his head in awe as he watched the TV. "A landslide."

She slammed the refrigerator door and did not ask him again.

A *click* followed by the thunder of contracting heating duct indicated that the thermostat, set by my father, had decided that we should be warm enough by now. We squeezed closer to the register, the dogs and me, aching for those last surges of tropical basement air. No matter how close you got to it, you were never warm enough.

"Sit down, Jack."

I had to stand up and make for the table. I had to have my mush. Mush was oatmeal, and I liked it. The only problem was, while I ate my mush, I had to listen to my father also eating his. I couldn't stand it. My mouth was unwilling to perform the task demanded of it. I tried concentrating on *Today* to the exclusion of all else, but he wouldn't let me. Like sloshing footsteps behind you in a dark wet alley, my father's mush-eating demanded to be heard.

He and all his brothers had great choppers. When he enlisted and got a checkup, the navy dentist told him he had the perfect mouth. Those teeth of his were designed to rend flesh and snap pilot biscuits. They were overqualified for mush. One eye on the TV, the other on the *San Francisco Chronicle* propped on his reading rack in front of him, he allowed a third of the milk-marbled Quaker oats to plop back into the bowl, a sound that worked in barbaric tandem with the smacking and gnashing of lips and teeth.

"Mom, could you turn up the TV, please?"

She ignored my request.

My father reached out and spun the crooked lazy Susan to the applesauce. This he smeared on his dry toast, producing another sinister sound.

The door swung open and the dogs made way for the shuffling slippers of my older sister. A compact sun bear in a quilted robe, she was never at her best in the morning. One shaking hand fluttered on the head of a dog, then rose to the counter and the cupboards. "What's for breakfast? Mush? Oinch juice?"

"Morning, Macie," I said.

"Morning, Jack. What are you having for breakfast?"

"Oh, mush, toast."

"No oinch juice?"

"Orange juice too."

"That's good. I wonder what I'm having for breakfast."

"Sit down and you'll find out." My mother was really cross.

Macie sat across from me with her hair flat on one side and round on the other. Once she fell asleep she never moved until morning. Her eyes were fuzzy and she carried a smell of sleep. One sateen elbow on the table, she flicked at her bangs with her tiny hand and yawned demurely. A sudden screech made her shoulders flinch as my father

7

lifted his chair to the left. Macie had been blocking his view of Barbara Walters.

"Four more years!"

Macie lit up and pattered her fingers on the table in greedy search for her spoon as my mother presented her with mush.

"Macie." I wagged my spoon low and silent, below my father's gaze. Her robe had peeled open to expose one of her breasts.

"What, Jack?"

I knitted my eyebrows in the direction of her chest, and she got the idea, tucking the robe in place and turning to her mush like nobody's business. I finished eating just in time, because Macie ate just like my father.

When I was little, before kindergarten, my mother and I walked Macie to her special school every morning, and in the afternoon, after I'd had a full day of playing at home, we would go back down the avenues and wait for her outside a pink building. Unmodulated, institutional shrieks came from the barred windows and rank smells mixed with the fumes from passing buses. I only went inside once and I never wanted to do it again. Macie never scared me, but her schoolmates, especially the older male ones, sometimes drooled and produced sounds that made my chest feel tight. There was a certain word I was not allowed to use around her.

When Macie turned fifteen she was too old for the pink school. She stayed home. So she wouldn't feel left out while I went off to school, every morning my mother packed her a lunch just like mine in a Mary Poppins lunch box with her name on it. When the noon siren blew, Macie would take her lunch out into the backyard, open it up and eat it, pretending that she was in school, too. My big sister was my little sister.

Something awful was happening over by the heater. The monkey was down there with the dogs. One of them growled. My mother moved to break it up, but she wasn't quick enough and my father lowered his paper in time to see the monkey mounting the smallest dog.

"Monkey, stop that!" said Macie.

The dog was old and compliant; she'd been through this many times before. I often wondered what sort of offspring this union would produce.

"Oh, good Lord," said my father.

The monkey rushed the job, his furry haunches a blur, but my mother swooped him up before he could finish. I learned a lot from watching that monkey.

"Good Lord," my father said again, crinkling the *Chronicle*, "can't we at least be civilized at breakfast?"

"Civilized?" My mother gave him a look. His entire face turned red.

What was she talking about? Not the monkey.

She headed for the door and my father called after her, "We could always sell him, you know!" But she was gone, whisking the monkey down to the basement.

I knew he wasn't kidding. For years he'd been trying to get rid of the monkey. He wanted to send him away, like he wanted to do with Macie. My mother just wouldn't listen to him.

My father stood up and motioned to me. We'd all gotten a late start this morning so I was getting a ride to school. He put on his hat and overcoat and I followed him out the front door.

" 'Bye, Mom, Macie. Good-bye, Pie."

Outside the fog was burning off but it was still cold, and I heard the rats waking up in the fat crowns of the palm trees. A military buildup had been announced right after the election, so planes were coming from down south to land on the carrier *Kitty Hawk* and be sailed over to Vietnam. I looked up at the silent sight of a swept-winged phantom flying by followed by its sound, leaving its white trail to cross another at a right angle, like high, vaporous telephone lines.

My father walked ahead of me to the car but I stopped. Something was out of place. A splintered wood cabinet sprawled on the sidewalk near the curb. Silvered glass sprinkled beside it crunched as I strayed over to investigate. I remembered the crash I had heard the night before. A volume knob nested in the sprayed cathode glass. A Magnavox. Judging by the damage, it had come from a second story. I guessed the point of origin was our next-door neighbor's window, which was at that moment occupied by a girl. She was standing alone, her hair parted down the middle. Watching me. Nothing else to do, so I waved. She waved back.

"Oh, jeez. Oh, darn it." My father cringed, backing away from his car. Election-night party guests had blocked the driveway the night before, so he'd had to park out on the street, which he hated to do.

His car was a convertible, clean and straight except for small dents and scratches all along the driver's side where he always scraped it while backing into our narrow garage. On the rear bumper was a sticker with the red, white and blue word NIXON on it. He'd been in such a hurry to see the returns last night that he'd left the top down.

"Oh, darn it," my father said again, his face screwed up tight. His nostrils flared. I put the Magnavox knob in my pocket and went to see what was up. He shook his head, took off his hat and waved it side to side.

About ten feet from the fender a smell hit me. I stood on tiptoe, gripped the car's steel flank and looked in. On the back seat was what appeared to be a pile of dog shit. When I looked closer, though, I realized it wasn't *dog* shit at all.

"What a thing for someone to do," said my father, pulling his ear, perhaps wondering at the gymnastics that must have facilitated the delivery of this unwholesome gift.

My mush came up.

When he heard me choking, he put his hand on my shoulder and steered me away from the car. Making sure not to get any on the tires, I splattered the sidewalk, sick so early in the morning. All my mush, gone.

When I finished and wiped my chin, I noticed that my father's Nixon bumper sticker had been amended. It now read: "FUCK Nixon." He hadn't seen it, thank God.

He took off his overcoat and jacket and looked around for a place to put them, his nose still snarled in righteous disgust. No place to hang them, so he folded them with maddening care, looked all around, and finally placed them on the front steps, frowning, a creature of thought. He slid the garage door up on its screaming springs. Inside, he scraped a shovel up from its cool concrete corner and cursed as a rake and hoe clattered together, tangling around his hand.

I heard a boom as my mother opened the upstairs window and stuck her head out, three fine paintbrushes clamped between her teeth. "William, are you still here?"

"Nothing, nothing." He stepped from the garage, head pivoting to take her in.

"What are you doing?"

"Nothing. Just something." The magenta in his cheeks and burning blue of his eyes indicated that the question quota had been filled for today.

"Well, see you tonight." The window slammed shut. I often found it hard to tell who was mad at whom.

He thought a moment, leaned the shovel handle into his crotch, and from his pocket shook a frayed white handkerchief. He tied it around his mouth and nose and then, shovel at the ready, approached the car.

I looked at our neighbors' house, a Victorian that they'd been painting all summer and fall. Fluted corbels, notched and swirled fascia, balustrades. Gingerbread, my father called it, bells and whistles. An eyesore, we thought. For months the new neighbors had been covering each part in a different color, using the kind of paints that glowed when you shined a black light on them. The whole thing was lumpy, though, since they hadn't bothered to first scrape off the flaking white paint that Mr. Wicker left behind when he died.

"Jackie, turn on the hose, please."

I waded into the ivy by the side of the house, crunching on snails, to find the hidden spigot. It took me a while and I knew I had to hurry because I felt him getting impatient. I found it just as he was about to blow up. I turned it on and heard a *spoosh* followed by water pounding vinyl, my father hosing down the back seat. I thought he might be overdoing it.

"Less! Not so high, please!"

I turned it down.

"I said turn it down!"

Now he was mad at *me.*

That girl was not alone anymore in her dirty next-door window. Two hippies stood beside her and watched my father, laughing into their hands.

"That's enough!"

They noticed me staring at them and ducked out of sight like little kids.

"Turn it off!"

I twisted the handle so hard it dug into my hand, then ran to help my father coil the hose. Swacking water from his trouser cuffs, he evidently hadn't seen the defiled bumper sticker yet and I was not the one to tell him.

We got in the car and fled the scene. Driving fast with the top down, it didn't stink so bad. He put the heater on MAX because it was November, after all.

Except for our house the neighborhood had really changed. My father said San Francisco was not the city he grew up in anymore. It wasn't just the people, he said, it was the buildings, and the stores with signs that you couldn't even read. Letters that melted one into the next, challenging you to decipher them. Psychedelic. "What's that supposed to mean?" was something he often said, looking around himself, letting the steering wheel slide insouciantly through the fingers of one hand. At every intersection, someone had used a stencil to spray the words THE WAR under the word STOP.

"Did you know that President Nixon never uses notes when he speaks? I first noticed that when I saw him speak years ago—"

The time he shook hands with him.

"—when I shook hands with him." He was practically shouting, since the top was down. "Even Lincoln needed notes!" he yelled. He thought for a moment. "People judge him harshly for his looks, that's all. And he's not really a bad-looking man."

My father's nose, broken twice, was chilled red in the wind and raised slightly to indicate that this driving required very little of his attention to make it work. Eyes wet and cold, black hair wisping from under his hat, he was there on the seat beside me, but talked as if he was somewhere else. I wondered who had called him the night before.

As we approached my school he said, "It's important to stand up for what you believe in. Even when people are critical."

He pulled up to the curb. I straightened the magnetic Saint Christopher that gazed up from the dashboard, then yanked the door handle. The latch clacked and I had to put my shoulder to the vinyl and push hard. The door was as long as I was and ten times as heavy. It swung out over the curb and I stepped down.

"See you tonight," he said.

I heaved the door shut. He drove on, hat straight ahead, and I got a last embarrassing view of the bumper sticker before he swung away onto Fillmore.

Fuck Nixon.

Two
Escape

I knew I was late because the crossing guard was folding his chair and packing his plaid thermos away, so I hurried inside.

The classroom doors were already closed and I heard voices winding up the Pledge of Allegiance as I climbed the stairs and arrived at 5B with liberty and justice for all.

The knob turned more quietly than I could have hoped. There, chalk in hand, was Mr. Ball. Cue Ball to some, Hairy Ball to others. He stopped blabbing long enough to make a check next to my name as I headed for my seat.

Jay and I sat in the back row, side by side, an oversight that Ball would have rectified if he could, but the rules said we must sit in alphabetical order and he didn't invent the alphabet. When I came down our row, Jay pretended to be reading from *Our Ancient World*. He was pretty fat.

Ball started in on the Romans and I rested my face on top of my binder, half-asleep with a boner. I was often tired in the morning because many nights I fought sleep for as long as I could. I heard Walter Peel's foot tapping spastically on the floor. Walter was hyperactive and took uppers for it, which for some reason calmed him down. Ball was the only teacher who wore a coat and tie and had a Triumph. With white curly hair and wallet brown skin, he had the habit of smacking his lips in wet punctuation to every sentence. Often, he was stoned. I'd heard that every year on the day Julius Caesar was supposed to have been killed, Ball came to school dressed in a white sheet and all the kids in class got to attack him with rubber knives and squirt ketchup all over him. I couldn't wait to see that. Imagine if someone brought a real knife and stuck it in him.

Ball woke me up with a smack of his lips. I lifted my head. The vinyl cover of my binder, stuck to my face, let go with a hiss. He was circling the room. His eyes met mine and I knew that he knew that I didn't do my reading the night before or the night before that, and furthermore would never get anywhere in this world. I looked down.

Ball continued to circle, smacking, asking, "Who was the Goddess of Wisdom?"

The name was on the tip of my tongue when suddenly there was a painful wrench on my ankle as Ball's shadow slipped across my desk then vanished altogether. Air was sucked from my ears as something heavy plummeted past me and into the aisle and then, finally, a noise emerged from the vacuum, crashing and final. Ball had tripped over my outstretched ankles. His loafers bounced once, lightly, on the linoleum, and then he was still.

The whole class burst into laughter. Not me, though. I wasn't that stupid.

"Mr. Ball, are you all right?" I held out my hand. He looked dead. "Mr. Ball?"

His yellow, bloodshot eyes fixed on me and his face turned red. "Costello, you tripped me." He looked around at the class. Some stopped laughing. "He tripped me," he repeated. Then he got to his feet.

Everyone watched us.

Now, I may have been late a lot and was certainly behind on my reading, but never in my life would I have even considered tripping Mr. Ball or any other teacher. It was just not something you did.

"No, sir," I said, "I just slump, see? I'm always doing that. I guess you didn't notice my leg sticking out, see?"

He grabbed my ear between his thumb and forefinger and pulled, his yellow nails sinking into the lobe. I stood quickly to reduce the pain as he applied more pressure and pulled me toward the door. No one said a word. I followed him, tears allowing me to see only straight ahead, the door rushing at me.

Then it was just the two of us, standing out in the hall, my ear still pinched in his nails. How could I tell him politely that he was a clumsy man with large ungainly feet and was so high all the time it was a wonder something like this hadn't happened earlier?

Suddenly, he slammed my head back against the wall so hard it bounced. I fell, landing on all fours, facing the lockers. He ran up behind me and gleefully slammed a pennyless loafer straight into my butt. At 8:45 A.M. That'd teach me. If I'd been in 5A instead of 5B, Mrs. Mark's boobs might have been floating before my eyes right now, stretching her turtleneck to the limit.

Ball pulled me to my feet, not difficult because I was a pretty small eleven-year-old. He lowered his voice. "Costello," he said, "if you ever do that again, I will kill you."

Jesus Christ, I thought, he's crazy.

"Yes, sir."

"But first, I will tell your mother and father what you have done." He saw me flinch at the word *father.* He smiled, saying, "Do you think your father would be happy to hear that you fall asleep in class every day?"

"No, sir." He waited. "Please don't tell my father."

"Good."

He let go. My ear burned. My head was ringing. Now his breath was on me. He was too close. His lungs panted ancient Roman air into my eyes. And wine, I thought. For a moment I had the feeling he was going to kiss me. Then suddenly he smiled. "Good," he said again, lifting his big head up and away from me like the wrecking ball on a crane.

"Go clean yourself up," he said, and walked back into the classroom. I turned toward the boys' room and then, out of the corner of my eye, I saw it. My eyes burned from the white of it, from the sunlight streaming through it.

The front door.

I had spent the better part of the last five years in this building. Each weekday morning I came in at 8:15, more or less, and left each afternoon at 3:05. I attended classes, kicked balls, washed my hands, all within these walls with their bus-rattled windows, and not once had I ever just walked out that door.

I wondered what my mother meant when she looked at him and said, *"Civilized?"* I understood that I would never find the answer to this kind of question in school. I walked toward the door.

"Hi, Jack," the front-office lady said. She smiled at me.

I found myself smiling back, waving even, saying, "Hi, Mrs. Knee," as I walked past. Had she stopped smiling? Said something else? What was she there for, if not to guard that door?

I placed my hands on the panic bar and pushed the squealing thing away from me. She didn't even notice. Could it have been so easy all this time? I could now hear my classmates up on the roof. For a moment my guilt turned their play sounds into shrieks of torment, but I was already outside.

Athena, I thought. Athena was the Goddess of Wisdom.

Something must have been going right because here came the 3 Jackson bus like a getaway car, just when I needed it. Before I knew it I spun my nickel into the slot, watching it roll down the clear plastic chute and into the mechanism, the parts transparent for all to see for no practical reason I could think of other than the simple pleasure of seeing it.

"Transfer, please."

The driver reached up above the windshield to a book of fluttering tickets and tore one off. He didn't hand it to me yet, though; they liked to make you wait, these guys.

17

Something inside me wanted me to go back. It was not too late. They probably hadn't even missed me yet. But then the driver twisted the handle and the accordion door slapped closed behind me. I thought, Why doesn't he just give me that transfer? He released the brake and I gripped the buzzing handrail as the dynamo sang an ascending scale beneath us. Finally he held out the transfer, gripping it just long enough to make me understand that he knew what I had done, then releasing it to me. Sometimes it seemed like everybody was stoned.

I careened down the length of the empty bus and onto the slashed back bench. We floated from side to side down Jackson Street on tires and springs, the driver and me, the two of us propelled by electricity, snapping and whirring yet somehow under control. I lurched forward as he let up on the pedal and slung us toward the curb at Presidio, where a guy about my father's age got on with a briefcase and paid a quarter, no transfer.

The driver and I were no longer alone. As we pulled out, the man looked toward the back of the bus. He saw me and smiled, almost fell, grinned at how lame he was, then shrugged and headed straight at me, alternately driven forward and pulled back by the bus's undertow as we traveled upward through the gears. He slammed himself down sideways on the seat right in front of me and looked around like he'd never seen a bus before.

I ignored him and checked the five numbers at the bottom of my transfer. Jay and Walter and I always played poker this way. I had two of a kind, but they weren't jacks or better. No cigar. The man eyed me, trying to get my attention. I refused to give it to him.

"Have you ever been on TV?" He snapped the latches on his briefcase and swung it open. I forced myself to look at its dark insides knowing they would be the last things I ever saw.

"How old are you?"

Two pencils, a Cross pen, manila folders.

"Do you like tuna?"

"What?"

"Ever tried Bumblebee?"

He pulled out a stiff color photo of a smiling fat bug and waffled it in the air between us. The driver's eyes were on us in his wide tilted mirror.

"We're making a commercial for Bumblebee tuna this weekend over at the polo grounds, in the park. Would you like to be in it? There's going to be a giant bumblebee and a pack of kids around your age."

He was a perv.

"You'll get to be on TV."

He handed me a business card. He had been put on that bus to punish me for the sin of leaving school.

"Here's the number of my office. Call by five today and you can still be in it, okay?"

I stretched up off the seat and snapped the bell cable. The driver swooped us in safe and sound at Sacramento and Presidio, two blocks early but I didn't mind walking. I timed it so the brakes pitched me forward, past the perv and out the door.

I slalomed around the white hydrant and up the street, no books or anything in my hands, the bus laughing away behind my back, sucking the guy's unwanted card away in its draft.

Gravity carried me down the hill, my knees kicking loose when I lifted them, feet wobbly in their sockets before they met concrete again. Garages on my left ran all the way down the block, different colored doors, each one a half garage lower than the next because of the slope. A glossy black one opened just a crack, its shadow a pool of blood curdling out onto the sidewalk, and I tacked to the right, out of the reach of any hand that might have tried for my ankle.

It was the Zodiac Killer again. He lurked in garages from the Great Highway to North Beach, and even though we'd heard his telephoned voice over our mush on Jim Dunbar's morning show and read his letters in the *Chronicle,* no one knew who he was. We thought we'd seen his symbol, the circle with a cross above, scrawled in the dirt behind the Julius Kahn playground where they found that girl. He promised to keep on killing. An invisible, famous man. I saw him all the time.

I headed down one more block to my usual transfer spot in front of the Vogue movie theater. While waiting for the bus for the past week I'd been studying this poster in a glass case that showed a red-haired woman with naked breasts and fringed pants gazing down from a red hill that could be on Mars. Alone now, I could stare at her until I was blue in the face, could even reach out and wipe a smudge from the glass. I closed my eyes, soaking up the cold sun, and the red-head began to move under my lids. I began to doze. Sleeping felt safe during the day. I heard grackles in the trees. They always whistled one time short, a second twice as long, and then let loose three to four warbles, like a bos'n's pipe. I squinted over the binnacle, her red hair veiling my view of the whitecaps ahead.

A shadow fell over her copper knees and I opened my eyes to see a lady coming toward me, pushing a stroller. I couldn't look her in the eye as she passed.

My bus was now two blocks away. The movie cashier's murmuring drifted from the booth. XXX. No one under eighteen admitted. Two dollar matinee.

I reached into my front pocket, maneuvering past the Magnavox knob. Nudged by my sunny boner was a leather Indian bag containing a rubber brontosaurus with the tip of his tail burned flat, also Eye of Terror, roach clip, shark's tooth, a tight roll of three ones, bus nickels and an emergency dime. My fingers settled on the dollar bills. If I could walk out of school whenever I wanted, then what else? XXX.

Forbidden didn't mean impossible. I stepped up to the ticket booth. With her orange eyelashes, talking there on the phone, she was not much older than me, that cashier. She stared at the two dollars I nudged through the chrome-lined half circle before her. The grackles sounded their bos'n's whistle. Permission to come aboard, sir. Her hand covered the phone receiver so no one could hear us. She was catching on, I saw. We were in this together. We both spoke at once, neither hearing the other, then she rolled her eyes and slid the bills back at me.

Thanks, but my bus had arrived anyway.

I didn't look back as I bolted across the sidewalk, took my seat, and the 55 pulled out.

All the nudie shows were up on Broadway. Whenever our swimming-pool blue station wagon passed that way, my mother made us lock all the doors. After the first block she covered our eyes if she could reach them. If not, she told us to cover them ourselves. So for me the length of Broadway between the off-ramp and Columbus Avenue was groups of soldiers on leave from the war cut up through my fingers, and sailors standing outside the Condor Club beneath the blinking red bulbs of Carol Doda's nipples, which looked just like Rudolf's nose.

The plastic sign featuring an enormous gangster, Big Al, faced Carol as sternly as a mortal enemy. They had done battle for years, one equipped with flashing breasts, the other a tommy gun. Women sat on stools in front of racks of faded photos, and on more than one occasion, when my mother timed it wrong and we got snarled in traffic right in the middle of all this, touts hollered into our car, "No minimum for the ladies!" We knew it was best to keep quiet then, a creeping carload of people with their hands over their eyes.

I got off the bus and headed down to the park. The noon siren blew, making me jump, the only fifth grader out there at lunch time while all the good kids were eating their Snack Packs in the cafeteria. My stomach groaned. Macie was in the backyard, a fifteen-year-old peering into her Mary Poppins lunch box, thinking that her brother must be eating now too. But my lunch was still in my locker, the embarrassing face my mother drew on it with magic marker grinning in the dark as potato chip grease spread over its brown skin.

I crossed the empty baseball field and behind the backstop

climbed a gentle slope of fallen chain-link fence, then dropped through the leaves into no man's land. This was lawless frontier, with adults hiding from their lives and children hiding from adults, lurking in caves formed by years of untended ginny juniper, sharp holly, and pyracantha with its poisonous red bird berries.

You watched your step in no man's land, because it wasn't just dog shit in there. Old Faded Label and other brands were the drinks of choice, and all bottles were hunted down and shot to pieces before the end of each day, so you couldn't sit just anywhere. We had routes that snaked through bowers so thick the hardest rain could not penetrate, leading to small rooms of filtered light and pine-needled dry floors, warm fastnesses that muffled all traffic, all aircraft, all of the city. These paths were not on any maps, like the tunnels under Chinatown leading from murder house to opium den, opening onto alleys no one ever bothered to name.

I did not look into the green room to my right where the mattress was and they didn't look up from each other and the dim flesh between them. I slipped down the packed clay slope, catching a view of the bay before changing course, bouncing over a trampoline of elastic branches and floating out of sight, fluttering fat pigeons out of my way.

The hours passed quickly in no man's land.

My tree was taller than any other. It must have been a hundred feet high. I could get to the top of it in nothing flat and had no idea what people meant when they said not to look down. I was small for an eleven-year-old and I was no great shakes at sports, but I could climb to beat the band. Another thing I could do was swim. In fact, if I hadn't been in my tree I would have been in the pool with the other team members. I once swam so hard in a meet I puked after the seventeenth lap, right in front of a bunch of parents. Even though I came in dead last, everyone told my father how much heart I had since I finished anyway, swimming through my bobbing vomit twice before the race was over.

The crow's nest at the top of my tree swayed in a pretty strong wind. Alcatraz looked like a long battleship with a yellow cell block the bridge and its water tank a conning tower. It dwarfed all other ships floating on the dark blue. The year before, when the Indians took it over, I wondered if they could have hijacked it like pirates and sailed for the open sea. Would it have fit under the bridge?

My tree creaked like a ship in the wind, and I caught myself sleeping. I shook my head to clear it and looked inland, where rail-grooved streets led up sharp hills, splitting rows of houses, and the fog returned from a day at sea. A man came out of our church, the Star of the Sea. I figured he'd gone to confession because that was the only reason anyone went to church in the middle of a weekday. Must have done something pretty bad.

He walked down the steps and put on his hat. A familiar hat. I swayed from side to side, my empty stomach feeling suddenly full as, taking one last look back at the church I recognized my father as he got into his convertible and drove away.

I looked down on the pearly backs of seagulls flying by and on the green froth of no man's land below them. If Ball hadn't fallen over and blamed it on me I would've been in P.E. right then and would never have seen my father. It occurred to me that the only reason our parents sent us to school was so they could do secret things all day. The moaning tree and all of its branches carried the electric wind straight into the trunk to make the palms of my hands buzz. I held on tight. What could my father possibly have had to confess?

Three
My Neighbor's TV

I uncrossed my fingers when I saw no station wagon parked in front
of our yellow house. No one was home. Maybe grocery shopping,
I thought, or taking Macie to see Dr. Root.

There was no way my father could have seen me. People never
looked up into the trees in no man's land. You could have hidden the
whole Vietcong army in there and no one would have noticed. I
looked both ways before I crossed, feeling God's eyes on me, bending
me to the black street.

The neighbors' discarded TV still sprawled near the curb. I
touched the volume knob in my pocket. What kind of person threw
their TV out the window? Someday I would find out what those hippies were up to.

I crouched beside the Magnavox and spread my arms to measure
the width. It was the perfect size. I would be able to fit inside it with
no trouble. Soon I would be on TV. First I had to get it into the
house, though, and it was too heavy for me to lift on my own. It
would have to wait for later.

I decided to sneak in through the back because the front door
looked too exposed. I did not want to be seen. Pie heard me coming
a mile away, and when I climbed over the fence he was right there on
the other side, his semaphore tail waving me in for a landing. I
dropped into the ivy and he greeted me. I fell to my hands and knees

and he and I fought through the dog door together. Sometimes, late at night, rats came thumping in through the same entrance.

Enveloped in dog breath, starving because I'd abandoned my lunch, I got to my feet in the washer room and rattled open the tin doors of the yellow closet. The tangy perfume of cleaning things rose from a nest of rags as my eyes flashed around, searching. The dogs milled around me, toenails clicking, the old ones making smells. Straight ahead I saw the green-and-yellow carton we all adored: Milk-Bones. An almost-new box. The large kind, for large dogs. Amen.

We all went back out through the dog door and sat on the step beside the garbage cans where we could hear anyone coming. Their licenses jingled hopefully as the first biscuit came out of the box, a doomed morsel tossed into a blitz of teeth. And one for me. I raised it and read the chiseled word, *SNACKS,* then crossed the line dividing our species and snapped off the end with my teeth. *Order a gold-plated ID tag for your dog, see details below.* I broke one in half for the old ones with their weak teeth and their forelegs tinted orange from repeated senile licking. I gave Pie a whole one and took him aside to tell him about my father going to confession. I told him that I'd decided not to tell anyone else; he thumped his tail and that was that. I crunched another Milk-Bone and considered going back inside and tearing into a Gaines burger, but it was too close to dinner. A car door slammed out in the street so there was time for just one more for me and one more for them. I put the tab in the slot and took a sip from the garden hose.

Back inside, I slid the Milk-Bones in next to the canned dog food, which was where I drew the line. I closed the cupboard and broke from the pack, crossing the kitchen fast enough to shut the door in the dogs' faces but not reaching the stairs in time to avoid being seen by Macie. She mashed her face against the glass and said, "Jackie," in a muffled voice as I flew up the narrow steps, startling the dozing monkey into baring his white fangs. I didn't want anyone to talk to me.

As I reached the second floor I heard the front door opening. Keys jingled and paper bags rustled as the front door swung shut.

"Hi, Jackie." Macie banged her way up the stairs. She was pretty big for fifteen. I heard something break and figured she must've dropped a Safeway bag.

My mother said, "Macie, what am I going to do with you?" then appeared like a gunslinger at the end of the long hall. "Did you have a nice day?" she asked me.

Something's out of whack here, I thought. "I guess so."

"You had a nice time?"

I didn't like her tone. What had I forgotten? "Sure."

"Well, your father didn't."

Good God, was it Wednesday already? My heart sank back into my chest, trying to hide. A yellow cloud of guilt floated past me, drifted downward, and pollinated the Stainmaster carpet with shame. It was Wednesday, all right.

"He went to school to watch you in the swim meet."

If I'd had leukemia, this wouldn't have been so bad. No one could get mad at an eleven-year-old boy who was dying of leukemia. And if you spanked him, he might die right then and there, stretched out across your lap.

My sister walked up to my mother's side, smiling, and asked, "What did you have for lunch?"

"Um," I said. Dog biscuits.

"Come on, Macie," my mother said. "Let's unload the groceries." They left me in the hall mentally retracing my steps, trying to figure out how my memory had betrayed me, how I'd forgotten the swim meet was today, Wednesday. I heard rain starting to tap the tar shingles on the roof over my head. He'd be home soon.

I walked through Macie's room to look down at the street. The first raindrops were collecting on the window pane and the gutted

Magnavox below. Macie's wallpaper had pale gray bunnies on a calamine lotion field, the same rabbit family repeated every yard. Inside a glass snow globe, an underwater Mrs. Claus sewed in her rocker, waiting all year for Christmas, and above her hung a painting of the saddest clown you ever saw. He cried himself into the thick oil background, melting away. I would have put that picture on someone's wall if I'd wanted them to eventually kill themselves, but it didn't seem to bother Macie.

On a chair sat her own red cat with purple diamond eyes, huge and faded, its head bowed ever since the sawdust settled from the neck into the fancifully elongated torso. She got it at a birthday party years ago, before I was born, when the other little girls there were her age. Now they were much older than her and did not remember the party, while Macie recalled perfectly the color and length of every guest's braided hair and what each brought for a present. A time machine had swept those birthday girls away, leaving only the red cat behind for Macie.

Lately neither of my parents met her eyes. My mother was always saying, "What are we going to do with you, Macie?"

It was a good question.

The room was dark, so Macie shuffled over the old baby blue carpet behind me and turned on the light. It flickered for a moment because her hands always shook.

"What'd you have for lunch, Jackie?"

"I forget." I'd never even looked in the bag.

"Did you have baloney?"

We went through this routine every day. She had to know what everyone ate. If you wanted to really mess her up you could tell her you had mush for lunch, or chicken for breakfast.

"I had baloney," she said.

There in the backyard, her lunch box on her lap, just like a normal girl. What were we going to do with her?

"Did you have baloney?"

27

"Mm hmm."

"With an apple?"

"Twinkie."

"An apple *and* a Twinkie?"

She knew what I really had. We always had the same lunch but she always asked me anyway. "Just the Twinkie." I knew this was impossible, and so did she, but I said it anyway.

"Wow," she said doubtfully.

She was making me nervous. I said, "Did you see that TV down there, Macie?"

She didn't answer right away. "Yes, I saw it," she said finally, sounding worried.

"Wanna help me bring it in?"

"*Jackie.*" Her voice mimicked a parent's astonishment. "That old thing?"

"Yeah. It's getting soaked."

"Mm hmm?"

"In a couple of minutes it'll be ruined."

This confounded her. "But it's already broken."

"Don't you want to be on TV?" I could almost hear her thinking about that. "Come on," I said. "Get your coat on."

She didn't really need convincing; she'd do pretty much anything you asked her to, but I liked to pretend sometimes. A teenager twice my size and strong, Macie was a big help around the house, though sometimes she broke things. They told me that when I was a baby and she was around four she used to climb into my crib with me.

My father's impending anger forgotten for the time being, she and I crept down to the shadowy front hall, our raincoats rustling. We listened as Pie and the others tucked into supper, their tongues propelling their dishes around the kitchen floor while my mother peeled potatoes with Walter Cronkite, who told her about the coming trial of the burglars of the Watergate apartments. The name *Watergate* was heard with greater and greater frequency since last summer—heard everywhere but in our house, that is. At least not when my father was home. He didn't want to hear about it.

I felt Macie trembling as I guided her outside. "Jackie," she whispered. She enjoyed pretending to be scared.

The view from the front porch was like peering out of a moldy stucco cave fringed with ivy. Swallows dipped in under the eaves to sip from the holy water receptacle beneath the plaster Virgin's hands. This was where the snails bred.

Macie used her arms like antennae, elbows pressed chicken-like to her sides, fingers flitting through the rain. Her instincts for balancing were different from ours. She leaned on things we couldn't see, appearing constantly about to fall but remaining somehow upright, her arms thin stems moving the air around her as if it could be woven. I held her shaking hand to hurry her along because our prey was growing soggier by the minute. If she fell, we both would.

We made it to the sidewalk, the traffic sounds raised to higher shining frequencies by the rain. First checking to make sure no one was watching, I pried my fingers under one side of the Magnavox and motioned for Macie to do the same on her side, telling her to be careful of the glass. I couldn't see her eyes in the shadow of her parka hood, but I heard the concentration in her breath. That TV had all of her attention.

It was heavier than I expected, but no problem with Macie's help. Soon I would be on TV.

Chips of the broken screen fell, loudly chiming on the wet pavement. Suddenly, our hippie neighbors' front door opened and a red light streamed over us. Strange oriental music came from the house as someone stepped outside, coughed, and closed the door. A figure came down the psychedelic steps, moving toward us through the dark. If those people would hurl a huge TV out a second-story window, what else might they do?

Nothing from Macie. Like all of us, she understood that the hippies were completely evil and so kept quiet as the intruder closed in.

We gave the Magnavox a heave and it levitated through the falling rain, revealing a herd of writhing worms driven from flooded gardens. Suddenly someone's large, dark shadow cloaked Macie.

I flinched and let the TV slip. In that terrible second the Magnavox rotated away from me with nothing between it and the crashing sidewalk but air, nothing between us and the stranger but rain. Was this theft?

Suddenly Macie wheezed as she took the entire load herself, knees buckling, back straightening valiantly. Flummoxed and panicked, I looked at her amazing lumpy outline and asked, "You got it?"

"Yes."

Not a trace of doubt there. No sign of strain or crankiness. I knew without seeing her face that she had on her perpetual smile beneath downcast goo-goo eyes. Heroic. If I asked, she would have carried that Magnavox across Death Valley in June, tubes bursting one by one from the heat, and she would never have complained.

"What're you doing?" I heard a voice, too close, warped by the rain.

Macie turned away in a fruitless attempt to hide the twenty-nine-inch diagonal. A face came toward us, its blond hair parted right down the middle over a high round forehead, its skin repelling beads of water. It was the girl who had watched my father and me that morning. Frail and thin, she slid between the raindrops and faced Macie.

"What're you doing with our TV?"

"It's broken," Macie said, regal and serene from under her hood.

I felt the start of the moment that always had to be endured in first encounters between my sister and others. Strangers would step forward, hands out and grins ready, expecting something which would never materialize. Instead of moving past niceties and into the future, they were forced to have a seat in the present, where they found themselves looking into a face as open as a well, indifferent, yet pleasant. Macie would smile for as long as strangers stayed and continue to smile long after they had departed.

The girl studied Macie. I watched her figure it out. She looked a couple of years older than me. Macie was older than both of us, sort of.

I stepped forward. "I've got plans for it," I said, placing my hand on Macie's arm, as if she needed my help.

"It's broken," Macie muttered again. She blinked in annoyance at the rain then slowly marched off toward our house with her burden.

"We had to get it out of our house," the girl said matter-of-factly. "It's the instrument of the Devil."

Macie was now halfway up the stairs with her impossible cargo. Stalwart hood shedding the rain, thighs working steadily, she looked like Tenzing Norgay, the first guy to smoke a cigarette on top of Mount Everest.

The girl watched her. I could see now that it was not a trick of the opaque street lamp or my own fright, but my neighbor's face really was pale as the inside of an onion and her eyes were black. Cold water trickled down my collar, giving me goose pimples as I walked away, feeling her stare on me, smelling her pungent perfume. When I reached the top of the steps, I turned just in time to see her bob out of the street light's circle and behind the hedge that divided our parents' properties. I heard her climbing back up into her bright old house, opening the front door, allowing that peculiar music to escape for just a moment, trapping it again when she closed it.

Macie, my silent sentry, spoke from the darkness: "She has long blond hair."

"Yep." I concealed my horror at the sight of my sister smiling as she cradled the instrument of the Devil in her arms.

Adjacent to the garage was a room too large and forbidding to accommodate any sane purpose. The concrete floor was painted the color of dried blood and had eggshell cracks throughout conforming to the earthquake-rattled ground beneath. Its rotting walls mirrored the layout of the living room above, but there was none of that room's light. The only heat escaped from cracks in the furnace duct. Because it was sunken below ground level, the windows were dark and high, ancient plate glass offering deformed views of passing tires and shoes. Now the loud rain battered those panes and leaked in over the sills. That misbegotten room. I had the idea that another family once lived there a long time ago and all died at the hands of demons who pressed the house down into the earth to hide their deed, then built an identical home on top of the old, whose inhabitants would meet the same fate. It was no place for children, and so it was the perfect place.

Macie installed the TV in the corner I chose. She sighed and plumped herself yoga style onto the cold floor, watching me pull the volume knob from my pocket and put it back on the TV where it belonged.

This room was where my mother kept her paintings: oil portraits of Greek priests, pink nudes and clipper captains with peacoats buttoned to the throat, their faces belonging to the coeds, actors, and itinerant blood donors who sat in costume for her and other art students twice a week. Some hung on the walls but most were stacked along the baseboards, leaning on their dusty predecessors like dominoes falling, slipping from the shadows toward the light of a single bulb that hung from the center of the ceiling. The canvases were used over and over again and I knew that many of my favorite pictures, ones she claimed to have sold, were actually still here. If you looked closely, you could see their outlines submerged beneath their successors. Beneath an elephant-riding raja a patriot still marched with bloody, bandaged forehead, and where once women dove for pearls Sacajawea now led Lewis astray with an umber glance. Each painting was a layered world of past and present confined by the dimensions of a five-and-dime frame, entombed in the basement.

Macie fidgeted. She had been quiet for as long as she could. "Do you remember when I had long hair?"

"Yep," I said as I used my emergency dime to remove the screws on the ventilated masonite at the back of the cabinet.

"Mom used to comb it."

"Mmm hmm. She still combs it."

"It's not long, though." Other teenaged girls had long hair, but she wasn't allowed to because she couldn't take care of it.

"She used to braid it," she said.

Macie sat among a group of portraits, all of children. People paid my mother to paint pictures of their kids, and for good reason: She could've made the devil himself appear a winsome cherub. Under her optimistic hand, all individualities were smoothed into passivity, all runny noses wiped, all frightened glares becalmed with a titanium white iris. Lacquered, framed, and hung, they reassured the purchasing parent that it was all worthwhile, this business of reproduction.

Macie stood up. "I used to get into your crib with you, Jackie, remember?"

"Mm hmm." As if I could remember back that far.

"I used to go to school."

She puttered around the room.

"Don't eat those." I caught her over in the corner, fingering a grape through the bars of the monkey's cage. He was confined to it when he was bad. It was big enough to hold Houdini. Macie let the grape roll back into the red plastic dish and fluttered her hands together behind her back, rocking on her heels.

"Maybe she'll let me grow it long sometime."

"Maybe."

The TV's back cover came off in rain-wilted pieces and rewarded me with a view of its singed guts. I saw that it would be a while before I could climb all the way inside and start broadcasting. It was going to take a lot of work, and tools. For now I just stuck my head between the transformer and picture-tube retainer so Macie could see my face. It was almost like being on TV.

"And that's the way it is," I said.

33

She laughed, holding her hand over her mouth. I saw the blood and went over to get a closer look. She had cut her middle finger.

"What, Jackie?" she asked. Often, she didn't feel a thing when she hurt herself.

She had cut it on the TV's glass.

Now she noticed it. "Oops. I'm sorry."

I told her to wait while I sneaked upstairs for Band-Aids. I told her it was all my fault.

I managed to return without being detected. I bandaged her up, saying, "You can't tell what happened to your hand, Macie, or they'll take the TV away."

"What?"

I looked at her. "Nothing."

Eventually, I knew, she would tell. She couldn't help it. There was no point in asking her to lie because she didn't know how. But she would if she could have, to please me.

My father's steps thundered on the front porch above. We both looked up. I felt my face getting red as his key turned and the old brass bolt popped. I pictured him kneeling in the confessional. I listened as the creaking of hinges was drowned out by the rushing toenails of the dogs as they mobbed him, the weary candidate, probably before he could even get his hat off. And it only got worse because he would have to sit down to remove his rain rubbers and so would fall victim to their praising tongues, recently perfumed with Alpo. A quiet hello to each as he rubbed their heads hard, then a loud greeting to the rest of the house. Returned by my mother, echoed from her tile-and-linoleum cockpit, distractedly, as she hid the monkey from his impending disapproval.

My parents were on polite terms, but were not really talking to each other. In itself, this was not out of the ordinary, but this particular silence had lasted longer than most. I wondered what it was they were not talking about.

"Where is everybody?" he asked.

This phrase, issued nightly, was usually earsplitting and scary, calculated either to provoke smiles or raise hackles, depending on what we'd been up to at the moment. But tonight it was beaten and sad, the voice of the smallest kid left alone in the middle of the house in his slippers.

Behind a dozen or so landscapes and still lifes, all the way against the basement wall, was a portrait of my father. He was sitting at his piano, his hands resting on the keys. It was from back when my mother was working, before they got married. It was unfinished, the eyes and mouth a blur, the background empty, but you could tell it was him. You could tell he was smiling. I had the feeling my mother had probably been smiling, too, when she painted it. I guessed that she started it around the time they first met, when she was still planning on becoming an artist, but then marriage and Macie had gotten in the way of its completion.

"Dinner!" yelled my mother, and Macie helped me conceal the TV behind a giant painting of the bay. No need to remind her to be quiet, to not give us away; she was silent and secret already. Because of this, I knew I was really in for it. The household barometer, Macie was entrusted with the measurement of our family's prevailing emotion, and though she didn't always welcome the task, her predictions were unfailingly accurate. Her special simple senses decreed that she must orbit outside the circle of intelligence, an angel enfolding us, unsuspecting, in her quiet mind.

I thought: What would we do without her?

We made it upstairs without arousing suspicion. Dinner was symmetrical in the yellow house: the four food groups, the four of us, the four dogs prowling the floor below.

Macie ate her portions strictly, one at a time, never mixing meat and grains in the same forkful, never moving on to peas until she had finished rice. My mother always had something different from the rest of us. Cottage cheese. Rabbit food. And she belched. A small woman, her size belied the resources hidden within that, when combined,

35

manufactured burps of shocking magnitude. My father wilted in his chair at their *basso profundo* onslaught. He grew ashen and quietly spoke her name, pleading by all the gods of decorum for her to desist. Then, as she put her lips together and whistled in awe at her own faculties, Macie and I would laugh with delight. But not tonight. She kept a lid on it tonight. And I kept my eyes on my plate, where one of these thy gifts, a chicken leg, lay waiting, bent at the knee, listening to my father say grace.

So far no one had noticed the Band-Aid on Macie's finger, but it was only a matter of time.

The bulk of the meal's business usually centered on my father's end of the table. From his chair, the only one with arms, would come a waving of wine glass and flashing of knife, a benevolent violence accompanied by questions directed at each of us in turn, his fork all the while conducting the music that played too loud from the phonograph in the living room.

But not tonight. Shrunken in his cardigan, he gnawed listlessly. Everyone else, dogs included, watched me, since no one could bear to lay eyes on his tragic face. And as far as anyone knew it was all my fault.

I wondered what the priest gave him as penance.

Pie's breath steamed my ankle. The backs of our chairs creaked and our forks rang high and lonesome. My father's music selection for that evening was Chopin nocturnes. He breathed them in and was transported, consumptive, misunderstood, to the Mediterranean shores of Majorca.

"Well," he said at length.

My father often uttered the first word of a sentence only to let it hang there for a long moment until the rest of his thought reached his lips. What occurred in his mind in the interim was open to speculation, but the scene around him in those moments was one of general, pained suspense. Arriving as they did between a series of somethings, his vacant moments were the essence of nothing, allowing a glimpse of the final void, which I imagined as just such empty junctures piled together in the dark. And he had been so happy that morning.

"Well."

My mother stopped chewing. Leaned forward. His "Well" held the promise of release for a moment longer, but then he bowed his head and the promise dissolved and we all knew that that would be it for the night. "Well" seemed to be all he could manage in the presence of his malignant male child. "Well" would have to do.

My mother stared me down. "Your father drove Dave Monk home after the swim meet," she said.

True to form, in the absence of his son, he picked the underdog. I pictured him on the tiled banks of the pool as he offered a ride to the spastic Dave Monk, who twiddled his pencil and hummed to himself like a turbine while compulsively figuring square roots in his overdeveloped head, interrupting whatever polite conversation my father attempted with automaton cries of "Danger, Will Robinson!"

Chopin filled the house like bad breath.

"Apparently Dave really turned the tide for the team by coming in third. It was what won it for them."

There was no stopping my mother now. Christ, I thought, Dave couldn't have come in third. He was too lame. She was making it up to torment me. I knew she'd be as surprised as I was to know that my father had been to confession that afternoon, but I wasn't telling.

Not listening, my father rowed a secluded dory, gazing into the eyes of George Sand, chewing on Rice-A-Roni. He'd stood and talked with other parents who carefully avoided stating the obvious, that the tall, graying man in the three-piece suit was politely watching perfect strangers, none of them his son, swimming race after race.

I wondered if he'd hoped I would still show up. Rushing in at the last minute, saving the day, pulling on my bulbous goggles, cinching up my Speedo? Held up on account of the good turn I'd done for the librarian? Better late than never, as he always said. Is that why he stuck around? Or had he, embarrassed, simply been unable to leave and admit that he'd waited in wet shoes for no good reason and that his son was not a team player? I could only wonder, because he would never say a word. He was too tired, too disgusted by more important things than me, things like his job, like the hippies that had crapped in his car. Those things earned his ire. All I merited was a wisp of disgust. I had to content myself with the careful isolation passed silently down from him, my haunted father, over dinner. If there was to be any punishment, I would have to inflict it myself. What did he think about all day? Where, besides to confession, did he go?

"My God," said my mother, "what have you done to your sister?" She grabbed Macie's hand and studied the Band-Aid. "I can't leave you alone with her, can I?"

Since Macie was not responsible for herself, blame was always easily assigned. I got the feeling it was more than the cut or the swim-meet fiasco, but I couldn't put my finger on what. Macie's little cut had suddenly become a federal offense. Another of the many mysteries of the yellow house.

After dinner my father reread the triumphant *Chronicle* Nixon headline, ignoring the *Washington Post* reprint in the bottom right corner detailing the arraignment of James McCord and the other four Watergate burglars. I hung around for a while, looking through *Life* magazines for pictures of dead soldiers, wondering if he would say something. He folded the paper loudly, put it down on the floor beside his open briefcase, and rubbed his hand across his freckled brow. He dozed, nodding so close to his reading light that the heat of the bulb awoke him. Then, vest unbuttoned, he rose and walked past me to the piano. It was like I wasn't even in the room. I heard the TV upstairs and rainy tires spinning on the street below. He and my mother were still not talking about something. She was watching *Hogan's Heroes.*

Over his head a pipe groaned with water and he looked up sharply, cocking his head.

Three years earlier, when Macie was twelve, she decided to take a bath by herself. She forgot to turn off the taps and as the water began to sluice over the tub's edge, she sang, "These boots were made for walking, and that's just what they'll do, one 'a these days these boots are gonna walk all over you," in perfect pitch, not finishing the song until long after water had seeped through the floor into the living room, drenching the piano with Mr. Bubble's indomitable suds. It had been a close one. I really thought he might've sent her away that time.

Now he pulled back the watertight rubber sheet. There it was, a Steinway concert grand, black lacquered like a clear night. The yellow house had been chosen finally because it had the only doorways wide enough to accommodate the piano's finely crafted hugeness. A square plaster patch, brighter than the rest of the ceiling, gleamed above him as he pulled out the bench, opened the keyboard with a velvet *thunk,* and settled in. Macie did not bathe alone anymore.

He hadn't had enough Chopin that night. In fact, Van Cliburn's records had only teased his appetite for pathos, so he left behind the canned yelps of *Hogan's Heroes* and began his favorite nocturne. I closed my magazine and sat there, all ears.

"I know *nothingk!*"

Startled by Sergeant Schultz's shriek, he fumbled, and the keys blurted out something Chopin never intended. I tried to look encouraging. He didn't notice. He stopped and took a breath, then began again, this time warming to the music, closing his eyes, fingers grounding him to the main circuit that buzzed in his head all day.

When he was finished, I began to clap. He nodded to me like Van Cliburn. I stood and clapped harder, but he'd just been leaning forward to adjust the bench, he had not nodded to me at all. I stopped clapping. Without looking at me, he began the same piece again. I might as well have been a ghost. Perhaps somewhere a person understood what went on in his mind, but not here, not in the yellow house.

I wandered upstairs, toward the TV's laughter. Just as I dove onto the floor between my mother and Sergeant Schultz, the phone rang. She said, "Could you get that, Jackie? I don't want to miss this." So I left those funny Nazis to their bawling and headed down the hall to answer it.

"Is Bill there?" The unexpectedness of the female voice caught me. In the background I heard the rain, and traffic. A phone booth at night denoted urgency, and I imagined her wearing a beret like the gal who had just climbed out of the tunnel with Hogan and said, *"Vive la Résistance!"*

"Just a minute, I'll get him."

"Who are you?"

The question stopped me from putting the receiver down. "Me?"

"Yes, you."

"I'm Jack."

I heard her breath cut through the pay-phone mouthpiece. Could she hear his piano behind me like I could hear the rain behind her?

"Jack Costello?"

"Yep."

She hung up. I hung up.

I leaned over the banister and was about to yell downstairs that someone had called when I thought about who she might be. I turned around.

"Who was that, Jackie?" my mother asked from behind the TV.

I wondered if I should ignore the question, like my father had that morning.

"Who was on the phone?"

"Nobody." Chopin soft-peddled up at me, liar's music.

"It must have been somebody."

"They hung up." For some reason I couldn't look at her.

"Oh, good."

She didn't want to be disturbed, I guess. Her laughs rose above the canned ones. I headed around the corner and down the long hall that led to my room. I was not large enough to contain this lie.

40

Macie was humming to herself and opening her wicker basket as I passed her door. I averted my eyes for, as my father always said, she was not decent. She was changing into her nightgown. Ever since Macie had become a teenager, this was a consideration, although she didn't notice.

I walked softly, but she heard me anyway.

"Did you really have baloney for lunch today, Jackie?"

"Yep."

She was on to me.

"And a Twinkie with no apple?"

"Mm hmm."

I mumbled another lie, hoping my mother wasn't listening, imagining gas wheeze from my rotting lunch eighteen blocks away, inflating the bag and expanding her hand-drawn smiley face.

Before stepping into my room, I reached around the door jamb and turned on the light. Once inside, I closed the door and got into bed without saying good night to anyone, leaving the light on in the bathroom to protect me, the radio on to keep me awake.

Bill.

Not even my mother called him that. "William," never "Bill." That name and the heat of her voice inside the phone booth had changed my father into someone never before imagined by me, his boy. Every morning he left, every evening he came back. Left and came back.

Every night he would kneel beside me on the carpet, our hands clasped on the red, white and blue bedspread, our mouths saying the Our Father, the Hail Mary, and then our own plea for ourselves, our animals, and relatives. After we prayed, I would climb into bed and he'd stand up, arms outstretched in front of his chest like the point of a spear, and he'd fall from his great height straight toward my face, only parting his hands at the last minute, stopping himself with them on either side of my head, saving my life as his dark cheek swept past mine and his beard scraped me hard and he kissed me, saying, "You're a good boy," then a comedic pause, "when you're asleep."

But not tonight. Tonight I curled up in bed, lies hovering between me and the radio dial.

TV and Chopin did battle down the hall, dwindling behind the increasing downpour over my head. I would not think about her, that woman on the phone. I would not think about my father going to confession on a Wednesday afternoon. I felt the fear and propped myself up. It was the same old problem: I was afraid to go to sleep.

I heard the rain on the garbage cans. I remembered the crib that Macie always talked about, the one she used to climb into with me. I grabbed the pillow and pushed it into my face until it was hard to breathe. Behind the enamel white bars of that crib, something had happened. But I wouldn't think about that, either.

I listened. The garbage can lids, private backyard gongs, were dented inward so that water pooled in the middle, making deep blips to accompany the raindrop taps that grew gently higher toward the edges, highest at the rims. And above all this, the tight ungiving tin of the handles on either side, all of it chiming and clanking, struck from the sky and never out of tune, singing right outside my window, right beneath my head. No other sound was as sweet as this.

Four
A Missed Opportunity

Friday night after dinner, I looked out the front window and saw a hippie lady in a purple skirt. She was standing next to the convertible, which my father had left out to take us to see the sequel to *The Computer Wore Tennis Shoes.*

Her hair hung over her face as she bent down by the rear bumper. I didn't tell anyone, I just watched her. She kept looking around to see if anyone was coming, and when she finished whatever it was she'd done, she straightened up and ran back into the psychedelic house next door. You hardly ever see adults running. She was barefoot, too.

Later, when we all went out to the car, I took a look at the rear bumper and found that the word *FUCK* had been almost completely erased from the Nixon sticker. She must've used Fantastic on it because you could hardly even tell it had been there.

My father didn't notice. I didn't think he'd even seen the FUCK at all.

If she and her people had defaced the sticker in the first place, then why had she cleaned it off? Had she felt bad about it? Had she decided that President Nixon was okay after all? I was really starting to wonder about those people next door.

———

On Saturday my mother and father were not talking about something again at breakfast so I went down to no man's land and climbed to the top of my tree.

My parents were highly skilled in their style of nonengagement, and an outsider wasn't likely to even notice they were fighting, but it was apparent to Macie and me through the smell of the air and the sound of the water in the pipes. Even the mush tasted different. We read the signs like ambassadors in wartime, when the clearing of a throat or the briefest hesitation to return a handshake could mean that your nation would be overrun before the dawn.

It was best to lie low at times like these. Anyone who stepped unwittingly between them might have lived to regret it, receiving a stinging measure of the animosity they concealed so well from each other. Usually Macie saw it coming before I did and would retreat to her room, foregoing television, since the set was in a hazardous common area, passing time until the skirmish had ended by crayoning over the normal faces in *Teen* magazine. I knew what was good for me, so I followed her lead and made myself scarce down in no man's land.

From my tree I saw Jay coming along with his Daisy BB gun. "Come on up," I called to him.

I knew he couldn't do it. I just said it to get him.

"You come down. I got some weed."

"Could you say it any louder? I don't think everyone heard you."

I was already halfway to the ground, swinging like the monkey counterclockwise down branches which had thoughtfully grown out into a kind of spiral staircase. Jay actually climbed this tree once, with a boost from me, but about twenty feet up he lost his grip. I watched him hit one branch full on the stomach, tripping it just off-center enough to flip him around so he hit the next one with his back. He continued that way the rest of the way down, an eleven-year-old boy fat as a badger flipping like pick-up sticks. It could've been a lot worse, but the repeated impacts slowed him down a lot. I moved out of the way just in time and he hit the soft ground crying. He had a nasty raspberry on his belly but otherwise was in good shape.

He'd brought two joints, one yellow and thin, the other stout and rolled in paper that scared me, though I didn't let on. It was a tiny American flag with full color stars and stripes that enshrouded his lumbo gold. The sight of this desecration put pins and needles in my toes. My head puffed with fear.

"What happened to you after history Wednesday?" he asked.

"Nothing. I just decided to leave."

"Ball scared you."

"Suck my dick, asswipe."

"Where'd you go?"

"The Vogue." Letting it sink in.

"To the movies?"

I could have told him about seeing my father going to confession. Instead, I punched him in the chest. "You ever gonna light that thing?"

He would never know that this was the first time I had ever smoked. He had gotten it from his mom's underwear drawer. She got it from Jay's father, the assistant deputy district attorney. They were getting a divorce.

"You know that lady with red hair?"

"The one in the poster?"

"Yeah. In the movie, she showed her tits."

"So?"

"They were huge."

"So what'd they do?"

"You know, they did it."

"Who?"

"Her and this guy. They were floating around in space."

"While they were doing it?"

"No. That was later."

"They have suits like on Apollo?"

"Sort of. No, they were silver."

"You see the guy's dick?"

"*No.*"

"You're so full of shit. They'd never let you in."

Turning his attention to his too-tight front pocket, prying into it with his noodly fingers, kindly Jay dropped the whole thing and let me off the hook with honor.

Safety matches rattled as he snapped one alight. "Ignition." He sucked hard on the starry end of it, hands flapping around his head in smoky concentration. Eagle has landed.

He handed it to me, saying, "Don't slobber all over it."

Before I'd even taken a hit I spluttered spit everywhere, giggling, releasing part but not all of my anguish. We had talked about getting high since September and, truth be told, I had egged him on to steal the weed from his mom. He glared at the air between us, coughing little wet coughs, sniffling. It smelled like someone lit a tire on fire.

"Good shit," said Jay.

"Yeah." I wanted to go home.

He shrugged, waiting for me to do my duty.

I touched Old Glory to my lips and drew the fire to life. The paper crackled and a seed popped, stabbing a hot needle into my cheek at the same time the smoke burned my guts from the inside out. I held it in so hard that barf choked up and hit the roof of my mouth, burning my throat a second time. I held it in until I couldn't stand it anymore then flung my burden out into the world, hot ropes of spit snapping out as far as they could before centrifugal force sent them flapping back into my face.

"Give it to me," said Jay.

Through fogged eyes I watched him anticipate my jerking hand like a defender in basketball: first left, then right, choosing his moment, plucking the joint from my palsied fingers.

"Oh man," he said.

My head whipped forward so hard my eyeballs threatened to eject. Tears pattered around my shoes. I took my first wheezing breath as Jay smacked my back enthusiastically. I hawked a lugie, stood up straight and wiped one sweatered forearm over mouth, nose, and eyes.

"You okay?"

"I'll live."

The next hit was easier and before long he and I were on our knees in the pine needles, laughing as the morons within us were shaken awake from long naps in bubbling wombs. Sun through our orange eyelids, we wondered aloud what sperm was. Mike Douglas, Merv Griffin, who were they, anyway? We saw stars in the blue sky, linked ideas best left separate and blew the thick purple brains out of banana slugs with Jay's BB gun. Each of us believed the tales the other told and we pounded Steve Miller songs into the trunk of my tree.

It seemed like we'd been there a very long time, our aboriginal chatter rising like our smoke from prehistoric no man's land, when suddenly Jay's red eyes bugged out and he stared, open-mouthed, at something behind me. I stood on tiptoe and saw it too, huge and far away, floating above the cypress and eucalyptus.

I rubbed my stoned eyes, watching. Strange black-and-yellow stripes fluttered loosely, then ordered themselves, growing rigid, taking shape above the faraway polo grounds.

I needed a better view, so I reached for my tree and started to climb. As I ascended, I gained perspective on the unknown enormity.

"Can you see it any better?" Jay looked up at me, using both hands to shield his eyes from the sun.

"Yep."

We listened. Music came drifting over the trees, a choir of children singing sweetly. In the foreground I saw a few dots: babies, dogs, Saturday afternoon people walking along the asphalt path. A hippie threw an orange Frisbee and it boinked off a tree. Past the white fence of the polo grounds—which were never used for polo, as far as I knew—that black and yellow and white thing floated. The children's singing grew clearer, taunting me.

"Yum yum Bumblebee,
Bumblebee tuna.
I love Bumblebee,
Bumblebee tu-oo-na."

I could have sung it better. That could've been me down there, running and singing, and the bee knew it. It leered at me, bobbing slowly along while its antennae flopped obscenely heavenward. Its fat, sexless waist grazed the ground behind a crop of tiny children who gripped ropes and held it earthbound in their pink fists, running gaily, tugging their insectile dirigible across the field while cameramen captured it all for TV, just like that guy on the bus had said they would. He'd been telling the truth, after all. I never should have thrown away his card. I could've at least *called.*

That bumblebee was a warning, I decided, an example of what could happen if you let things pass you by because you were scared. It made me want to fix everything. I made up my mind right then that I would straighten my father out. I would make everything right in the yellow house.

I heard the dull *slak* sound of the Daisy being fired. Through the veil of branches I saw Jay standing by the drainage ditch, cheek pressed against the stock, aiming at the bumblebee. He fired again and I watched the BB blur, then decelerate and arc downwards, falling coppery into the grass not even halfway to its immense gas-filled target.

Not on television, I hid in the top reaches of my tree, alone and swaying, filled with regret.

Later, with my cotton mouth, I said good-bye to Jay. I watched him slowly climb the steps of his divorced duplex, feeling the stoned secret shroud that had protected us now torn in half.

What he'd said about getting divorced was that at least in the future he would only have to deal with them one at a time. I still didn't like the sound of it. I almost followed him up his stairs, wanting to move in for as long as they would keep me, but instead I turned north toward the avenues, grackles whistling me home to supper, stupid dogs yapping at me through their walls. I ducked my head, knowing that I would say nothing to my father, or anyone else. I would keep his secret.

Still stoned, I slipped down the last hill as the first few wisps of late afternoon fog cooled my face, leaving my cheeks spotted red to match my eyes, and I approached my block like a half-witted crab, working equations designed to fit my deformed thoughts into the level corridors of my father's house.

Five
My Grandfather's Deck Chair

On Christmas morning, over mush, my father leaped up savagely from the kitchen table to turn off the TV. His momentum threw him off balance so one hand hit the volume knob the wrong way, causing a distorted voice to blurt from the speaker before he could click it off, before he could extinguish the face of a shot-down U.S. pilot in striped pajamas held up by the enemy for us to see. Switched off, the POW's sleepy face dwindled from our kitchen, draining down to a white dot that watched us for a moment, then winked away.

In church, I sat with my mother and Macie on either side of me. Macie fidgeted with the buttons on her coat while my father reached over and turned the pages on her hymnal so she could follow along with her uncomprehending eyes. He liked to pretend she was a normal fifteen-year-old.

We were not allowed to open gifts until after church, and Macie would not be happy until then, for each year she grew more certain that this would be the Christmas with no presents. She mistrusted the generosity of the occasion and awaited the day when Walter Cronkite would loom up evilly on the TV screen to announce that the exchange of gifts on Christmas had been canceled, replaced by some other ritual, like the infinitely less satisfactory Ash Wednesday smearing of charcoal on one's forehead. For Macie, Christmas was complicated.

The words of the priest were repeated by the worshippers in a monotonal din that, combined with the close warmth of my family, conspired to send me off to sleep. I had managed to stay awake until past two the night before. Now shaking my head, I shoved myself up against the back of the pew and looked around.

Past where a sleeping man's red-creased neck billowed over its Christmas collar I saw Mara Oliver. She was twelve, a year older than me. I watched her blond head until it began to blur into the votive candles off in the red distance. She sensed something on her, but didn't know it was my eyes, and in response took one pink finger of her left hand, slid it under her hair at the temple and draped the hair back, pinning it behind her elf-like left ear, revealing the blond fuzz on its tiny lobe. I felt a boner under the warm folds of my coat.

Mara was the most beautiful girl in Catechism, and instead of a right hand, she had a two-pronged stainless-steel claw at the end of a flesh-colored wooden cylinder. The claw was controlled by wires that led mysteriously up under her sleeve. Mara's hair was so fine, her skin so smooth, and her eyes so deep and green it was as if, in the great accounting of things, the deficit of her hand had somehow been re-allocated toward another purpose, the perfection of her features. Somehow, that absent hand became an extra something distilled into the rest of her, washing her with the kind of beauty each of us may see once before we die. By the way the side of her cheek moved, I knew Mara was repeating the words, "Lamb of God, you take away the sins of the world."

I felt my father's deep voice vibrating through the back of the pew, "Lamb of God, you take away the sins of the world."

I hoped so.

Something clanking whooshed through the air as incense billowed from Father Tracy's censer, a silver orb he swung before him on a long chain like a giant smoking yo-yo. The smoke rose toward the rafters, driving out the evil spirits, and I breathed it in with enthusiasm. It caught in my throat and started me coughing. I covered my mouth. My eyes filled with water and the back of my throat tickled dangerously, threatening eruption.

"Lamb of God, you take away the sins of the world, have mercy on us."

My father leaned over and shook his head at me, his expression cross. I couldn't look at him, knowing what I knew. I couldn't stand it. I struggled past my mother's knees, clasping my upright boner behind my hymnal, and fled to the back of the Star of the Sea, where I clutched the cold marble baptismal font, coughing and hiccuping while everyone said, "Lamb of God, you take away the sins of the world, grant us peace."

Macie came back and joined me.

"Careful coughing, Jackie," she said, "you know what can happen." She said it with strange, dark purpose. I suddenly felt as if everyone knew something I didn't. I couldn't stand the idea that Macie knew more about something than I did. I wanted to ask her about it, but all I could do was cough.

She looked away, twiddling her fingers in the holy water. "Santa came last night. Right, Jackie?" she asked, worried now, unable to whisper, patting me on the back and tilting her head to look down into my face.

I had the feeling she'd deliberately changed the subject, which was a real feat for Macie.

"Right?" she repeated.

"Yep," I said, choking on the purple smoke, and I couldn't stop myself from looking around to see if anyone had heard her, a teenage girl bending down and asking an eleven-year-old boy about Santa Claus, in whom she still believed.

B ack at home Macie was at last allowed to get at her stocking, then at her presents, and it wasn't long before she had eviscerated them all, and one of mine as well, and was looking for more, greedy and dangerous, not to be trifled with, head down and serious as she went about the business of Christmas. The smell of the tree was drowned out by eau de cologne, a gift from Aunt Jerry, which Macie applied much too liberally to her throat and hands, trying to smell like a normal teenager. The monkey wailed, lonesome, from down in the basement, not allowed in because of what he did to the tree the year before. My father turned the phonograph up louder to drown him out and conducted Handel from his chair.

I sat in the corner and read a book about space, a present from my mother. Occasionally I peered over the top of it, over Gene Cernan floating outside of Gemini 9 at an impossible 17,500 miles per hour. Once I looked up just in time to see another of Macie's gifts stripped of its Noah's Ark wrapping paper by her shaking hands. A chromatic harmonica. Pie's eyebrows rose when Macie lifted it to her lips and blew. He crossed the living room in a flash, seated himself reverently in the wrapping paper before her, and raised his voice in sweet torment. Macie laughed and blew nonsensical notes while Pie's eyes rolled around in their sockets. He pressed on with his instinctive howling, attempting to harmonize with her impossible scales. Occasionally his eyes met mine and I had to look away, never having seen him so out of control. He sat on his tail, his lips forming a gentle O, ears flattened on his head, answering some mysterious call from his absent pack, alone in the middle of a forest floor of colored torn paper and ribbons.

"All right, all right," said my father, wincing, losing Handel's thread. "Don't encourage him."

But Macie kept at it, and Pie's voice, by now growing raw and low like Patricia Neal's, drowned out the hi-fi.

"Who gave her that?" he asked.

"Madeleine." My mother didn't sound entirely sure.

"Well, I don't think it was such a good idea."

"Madeleine doesn't know any better, Dad." She called him Dad when the children were present. "She hasn't seen Macie in years."

My father squirmed in his chair for as long as he could take it then finally stood atop his huge feet, waded through the wreckage of our celebration of the Virgin birth, and snatched the Hohner from Macie's hand. At which point his simple daughter looked up at him and asked, "Am I annoying you, Daddy?"

He turned away, looking up at the gold angel that sat atop our tree. Sometimes, no matter how hard he tried, he just couldn't pretend Macie was normal.

M y mother was in a high state. She leaned against the yellow kitchen sink and called the turkey a bastard as she rammed her fist deep into its body cavity.

Around four o'clock they started arriving. Macie and I were ready, dressed in our monkey suits, making the rounds from relative to relative as Burl Ives sang "Frosty the Snowman" from the hi-fi.

They all milled around the living room. Uncle Pat, who had amazing bat ears and a perpetually crimson face. His odd, slouching proportions could have made the finest silk suit look like sack cloth, but he had a surprising, elegant way of gliding across a room to fetch a drink. Though he was the smallest brother, his laugh was the loudest. Away from the group loomed Uncle Regan, the oldest and largest, whose hair stuck out from his temples like the fuzz on a cotton-topped marmoset's head. He stood quietly staring out the front window with his hands folded behind him, like a detective about to whirl around and reveal the murderer among us, while in reality he was merely rearranging his boxers. His brother Connie, wide and tall, my godfather, riffled aimlessly through the sheet music atop my father's piano, which shone that day, uncovered and bright for all to see.

The four sons and their quiet, unobtrusive wives were watched from the most comfortable chair in the room by my grandfather, so tiny and old you wondered how all those large men had been ferried from his wizened loins to that carpeted island of adulthood. He sat, small and bald and bandy, a vest the color of his eyes stretching over his tight belly, a thirty-year-old tweed suit covering his eighty-year-old body, and woolen underwear underneath all that.

"Where's my child bride?" he sang between sips.

"She's right over here, Dad." Uncle Pat stepped away from the couch to reveal my grandfather's second wife, a youthful seventy-five.

Satisfied, my grandfather searched for fresh prey. "William," he said, looking up from the small dog that sprawled in his lap, languorously licking the salt from his hands. "William, the liquor in your house flows like molasses." He shook the ice in his empty glass accusingly at my father, who left Uncle Connie with a pat on the shoulder and went to get a bottle.

"All right, all right, Dad," he shouted, happy to be a son again, with older brothers. As he passed me, extra loud and jaunty, he roughed up my hair with his strong, atta-boy hand. He leaned into the curve that led to the kitchen door, bending his head to the left, the centrifugal force exerted by his enthusiasm pulling his coat flap to the right, his shiny feet rolling him along like a locomotive. In the time that it took for him to ram the door open and for it to whoosh shut behind him, I heard the sound of some movie on the little TV, and pots clattering in my mother's hands.

"Jackie." My grandfather was looking for diversion in the interim between White Horses. "Did you know you're lucky to be alive?"

"Nope," I lied, playing along.

"It's true. If it wasn't for a deck chair, you'd have never seen the light of day."

I took my place on the hassock in front of him and Macie joined me, smiling and listening, even though, as usual, my grandfather was ignoring her. He repeated by rote a page from our family's private book of Genesis, as he did each Christmas. He always told it to the youngest of the youngest generation, so that by inference all those in between were gathered up in the tale.

Just as the story was getting under way, my father returned with the bottle. The phone rang and he stopped in his tracks. He shuffled toward the kitchen, then toward my grandfather's empty glass, finally made up his mind and dashed away up the stairs. Everyone looked at everyone else. We all heard him answer the phone, but not the conversation that followed. I wondered why he hadn't just let my mother answer it in the kitchen. My grandfather gazed sadly at his empty glass, then went on with his tale.

He told us how on a rare, sunny San Francisco day in 1915, he carried his valise down the hill to one of the piers, at the end of which waited a deep-water steamer bound for Peru, where he would join his brother Francis in a mining venture high in the airless Andes. After showing his ticket he ascended the gangplank. At the top the purser informed him that if he felt need of a deck chair—at the mention of this word my grandfather leaned forward for emphasis, squeezing the tiny dog between his thighs and belly so the creature squeaked and hopped to safety—if he felt need of a deck chair for the long voyage ahead, he would have to purchase one himself.

He found one in a dry goods store in the Italian section, not far from the present-day location of the Condor Club, home of Carol Doda. Stowing it under his arm, a single young man on the way to Peru to make his fortune, he strolled down a steep street above the as-yet-bridgeless Golden Gate, his future as wide as the shimmering bay below him.

But as he walked he sensed disturbance in the air. He heard voices raised in panic and quickened his step. As he approached his pier, he found that the hubbub centered on his ship, or rather on the place where his ship once had been, for his steamer lay capsized in the water, sinking, rolled over as the result of incorrect placement of cargo in the hold, presumably more to starboard than to port, or vice versa.

Scores perished in this inane tragedy, but my grandfather was not among them, thanks to a convenient purser and a folding hardwood chair, and he made it clear that I owed each day of my life to the intercession of that fabled piece of furniture. Through the telling of this tale he satisfied his need to claim authorship of all the generations present in that living room. I supposed he was entitled, though I knew his urge was selective. I had never seen him claim responsibility for Macie.

My father returned from talking on the phone, unscrewed the bottle, and shooed Macie away. "Don't bother your grandfather," he said, though she hadn't opened her mouth. My grandfather sat back, his story finished, watching the scotch splash into his glass. Then Connie came up behind my father. I saw him secretly pinch his elbow. He steered him into the corner. I pretended to pass the Triscuits so I could get near them and I heard Connie whisper in my father's ear. "Not on Christmas," he hissed, and my father's face turned red.

I pictured the blond commando in her beret, standing in a pay phone, shouting, *"Vive la Résistance!"* When my mother came out of the kitchen, smiling, they broke it up.

Two White Horses and one turkey dinner later my grandfather gazed across the living room, through the leaded-glass windows and into the past.

It was a quiet Christmas crew now gathered in that room, so stuffy and warm. All our preparations, our baths, perfumes, and Wildroot pomades, our suits and smiles had by evening's end lost their luster, but together we hummed with satisfaction. If I listened hard enough I could hear the TV upstairs, watched by Macie, whom everyone had run out of things to say to a long time before. My father was more relaxed now that she was gone.

The dishes were all cleared and I crouched behind the tree, below the window sill, with Pie, who wore a red ribbon. Cool air radiated from the street through the window pane and all the gifts were gone from under the tree. Everyone had forgotten how Connie bawled my father out. Everyone had forgotten the phone call.

We all thought that my grandfather had fallen asleep, his chin rising and falling on his gnome-like chest, when he placidly opened his eyes and said, "Play something for us, William."

"All right, Dad."

"He plays beautifully," my grandfather confided to his child bride.

I heard the clunk of the keyboard lid opening, then my father playing that sad *Nocturne* by Edvard Grieg that I wished I could play myself.

Five and a half blocks to the west stood the pink house where my grandfather and his first wife raised their sons, and where, up in the attic, my father practiced the piano every single day starting at age four. While his brothers played ball on the streets, my father's metronome clicked along, orderly, as he ran through his scales. Alone with the low afternoon light spilling across the pine floor and the door closed at the bottom of the stairs, his joy had no limits. He felt his life blossoming inside his chest as he learned his preludes, nocturnes, and audition pieces, each carrying him closer to the standing ovations for which he sometimes practiced humble bows, with the curtains drawn. In his twenty-second year something happened, though, and he stopped, stranded in time by the overarching hope of his childhood, and got himself a job.

Her shoes off now, my mother got up from the floor by the fire and put her hand on my father's shoulder. He missed a note, swore gently under his breath, then went on playing, softly. If my grandfather hadn't bought that deck chair I might never have seen the light of day, and if my mother hadn't been so involved with *Hogan's Heroes,* I might never have picked up the phone that night. I would never have known what I knew.

With my arm around Pie I felt safe enough to sleep. I laid my head on the floor and the ornaments grew large as the music filled the room and the family talked about things that didn't add up to anything except the sound of their voices and the feel of the words in their mouths. I could see them all reflected there in the colored glass balls, their round skins coddled by green branches, warmed by tiny electric lights, and in one of the ornaments I saw myself, hanging there among them.

Six
Summer Reading

Winter and spring passed, and at last the fog grew heavier, a sure sign, in San Francisco, that summer had arrived. I began working my way through the classics: *Frankenstein, The Time Machine, Moby Dick,* all of them trimmed down to reasonable lengths and colorfully depicted on the pages of *Classic Comics.* Featuring stories by the World's Greatest Authors. *Endorsed by Educators.* Jay and I exchanged them, as well as our *House of Secrets* and *House of Horror* comics. No superheroes for us. Blood and guts, men with sideburns and brandy snifters. Impossible impalements and cranial eruptions—presumably drawn by LSD-gobbling schizoids—were presented to us each month. The rich smell of their inks drifted up from the swaying stack beside my bed, enticing me.

Toward the middle of each *Classics Comics* was a page of advertisements completely unlike those found in any other comic. There were no X-ray glasses for seeing through bikinis. No offers for sea monkeys, which I had ordered two summers earlier and dutifully attempted to train even though it was painfully obvious to me, present at their birth, that they were just brine shrimp and did not wear crowns. No, the ads in *Classic Comics* were more serious than these. They seemed as if they should be illegal. Tools for picking locks, both "novice" *and* "professional." Tools for hotwiring cars and the instruction manuals to go with them. Blackjacks. Brass knuckles. Spanish fly, about which we had many times retold the story of the woman so affected she was forced to pleasure herself—with disastrous results—on a stick shift, while the guy who had given her the potion was in the drugstore buying rubbers. These advertisements hinted enticingly at a nether world in which men stole from each other, beat one another, slipped women dangerous potions. Besides Jay and me, what other kinds of people were out there in the land, reading *Classic Comics?*

Halfway through *Lord Jim* I saw an ad for the Record-a-Jac. The room grew silent around me as I was guaranteed:

CRYSTAL CLEAR RECORDING
OF BOTH SIDES OF YOUR TELEPHONE
CONVERSATIONS.
GET RESULTS EVERY TIME.
ONLY $4.98

It jumped right out at me. I was about to show it to Jay when something shut my mouth. I had a strong feeling about this Record-a-Jac.

I took *Lord Jim* home that night and carefully cut out the order form, knowing it was wrong, that *Classic Comics* were never to be defaced. Nevertheless, I filled it out, taped the exact change to a piece of binder paper, and sent the envelope off to Lake Forest, Illinois, telling no one, not even Jay.

That summer Jay's mother had become more and more scarce. His father had quit as assistant deputy district attorney and was now seen only every other weekend. Both his and my parents thought that since Jay's older brother had moved out and no one else was around, I should spend a lot of time over at his house. My job, as outlined by my well-meaning mother and father, was to keep Jay happy,

61

immersed as he was in the midst of his family's demise, and I took that job seriously, making sure that our days were filled with adventure and delight. Presented to me as an act of charity and sacrifice, I made it my paradise. Jay and I faced each day with a house empty of adults, and the long summer awaited, a world without limits.

Jay had the entire upstairs flat to himself but felt compelled to move all his important things into the crawl space between the roof and the ceiling. Though it was hot in the daytime and we occasionally had to shake each other out of an oxygen-deprived stupor, the secret splendor of the location was incentive enough to remain. Frayed plywood sheets—from a construction site down the block, stolen under cover of night—were laid across the joists. We pulled the antique electrical conduit from the ceiling sconce below up into the crawl space. A neat twist of the bulb turned it on and off. The only outside light came from a slat-louvered grate, which also offered a useful view of the street.

We entered this space through a trap door in Jay's father's closet via steps of opened drawers in an empty old dresser. We shut each drawer behind us as we climbed, and left not a trace. Sleeping bags were crammed through the opening and spread on the plywood. Within reach we always had a flashlight, a transistor radio tuned to KFRC, and matches, for making fart-driven streams of flame and for igniting our bong.

Some nights between comics we just lay there, silent. One of us would twist off the bulb with sizzling fingers so only the street light outside threw shadows through the ridge vent. Holding our breaths in the crawl space, brows dripping like sub commanders, we listened as the building's turn of the century frame, responding to changes in temperature from day to dark, popped and creaked. Alive, it transformed itself into a Death House, with the Manson Family or the Weathermen creeping through the rooms below, searching for the boys they knew had to be there somewhere. With the BB gun loaded, we were always ready.

In the daytime Jay and I walked everywhere. Pigeon-toed from birth, Jay frequently got his feet mixed up and fell down in a heap. We'd be going along, talking, and I'd look over to say something, and see nothing there. A few yards back there he'd be, flat on his ass. You never knew when it would happen. One minute he'd be there, the next he'd be gone, a silent, vanishing boy. I learned to stow away my giggles and wait while he, red-faced, not possessing so much laughter that he could afford to squander it on himself, stood up fast and rejoined me, closemouthed and mad.

One afternoon we came into Jay's kitchen through the preferred, secret back door to find his father by the refrigerator, watching the small black-and-white TV. I entered warily, behind Jay, for I could almost touch the vengeful atmosphere floating between Mr. Herman and the television. On the screen, flashed across the country from Washington, D.C., sat a man with eyebrows like the horns of a minor demon and half glasses slipping to the end of his nose. He leaned, hell-bent and wry, over a microphone.

"Sam Ervin," said Mr. Herman. "He's going to bring the bastard down."

I had no idea who the bastard was, but hearing the word and the venom behind it gave me a thrill.

Jay's father was a Democrat, drove an Econoline van, and when he visited, always seemed to be returning from the mountains or the desert. He usually came and went under cover of darkness. On those rare occasions when he stayed the night, we would hear him down in the garage, battling drug-induced insomnia by means of the fierce rhythm of his punching bag. One night I was sleeping over and a neighbor called to complain about the racket. Mr. Herman spoke to him calmly, his voice almost soothing as he said, "Why don't you leave me alone and go back to beating up your daughter?" Then he hung up the phone and returned to his punching bag as if nothing had happened.

Now here he was in the daylight, the only father I ever saw who dressed like a cowboy, with an oily sheepskin coat, faded jeans and boots, and a crooked tan hat that when removed revealed a head bald as Mr. Clean's. The warm smell of sweat and Camel nonfilters floated off him. He was pigeon-toed, like his son, though he had somehow come to grips with the condition, walking like John Wayne did. I never saw him fall. Some kind of septum condition caused him to hiss through his nose when he wasn't talking, which was most of the time.

"That's John Dean," he said.

On the TV, John Dean spoke: "He said that we can sell the story just like we were selling Wheaties."

"The President said that?" asked Sam Ervin. My ears pricked up.

"Ha! Now we're getting somewhere." Mr. Herman slapped his palm against the refrigerator, wincing as he waited for the dented metal to rebound. When it finally popped softly back into place, he interrupted Sam Ervin to ask John Dean, "What else did the bastard have to say?"

Dean: "He said that, for now, to keep the cap on the bottle."

Ervin took over for Mr. Herman. "These were the President's exact words?"

Dean: "That is from the tape's transcript."

Suddenly the kitchen felt too hot.

As Dean's incongruously beautiful wife, with her pulled-back blond hair and proud chest, watched her bespectacled little husband read his statement, I felt myself coming loose from the kitchen and its clean tiles and saw a wall of linoleum stars falling away from me. It was June 25, 1973, and President Nixon was the bastard.

I could feel my face sweating. The need for sleep suddenly hit me. I yawned and when I tried to make fists, my hands felt so funny I giggled.

Jay wouldn't stop staring at me.

I couldn't follow all that Dean was saying, but there was no question as to whom he was fingering with his testimony. "I began," he said, "by telling the President that there was a cancer on the presidency, and that if it were not contained, it would certainly kill his administration."

Wiping my eyes, looking at Jay's father, I realized that what I had taken for anger was in fact a kind of joy. His eyebrows rose, rumpling his forehead all the way up to the bald crown, and he smoothed the wrinkles affectionately downward, back into place, a hissing bald cobra. What he saw on that TV made him happy. It occurred to me that if he knew that my father had once shaken hands with Richard Nixon, he would kill me. He looked at me, and I felt sure that he could read my mind. I must have looked pretty bad because he laughed, a big man, and held out a chair for me. I sat down, put my elbows on the table, and watched. It didn't feel real, it felt like a dream.

Mr. Herman put his hand on my forehead. "Feverish," he said. I pushed his hand away. It had been blocking my view of the TV.

From here on out, I realized, this summer would have to be devoted to the Watergate hearings. I would get to know all of them, all the players, identifying them by their bald spots and crew cuts, their glasses, cigarettes, and quavering jowls. Soon I would even recognize their voices from the bathroom down the hall. From here on out, much to Jay's annoyance, it would be Colson and Dean every afternoon instead of *The Little Rascals,* Haldeman and Ehrlichman in lieu of *Speed Racer.*

Watching and listening to the rustle of papers and clearing of throats, I saw the approach of something that scared me, yet also filled me with an inexplicable joy. This was something I could never discuss at home, something forbidden and destructive, and though I knew it brought with it nothing but sadness and ruin, I couldn't stop watching.

Jay drew away, getting out the cereal bowls with a clatter. The long tables and gray-haired men on the screen held no attraction for him. But Mr. Herman knew that the same was not true for me. He looked down and smiled at me in the way he had of conveying both menace and a complete understanding of who you were and how hard you thought it was to be you. It was an odd combination. That summer I chose him for my idol. I didn't know that, in general, children are poor judges of character.

Two weeks later I had the Herman's kitchen to myself. Jay frowned on guys who wasted sunny days indoors and was outside, slamming his ball with regular anger into the garage door. I ate my cereal, dangling my feet under the kitchen table, watching the TV, when Alexander Butterfield, former assistant to H. R. Haldeman, testified to the committee that the Oval Office had a taping system.

Sam Ervin's huge eyebrows trembled. His hands shifted sheets of paper on the table before him. He couldn't believe it. Nobody in the hearing room could believe it, and neither could I. A taping system recording the President's every word. It was like *Mission: Impossible.* My interest in Watergate had been sparked by John Dean, but Butterfield's testimony and its implicit promise that one day we might all get to hear actual recordings of the President's secret life now held me spellbound.

Later, over dinner, my father laid it all out for me.

"He wasn't the first, you know. They've been doing it for years."

As he ate his chicken, he explained that the first known in-house surveillance of the White House had been conducted by Franklin Roosevelt, who, he reminded us, was a Democrat.

"Read your history," he said.

It seemed FDR had the Army Signal Corps install a concealable RCA microphone in a table lamp and placed it in the Oval Office, where it apparently remained through Harry Truman's administration. "You can still see it there," my father told us, "in photographs of Truman, in the background."

I wonder if Truman had known about the lamp.

"It wasn't there with Eisenhower. He had it removed." Eisenhower, the Republican. "Of course, Kennedy had bugs everywhere."

I asked, "Where is it now?"

"Where is what? The lamp?"

"Yep."

"Well, I don't know." His eyes rolled toward the ceiling. "That's not the point. The point is, the President has done nothing wrong. Years ago, when I met him, I could see in his eyes what kind of man he was . . . a decent man."

As my father launched into his millionth retelling of the story of how he shook hands with Richard Nixon, I stared at my chicken and wondered if Mrs. Eisenhower had sold the bugged lamp to an antique shop or something. Was it purchased later? Maybe it sat in some unsuspecting family's living room, having reentered civilian life while its hidden microphone, whose diaphragm had once quivered to the decisions of the most powerful men on earth, now rested, becalmed. I couldn't wait till the Record-a-Jac arrived.

Later that night I woke up, relieved as usual that nothing terrible had happened in my sleep. I saw my father down the hall, just standing in his robe. As my eyes adjusted to the darkness, I saw that he had started using safety pins to hold the robe together at the elbows and other stress points, that the dark blue and black threads of the plaid were apparently made of stouter stuff than the lighter shades; they were holding on longer, bridging the gaps left by the long-eroded, frivolous reds and greens.

He was staring at the house next door. Someone was singing.

I got up and sneaked over to my window. In the neighbor's kitchen I saw the hippie lady who had cleaned off my father's Nixon sticker. She was frying up some eggs, feet bare below her gauzy skirt, singing "Amazing Grace" in a sweet voice. What was she doing having breakfast in the middle of the night? Someday I had to find out what was going on in that house.

I peeked down the hall. My father still stood there, listening to her sing. His eyes were closed. Neither of them could sleep. I wondered if they were afraid, too.

Seven
The Rat Patrol

Back when he'd been working in the district attorney's office, Mr. Herman watched the hippies come and go, confiscating their best weed, and began to smoke more and more of it until one day he'd found that he envied them. So he quit his job and moved into a cave somewhere to the north, where he began to execute gigantic paintings of satyr-like creatures with bowl-cut blond hair and thin, tan chests, not unlike the race of morons found in the future in the movie *Time Machine*. Sometimes they rode dolphins, these creatures, while at other times they just sat on the grass, picking lice or something from one another's hair. They represented some kind of paradise to Mr. Herman, who, though unable to kick his Camels, had turned vegetarian and to whom blondness, tanness, and large eyes apparently embodied ideals to which we should all have aspired.

When Mr. Herman moved out, an artist now, he left a hall closet filled with things that had no place in his utopia, costumes that he had tried on and shed before arriving at his present one. Scuba gear, golf clubs, surfboard, Ouija board, second-hand tailed tuxedo and folding top hat, underwater speargun with its rubber bands unfortunately corroded, seven three-piece suits, jazz records, rock records, classical records, a saxophone, books on organic gardening, real estate management, and social revolution, a Twister set, a fishing rod, and three enigmatic masking-taped cardboard boxes labeled: TAX RECEIPTS, 1960–65.

It was the boxes that attracted me the most. When Jay said he couldn't understand why anyone would want to look through old tax receipts, I replied, "Exactly."

I began lobbying Jay, seeking his permission to open the boxes. At first he refused, either out of respect for his father's property or out of a basic fear of the man. The latter was the more likely explanation. Mr. Herman seemed dangerous; his cheeks at times turned an angry red below blue eyes that guttered with the dim fire of dubious intelligence. In either case, Jay was hatefully resistant to my pleas, and it was only through the kind of pressure that makes the exerter feel more than a little shame that I finally received his permission to open the mysterious boxes.

Jay watched from the hall, beside the closet door, his left hand twitching nervously behind his back. I tipped the top box from side to side. Inside, something heavy lurched and my stomach growled. Through a small, dirty window at the rear of the closet came the sound of the neighbor man shouting at his daughter. I guessed Mr. Herman was right about him. Jay rocked to and fro on his heels. Printed on the box was an ad for navel oranges. The sides swelled from an unknown pressure within.

"Come *on.*" Jay was losing his nerve. He feared his father a lot more than I feared mine.

Using the sharp bumpy edge of my house key, I slit the packing tape between the top folds of the box and pulled them open. I was welcomed by the scent of oranges past, and something else.

Inside the box, bliss.

I tilted my head to the side to eliminate the glare from the bare lightbulb, and there she was, shrouded by blue folds of a fabric so thin it must have been living, like seaweed, rumpled into channels radiating away from her, well suited for the runoff of her vast love. She had a severe dark line over each eye, just like Cat Woman, and a little pink mouth so tiny you wondered how she could have breathed through it, yet breathe she must have, and when she did, the lovely blue shroud rose and fell over her nipples, pulling the cloth tighter into the darkness between her thighs. Tax receipts, hah! Oh, the clever man.

"What's in it?" Jay saw how still I stood. Craning his neck to see past me, afraid to come in, he sniffed the air for danger. "Jack?"

I found that I was unable to find words for what lay before me. All language left me, leaving in its place nothing but total, unquestioning gratitude. It was a treasure chest, this box, containing a dream so welcome and bright that I wondered what I had done to deserve it and what tortures I would suffer for usurping it. And there were two more boxes.

"Come on," he said, all out of courage now, turning to go. "Someone's coming."

For a moment, I thought I heard footsteps too, on the steps outside, and I knew then that I must protect the dear, orange-scented contents of that box, contents that offered so much, yet had already consumed my peace of mind.

"Just a sec" was all I could say.

"*Why?* Come *on*, man, what's in there?"

From deep in my belly came the word. "*Playboys,*" I croaked. I heard his sneaker turn and stop breathlessly in the carpet. "*Playboys,* Jay."

In those moments before I'd finally spoken, I had been calculating ways that I could have ensured his ignorance, protecting her and all her sisters, my wards, stacked in the darkness beneath her. "Tax receipts," I might have said, "that's all." And then I might have somehow snuck her out, placing her on the window ledge outside, sneaking into the alley later and climbing up in the darkness, eloping with my newfound love. But the sincere nakedness staring up at me would have frowned on that, and so I had spoken the truth, testifying to her power as if upon a courtroom Bible. Now I'd have to share her. There were unjustly few outlets for the passions of eleven-year-old boys, and when one came along it was to be cherished jealously.

"Oh shit, he's got tons of 'em," said the jaded Jay.

How long had he known? Why hadn't he spoken up? Did he have any idea how many precious moments he had wasted?

"Come on, man, someone's really coming."

I turned to face him and he saw the passionate vacuum in my eyes. At once, the fear of getting caught vanished from his face and in its place there spread a smirk. Anger clotted at the base of my tongue. I would kick his ass.

Keys jingled in the corridor outside. Jay reached past me, shutting off the light, pulling me out of the closet and swishing the door shut. We bolted down the hall, sneakers squeaking as we rounded the corner into the master bedroom, slamming into the closet there, climbing up into the crawl space and lowering the trap door back into place behind us.

We listened.

Up there in the suffocating heat I felt woozy, terrified. Lustful. Something crinkled in the darkness and Jay, hearing it, clicked on the flashlight. The beam flew unerringly to my guilty package.

"You took one?" he hissed. "Man, you fucker, I didn't say you could take one."

The front door closed downstairs as she squinted into Jay's interrogatory light, watching us with her unjudgmental affection.

"It's no big deal," I whispered, but when all you had was an older sister who collected *Teen* and *Tiger Beat* magazines, this was a big deal.

His face softened at the sight of her. He held out his hand. I realized that I would have to give a little, so I handed it over. He snapped through the magazine like a pro, fingers stopping unerringly at the thrice-folded center, thumbs coming into play now to spread it callously open, index finger looping underneath and flipping over the jokes, revealing a set of tan calves and above that two stapled knees and above that the heart of the triptych, breasts swelling monumentally below a face framed with shiny brown hair. She knelt on a chair on a bright beach. Beside her right knee on the creaking wicker, swaddled in a beach towel, was a tiny striped kitten with blue eyes that looked right into the camera, just like hers.

Downstairs, someone called, and Jay snapped the magazine shut, shoving it—too roughly, I thought—over into the tight angle of the eave.

"Jay!" Mr. Herman was staring into the fridge, from the muffled sound of his voice. "You boys up there?"

Jay ignored him. "You have to put it back," he told me. "He'll kill me if he finds out. He'll kill you."

"Okay, sure," I lied, stalling, plotting to somehow spirit her away from this unappreciative house.

"You up there?"

"Fine!" shouted Jay incongruously. Then, whispering to me, "Soon as he's gone, you put it back."

"Come on, man."

"It's just a magazine, jack-off."

"So let me have it."

"It's my father's."

"If he wanted them, he would've taken them with him, wouldn't he?"

"Well."

"Come on. Like he's gonna notice one's missing."

"Was it on top?"

"Yeah."

"Then he'll notice it's missing." All of this in spastic whispers.

"It's not yours to let me have, anyway," I was groping for any stratagem.

"It's my dad's, though."

"So what?"

"So," he thought for a moment, "it's more mine than yours." This kind of standoff made the inside of my head itch.

"Agnew's on the take! How about that?" Mr. Herman reported, mouth full of food—bologna, most likely—from down in the kitchen. Ordinarily, this news would have filled me with excitement, but not right then.

"What if I trade you for something?" I said.

Jay's eyes flashed across the darkness. Now I was getting somewhere. I had hoped it wouldn't come to this, but he held the advantage, and my need was overpowering.

"Come on," I said, "name it."

Jay's eyes were unnaturally calm.

"All right," he said, "I want the Rat Patrol."

Shrewd Jay, much smarter than I who had been made daft by desire, was putting me to the test. The Rat Patrol was my favorite thing, and he knew it.

Sand-colored and weathered, a televised creation manifested in die-cast metal, the Rat Patrol was a modified Jeep six inches in length with three windblown, khaki-clad soldiers: one driving, one hanging on for his life, the third manning the .50 caliber machine gun in the rear. The Rat Patrol flew over dunes and across hard-packed mud, seeking out and destroying gun emplacements, liberating Bedouins, spilling Nazi blood over the hot sand, handling what no other soldiers could handle. When the Rat Patrol looked out over their filthy windscreen, it was always 1944, and they were always engaged in combat with the elusive Desert Fox.

Downstairs, Mr. Herman turned on the TV and Spiro Agnew's denials bounced around the kitchen.

"Let me think about it," I said.

"Okey dokey, artichokey," said Jay nonchalantly, making sure I saw him flipping through the magazine. I had to close my eyes.

I pictured the Rat Patrol, there on my shelf at home. The Rat Patrol had spent countless hours spinning over my red carpet, crashing barriers as my eyes watched from the desert sky, my mouth providing sputter-lipped motor and artillery noise. I rode with the Rat Patrol, taking the same knocks that they took, feeling the same triumphs they felt, and without me they were nothing.

I had almost the same fondness for the Rat Patrol that I once had for those rubber toys I used to steal from the dogs, who did not hold them in the same reverence as I. It had pained me to see how they tore at them, puncturing and bespittling them.

There had been squeaking ducklings in midhatch, eggshell still stuck to their heads. There were rubber shoes and newspapers, fire hydrants, femur bones, and whole racks of lamb, all rendered in resilient rubber. They had been wonderful, but of them all, Jerry the mouse had been the best, Jerry of *Tom and Jerry* fame. With his round belly, black tail, whiskers made of fishing line, and cheerful smile, he became my favorite companion. Only seven years old, I had become already maudlin, sentimental for things so cute they could never exist, and by their very impossibility were all the more poignant. I would hold Jerry, smelling his pungent rubber, and bemoan the loss of my childhood, which had only just gotten under way. I had taken him everywhere with me and he began to dry and crack as he grew older.

"One *Playboy* for the Rat Patrol, okay?" said Jay, punching me in the arm. He waited, wondering how far I would go. Neither he nor anyone else knew about Jerry, and that was fine with me.

I found myself momentarily shocked at how easily my answer came. I sensed that I was moving on to other pastimes, other recreations embodied by that glossy magazine. Just as I had left the squeaking Jerry, I would leave the Rat Patrol behind to bound over dunes, their wheels whirling without me. Having made my decision, I dusted my rugged hat off on my knee and turned to go, leaving them in a dry wash, the cooling engine's ticking the only sound in this foul Sahara. I could feel their eyes on my back as I trudged to the high crest of a dune. We had seen so much together. At the top I turned and looked back at them for a moment, and waved heartily, ignoring the looks of betrayal on all of their leathery faces. "Sure," I told Jay, "you can have them."

In the cool afternoon we left Jay's house, and grackles noticed us as we shut the door, and they took flight, whistling and dark against the white summer sky. Each day contains a world.

Jay carried the *Playboy* in a Safeway bag, swinging it against his knee, a little too carelessly for me. Just to spite me, he made the walk last forever. He whistled, which he never did, picking up anything shiny that he saw on the sidewalk, a curious crow.

At last we approached my house, cool fog passing over our heads. My tongue was dry. We made our way over the fence on the right side of the house and Jay asked in a loud voice if he could have something to eat. I shushed him, looking warily up at the second-story windows. He knew very well he could have a Ho-Ho or something; he always did, unrolling them so that he could get at the interior first.

My greeting to Pie was terse and he turned away, offended. I would make it up to him later. I couldn't help it; my mind was elsewhere. My eyes were on the bag and my ears were tuned to the highest frequencies. We pushed through the swinging kitchen door and out into the hall. We paused there, listening like burglars, and then started up the steep stairs.

I heard the grackles outside, making that warm burbling sound that meant the sun was about to come out. I heard the TV muttering anxiously about Spiro Agnew. My mother was napping down the hall, lying on top of the bedspread. When the grackles stopped singing, the sun came out, finding its way through the back of my mother's ear and lighting it up so that it glowed, peach fuzzed and orange. Lighting the monkey's smaller ear in the same way, catching the white hair that grew to a point there like Mr. Spock's ears. He crouched, sleeping, on my mother's chest, rising and falling with her breaths.

Jay caught a sneaker on the top step and cursed, surprised, as if he didn't trip ten times a day. The monkey stirred at the sound, his little eyelids fluttering just like a person's, and his long hand gripped my mother's sweater, waking her.

"Ohhh," my mother said, stretching, "Jackie, what time is it?" She hadn't opened her eyes yet.

"Maybe four," I said, watching the monkey. His black eyes looked from me to the bag in Jay's hand, then back at me. He knew.

"Don't wake your sister up. I'm not ready for her yet." The only rest my mother got during the day was when Macie went to sleep.

"Okay," I said, motioning for Jay to follow me to the safety of my room. Then he blew the whole thing, saying, "Hi, Mrs. Costello."

And we'd almost made it.

Now that my mother knew we had a guest, she felt obliged to sit up and look at him.

"What's in the bag?" she asked, getting right to the point, setting the monkey on the coverlet so she could swing her legs over the side and stand up.

For a moment it looked as if Jay was going to obey his usual impulse to spill the beans, telling her that within the Safeway bag a woman cavorted like a lioness on grassy plains. I prayed that he could keep his fat mouth shut for one minute longer as I answered, "Comics." My tongue wrapped around the word, transforming it in the way that lies do, so that "comics" would never mean comics again.

"They will rot your minds, both of you."

She looked at me sternly, but not for any reason that mattered right then, then stepped into the bathroom and closed the door. This left only the monkey, rubbing his grape-sticky hands together, watching me with his tiny, judging mind.

We made our way past Macie's door and into my room.

Before I'd even closed the door Jay had seized the Rat Patrol from the shelf. I was about to object when I saw that he had finally let go of the bag. It waited on my desk. The exchange was complete.

He turned the radio on to KFRC. "Muskrat Love."

"Turn it down," I told him. "My sister's asleep."

"So?"

Jay didn't like Macie much. He was always asking me how old she was and when I said fifteen, he would laugh. One time he even called her a retard. I had to have a word with him. He didn't do it again.

Now that the Rat Patrol was his, he was feeling his oats. He felt the same way I had when I'd first rolled it across the floor. You could press it down with your full weight and it could take it.

I turned the radio down myself and crawled under my desk, into the space where your legs went, reaching up to take hold of the bag, pulling it down after me. I unrolled the top of the bag and looked into the darkness. I savored the moment.

I spread her on the red carpet and listened to the high dry grass whispering against her brown thighs in a field somewhere to the south. I held on tight, sitting beside her on that catamaran as she guided it through choppy Hawaiian seas, her blouse fluttering open in the wind.

"Jay," I said over the desk, "I'm going to marry one just like this."

"You idiot," he said, "you don't marry playmates. Nobody marries playmates."

But I would.

Eight
And That's the Way It Is

When I was growing up I thought we were always at war. From the time I was old enough to understand the TV, that's what I saw on the news. War, to me, was our country's natural and constant state, as unchanging as the forty-hour work week, as essential as oxygen. Once, when I lay inches from our TV, my wonder at the Apollo 11 astronauts bouncing around in their cool white suits was interrupted by a bunch of Army men who had killed a few hundred women, children, and old people in the village of My Lai. Another time Bing Crosby's *Christmas Special* was violated by the sobbing survivors of the bombings of Hanoi and Haiphong. And on more than one occasion my beloved Watergate hearings were interrupted by news from the other side of the world. Men in sweltering khaki shirts with microphones confided in us nightly, showing us red mud and rail-thin boys in uniforms so sweaty they seemed to merge with the wet air. They smiled and smoked when they weren't laid out on stretchers screaming like babies.

The word *Vietnam* was not welcome in the yellow house. It made my father cringe. "Isn't there anything else on?" he would say, squirming in his chair as my mother held her tongue and changed the channel. But down in the basement, where Macie and I would broadcast from our own insurgent station, Vietnam was fair game.

Once I had finished removing all the parts, I could actually fit inside my Magnavox, a pajama-clad anchorman. I honed my Walter

Cronkite voice on names like Saigon, Hanoi, Ho Chi Minh, and Premier Diem. And they were always good for a laugh. Words like An Loc, Ap Bac, Dien Bien Phu, and of course Du Quoc Dong never failed to reduce Macie to helpless fits of giggles. From inside the Magnavox, furrowing my brow and holding my notes just like Cronkite, I'd say, "Four hundred casualties were sustained today at Phan Dinh Phung," and she'd just die, cackling, rocking back and forth in the lotus position. It hurt so much she'd have to hold her stomach, but I'd keep going, relentless. "Phu Bai," I'd say, "Pol Pot," and she'd roll over on her back, yelping, "Jackie, *stop* it!" We were at war with a land of funny names.

On the last day of June, just when I was about to give up hope, an anonymous brown package addressed to me appeared on top of the mail on the table by the front door.

My mother regarded it. "You didn't buy more sea monkeys, did you?"

"No way."

"Well what is it?"

"Nothing bad."

She understood the truth to be the reverse. "It better not be anything like that foaming sugar. You made your sister sick with that."

In my room with the door shut, I opened the box. Inside, accompanied by a single sheet of mimeographed instructions, was a three-foot-long vinyl-insulated wire with an RCA jack at one end and a suction cup at the other. A device of elegant cunning, it would mate well with the old reel-to-reel recorder my father had kept in the back of his closet until two weeks earlier, when I had stolen it.

I crawled under my bed, hissing in three/four time, providing the snare drum accompaniment to the *Mission: Impossible* theme. Above me, slipped between bed frame and mattress ticking, was my favorite girl, smiling down from sky blue sheets. Beside her was a chisel, filched from my mother's paint box, which I now took down.

I pressed my ear to the floor and listened to the kitchen below, making sure that my mother was busy watching *Dialing for Dollars,* then I resumed the *Mission: Impossible* theme, slipping the chisel between the top edge of the baseboard and the peeling wallpaper.

The search for the perfect hidey-hole had been long and perilous. Many treasures had been sacrificed to my mother's unrelenting eye. By the time I was eleven my secrets had grown darker, the accompanying paraphernalia more incriminating. The need for a tamper-free storage place had become critical. I'd tried putting myself in my mother's place; if I were her, where would I look? But time and again she would foil me and I would forfeit something forbidden and precious. My mistake was always in underestimating my opponent; she could have worked as a border guard, so highly attuned were her suspicions and aptitude for detection. And although I knew better than to believe any hiding place inviolate, this one was as good as they came.

I pulled back on the chisel and pried off the baseboard. It came off easily because I had reamed out the original holes so the nails could move smoothly in and out, a technique learned from *The Great Escape.* Inside was a space fourteen and a half inches wide from stud to stud and three and a half inches deep between trim and exterior lath. Inside was my bag of lumbo, a brass pipe, a chunk of hash, and the reel-to-reel.

I unsnapped the leather case, found the *mic* hole, and plugged in my new device. It fit perfectly. Replacing the baseboard, reinserting the chisel into the bed frame, I held perfectly still and listened to the house.

The time was right for the Record-a-Jac.

At 3:00 P.M. the phone rang one and a half times. My mother picked up the yellow wall model in the kitchen.

In my parents' bedroom, I stuck the Record-a-Jac's suction cup to the handset on the obverse of the mouth piece, just as the instructions had described. It held tight, as promised. I lifted the handset slowly, watching the spring-loaded plugs rise with it. I did not do the *Mission: Impossible* music now. I did not make a sound. My hand was steady. The plugs stopped and a sliver of air appeared between them and the handset. Immediately that space was filled by tinny female voices.

I raised the handset no further. With my left hand I switched on the recorder and the reels began to spin. Now, holding my right hand utterly still, not allowing the handset to touch the twin forks of the cradle—the same way you do when playing the game Operation—I slipped a folded piece of shirt cardboard into the gap, an idea suggested in the instructions under the heading: *Professional Surveillance Techniques.*

Ever so slowly, I released my grip on the handset. The cardboard held, suspending the heavy handset just above the pegs, and I let out my breath, wiping imaginary sweat from my forehead.

The ladies chattered away. There was nothing to indicate that they were on to me. So far, so good.

Later, back in my room, I rewound the tape, plugged in the white plastic earphone, and turned the playback mechanism on. There was no sound for a long time, just some scratching and popping. I was getting worried. Had I been ripped off? Nothing. Not a peep. If I was ever in Lake Forest, Illinois, I would be sure to visit the men who had made this stupid contraption, and they would be sorry.

Suddenly a voice howled into my right ear and I scrambled to turn the volume down. Apologies were in order to the honorable technicians of the Record-a-Jac Company.

As I had suspected, the caller was my mother's friend Mrs. Palmer. She had known my mother for years and neither of them could understand why their sons had just never hit it off. If they'd only known.

82

First off, her son Gary told everyone who'd listen that he did it with his sister. While there was no way of knowing whether or not this was true, there was one other thing about him which had never been in doubt.

One day after school Gary Palmer sat down on the front steps of his house and displayed a striking talent.

Me and Jay and Gary and some other guys were shooting at each other in the street, zigzagging between parked cars like Steve McQueen, cap guns blazing, when Gary put down his pistol and walked up the steps of his house.

"Watch this," he'd said, looking down at me and the other guys. Then he turned around, sat down on the steps, and unzipped his pants. As long as I lived I would never forget what I saw next. There, on a flight of steps made of bricks twisted and blackened by the 1906 fire, Gary Palmer blew himself.

Now, you might think that you'd need a pretty big boner to pull that one off, but Gary's had been only about average for a nine-year-old. No, the magic lay in his ability to bend himself right in the middle, like a lawn chair.

I stood there with Jay and the other guys, my Colt revolver dangling in my hand, and watched him. I felt woozy. Things like that just did not happen in the middle of April afternoons with the distant sun shining in your eyes and sirens singing two streets over. Boys did not bend at the waist like yogis and fellate themselves. On that day, Gary Palmer committed social suicide, and he paid the price for his brazenness in the sum of hundreds of lunches eaten alone in the cafeteria for the next five years, even if he *was* the fastest runner in the class.

With one ear on the phone and the other on the door, I listened closely. I was surprised and disappointed to find that they were not talking about me. Eavesdropping teaches humility.

Mrs. Palmer said, "I saw on the morning show how these sea elephants meet on the same beach every year at the same time."

My mother cut in. "Oh, you mean elephant seals. I saw it, too. They come to mate, don't they?"

"Elephant seals. Okay. I thought since Gary's birthday is around that time I'd just put them all in the car and drive them down to see it."

Mrs. Palmer sounded dreary and bored.

"What a great idea." My mother, bucking her up.

"Well we can't afford to take them to the movies this year."

"I think it's a great idea."

"He's only twelve, for Chrissakes, what's he expect?"

They swore when I was not around.

"They'll love the elephant seals. I wish I'd thought of it." My mother was a kind of genius when it came to polite chitchat.

They went on this way for exactly nineteen-and-a-half minutes by my stopwatch. Gary's birthday was still several months away, and I was in possession of intelligence indicating that he would be treated to a trip to the beach in his mother's Country Squire to watch some kind of sea elephants along with ten of his pals, if he had that many. This was useful information. I laughed aloud from my listening post, contented. My operation had been a success.

At dinner, Arthur Rubenstein played a Beethoven sonata while we ate chicken potpie and Marcie asked us each in turn, earnestly, what we had for lunch that day. My father hardly ate a thing. He fell in and out of the conversation, slumping in his chair, abandoning us for Beethoven's cool sympathy. He had not been sleeping much at all and this deficit manifested itself in his repeated dozing off at the dinner table, behind the wheel, in front of the TV. Someday I would ask him why he wandered through the house at night, why he couldn't sleep. I would tell him how I was afraid of sleep myself. But for the moment I skewered up to twelve lima beans on a single fork and pictured my secret tape, safe inside my bedroom wall.

Just when we thought my father was fast asleep, his right hand darted up from his lap, startling Macie, and formed figures in the air, his arm an expressive limb attached to an unconscious conductor. His eyebrows ascended the creased expanse of his forehead. The music had enchanted him.

At that precise moment, my mother said, "Katie Palmer told me the funniest thing today." My father winced, his conducting hand forming a fist as if to grip the elusive a minor thread that was winding away across the front hall, back into the hi-fi. He nodded to let her know he had heard her and was fascinated, then snatched back the thread just as it was about to escape.

She went on: "She's going to take the kids to see the elephant seals mating as a treat on Gary's birthday."

Now he opened his eyes. The music had left him behind at the head of a mutinous dinner table. He released a breath, his chest deflating inside his shirt. He looked at her so absently you would never have known that he was seething.

"That's nice," he said, perhaps amazed for the hundredth time at what he perceived to be an uncanny ability of hers to speak at exactly the moment a piece of music reached its greatest heights. Either she didn't hear it at all and it was just coincidence, so he was overreacting, or she did hear it and, sensing its power over him, acted swiftly to pull him back to her bosom, to reality. Stranger yet, perhaps the music itself somehow compelled her to talk, conversation being her soul's particular response to beauty. He tipped his head back, considering the ceiling, musing at the many different ways music affected us.

After a moment, he returned to us. "Can she do that?" he said, attacking the problem.

"Do what? What're you talking about?"

"I mean, the elephant seals . . . they're there to mate, aren't they? Should she put a bunch of children through that?"

"They're just *seals*, William. You can't see all that much."

They talked on, taking my secret with them. My cover had been blown by my mother's instinctually open nature, and the taped conversation, whose only value had lain in my secret possession of it, became worthless the moment she'd immersed it in the stream of everyday discourse. Still, it had been a fairly successful first effort, and boded well for future clandestine assignments. Like Sam Ervin, I would get to the bottom of things.

Nine
We Interrupt This Program...

Before breakfast my father crouched in front of the TV. Dan Rather had a special report: The White House announced that morning that Vice President Spiro Agnew would resign. As near as I could tell, Agnew didn't pay his taxes, took some bribes, and got free liquor and groceries delivered right to his house. Dan Rather said he could even go to jail for it, which caused my father to pull back his lips, exposing his enormous teeth. He pushed closer to the screen, a giant who might have torn that tiny Dan Rather limb from limb at any moment.

"Could you turn it down, please?" my mother said from the stove.

Pained, he knit his eyebrows in her direction and made sure she noticed him switching it off.

"You didn't have to turn it off."

"Oh, it's all right," he said bravely.

They were not talking about something again.

No one made another sound until breakfast was well under way and Macie said, "Remember when I used to climb into your crib with you, Jackie?"

"Yep."

"You used to hug me, remember?"

"Yep."

My father looked at me and narrowed his eyes. He looked at Macie, and by that time his face was just awful.

"Macie, look me in the eyes," he said. This was the only way to get her to really understand something. "Do you remember what we said about the crib?"

"Yes, Daddy."

"We said we would not talk about it, right?"

"I'm sorry, Daddy."

"You won't do it anymore."

"No, Daddy."

I noticed for the first time that Macie was now almost as tall as he was.

He leaned forward and said, "Macie, use your napkin."

Now, Macie often got a good deal more food on her face than in her mouth and it was usually best to just wait till she'd finished to wipe it off, but today he was in the kind of mood where the sight of Quaker oats smeared all over his fifteen-year-old daughter's face really burned him up.

Macie dabbed at her chin, missing the mark entirely. Suddenly my father's hand fired across the table, snatched the napkin, and rubbed her face hard.

"William," my mother said, trying to calm him, but he didn't listen. When Macie's hands floated up to rescue her poor face he pushed them back down into her lap. All of his anger at Dan Rather was in that napkin.

"Almost got it," he said.

If you didn't look too closely, my mother might have seemed fine, but if you did look closely you could actually watch her eyes get bluer, darkening. Lately, when my father spoke to her, her face would blanch with the effort of swallowing some savage response. She was climbing the walls.

She'd been watching the hearings too, though she would never admit it, and always turned them off when I came in. With the shutters drawn and the industrious birds calling to us from outside, she and I opted to stay indoors and watch Watergate unfold for as long as it took. I suppose we both had our reasons.

"William, stop," she said as she took the napkin from him.

Macie was crying now. I figured it would have to end soon, but then my mother started in on Macie's face too, even though there was no food left there at all.

If Macie had just kept quiet about that damned crib, this never would have gotten started. It always made him mad when she babbled, but for some reason that crib would really set him off.

I stared down at my plate. Ordinarily, I would have tried to lighten things up with a little humor, but not this time. I didn't even say anything when Pie cut a ripe one over by the furnace register and it drifted over all of us in sour counterpoint to our thoughts.

"Missed a little there," my mother said, still rubbing away.

Finally it was just too much for Macie and she started to hiccup, which was what always happened when she cried too hard.

"There," my father said, "that's better."

The thing they were not talking about was Macie.

Ten
The Break-in

The whole idea came to me one day in early July. I was down in the basement, working on my Magnavox. I was making a sign out of construction paper that, when complete, would drape over the back of the set, so that you could read the word NEWS over my left shoulder. I had taken to wearing my First Communion coat and tie while I was on the air. I hadn't decided which station I would be on yet, but I was leaning toward Channel Five, because that was Walter Cronkite's channel.

I found myself wondering once again what kind of people would throw their TV out into the street in the middle of the night. Our neighbors were strange people, we knew that. Hippies. Some of the last of their shaggy breed to roam the seven hills of San Francisco, somehow having missed the migration back into the forgiving mainstream of society. Rogues.

I had been observing them. The guy who seemed to be the man of the house had greasy black hair that hung to the middle of his back and a bearded face that always looked somehow out of focus, like he was peering through a grimy window. I watched from my bedroom window as he worked fitfully on a Volkswagen microbus he'd somehow gotten into their back yard. I wished I'd seen him bring it in because I really didn't think the space between our two houses was wide enough. I don't see how he could've done it. Maybe he disassembled it and carried the components in at night, then quietly reassembled it back there. But why? I couldn't understand what the lady of the house, the one with the pretty voice, saw in him.

And then there was the girl.

My interest in the hippies, born when their colorful house vomited forth that twenty-nine-inch Magnavox on election night, had grown steadily ever since, encouraged by their dark comings and goings, nourished by the absence of any solid information. I needed to know more.

Obviously, I couldn't just go over there and knock on their door, like you would've done with normal neighbors. If I did that, I might never return. No, if I was ever to find out what they were up to over there, it would have to be a clandestine operation.

Outside the basement windows, cars slipped past at eye level while my dull scissors crunched through the thick red paper and one thought led to another until I found that I had decided to sneak into the neighbors' house.

It took me forever to convince Jay to join me. I assured him that we wouldn't be stealing anything, that we'd just be gathering intelligence, like the Watergate burglars. He kept returning to his original sticking point, though, saying serenely that it was still just plain *wrong*. He was always saying things like that. On more than one occasion I found myself wondering what I was doing with such an uptight friend. But he was only a human boy after all, and so had a normal appetite for cruelty and adventure. All I had to do was tell him that I had heard rattling chains over there, presumably from a child manacled cruelly to the attic wall. I told him stories of screams past midnight, of pools of blood, and most titillating of all, of a mysterious ghost girl with anesthetic eyes who only came out at night. By the time I finished, he was so excited that the whole thing might as well have been his idea.

So it was that on a Saturday night in July, long after my parents had gone to bed and after the first Creature Feature had ended, Jay and I prepared to go forth, the tips of our ears cold, our faces hot

91

with anticipatory guilt. It was never easy sneaking out at night when your father was an insomniac and might have been bumping around the house at any and all hours, but I had some experience in this. I had not been caught yet.

I turned off my bedroom light and we watched two minutes pass on my clock's luminous dial, silently, letting our eyes adjust to the darkness, also ensuring that anyone who might have been just idly watching my lit window, as I was sure people often did, had now found something better to do with themselves.

I adjusted my commando cap, which was actually a navy blue ski cap from which I had excised the offending snow white fuzzy ball that sprouted from the crown. I felt guilty as soon as I had performed the amputation. I felt guilty now. My mother had given me that hat.

The night was cool and foggy.

I went first, slipping under the screen and swinging my leg over the sill. I made my way down the drain pipe, but Jay didn't budge.

"Come on, man," I hissed at him, and then I felt the pipe shudder and it occurred to me that it might be a good idea to get off of it before he applied his entire weight. Jay must have weighed a hundred pounds and I didn't want to end up crashing backward away from the house, the drain pipe still clutched in my hands the way Don Knotts did in that stupid movie. So I shinnied down past the dark kitchen window and let go.

My sneakers slapped silently onto the concrete.

I looked back up into the narrow slot of sky between fence and house. Past Jay's descending bulk and the outcrop of the eave, the fog was flying by really fast, illumined from below by our city, endless shades of dark passing, light passing. This fog's momentum was so great it tried to pull my eyes along with it and for a second I lost my balance. Right then, up past the fog, the first Skylab crew hung in low earth orbit. There were no more Apollos.

Jay landed beside me, just the way I'd taught him.

"Phew," he said.

Our plan was to scale the concrete retaining wall that divided our lot from the Little Sisters of the Poor, then inch our way along it, carefully straddling the barbed wire until we had crossed the property line.

We climbed, the dark spume of spider webs trailing across our throats. Through the concrete, we felt the rumbling of Saturday night cars out on the street. When we reached the top, Jay giggled at the sound of a neighbor man pissing obliviously into his toilet and I stood up straight like a tightrope walker.

I doubt that anything could ever carry as much weight or as much joy as that secret midnight voyage of ours. On top of the wall, the fog whipping past us, we were forbidden commandos, immortal and cruel. Though I knew it might endanger our mission, I couldn't help but whistle aloud the theme from *The Great Escape*. I thought that it was too bad that our school didn't offer a sport where you had to climb trees, houses, walls. If it did, I would have been the team captain. I was sure that Jay's tendency to fall flat on his face at the drop of a hat would have disqualified him, though.

"Sorry, man," he whispered suddenly, having stepped on my left foot.

"It's cool."

We had crossed the property line. Time to be still and observe. We were now trespassing.

The neighbors' house was pretty quiet that night. It looked as if they'd gone out, even though there was a light on upstairs. Most people, even hippies, left a light on when they went out to discourage burglary.

I glanced at Jay. The upstairs light shined a perfect rectangle onto each of his eyes, which were wide. "What if there's someone in there?" he stuttered.

"What if there is?" I growled. Then, before he had a chance to answer, I slapped him on the knee and said, "Let's go." I dropped into their yard, landing in a heap, but A-Okay. I looked back up at Jay.

"Hey, Jack," he said.

"Come *on.*"

"Jack?"

"That's my name, moron. Come on." I talked fast, trying not to give him a chance to say what I knew he was about to say.

"I'm not going." There it was.

"What?"

"I'll wait for you here, okay?"

"Pussy."

Even as I said it, it was clear to me that a hundred scornful *pussies* couldn't change his mind. He wouldn't budge. "All right, gay boy," I spat, since we were obviously past the *pussy* point, "Wait here if you want."

I had nothing more to say to him.

Alone now, with the determination of one betrayed, I set out on the long trip across the back yard.

It was like *Sanford and Son* back there, a real dump. I had to step over craters lined with broken glass, past heaps of bottles of all shapes and colors, threading my way between silent engine parts and a kid's old red wagon, past the man-of-the-house's gutted Volkswagen. Everywhere were dead brown potted plants that may well have been loco weed. I kicked a bottle and cursed myself as its *clink* escaped across the yard.

At last I reached the back porch, the point of no return. I looked back at the wall and Jay waved at me lamely. He hadn't moved an inch, the pud. I looked forward to rubbing his face in his cowardice for the rest of the summer. He'd probably try and make me promise not to tell anyone else, but there was no need; I wouldn't have told a soul.

The hippies' house loomed over me now and I could smell it, smell curry and fish sticks and onions and coffee. I heard the solid creakings of its pre-Earthquake frame. I walked to one side of the steps, where they were more solid, and my ingenuity was rewarded with silence. I was not so fortunate with the rest of the porch, though;

its boards groaned so loudly with my first step that I decided just to make a break for it. I dashed over a mine field of cracking lumber, stopping directly beneath the window I had had my eye on, the one just to the right of the back door. Now it was quiet. Now I was really spooked.

A nervous fart escaped me.

With shaking hand, I reached into my back pocket and pulled out the hand trowel that my mother used to root around in the garden. A foghorn blew and no light reflected off the rusty old trowel. The Zodiac lurked around the city on nights like this one.

I inserted the trowel blade between sash and window and pink paint crumbled away, revealing Mr. Wicker's old white paint beneath. It was unlatched, all right. Why should they have latched it? They were, after all, the kind of people the rest of us locked our own windows against each night. I pried downwards on the trowel handle and with a screech the window slid upward enough for me to slip my fingers in. I stuffed the trowel back into my pocket and used both hands to lift the window. It crunched and the lead sash weights rang, heavy bells tolling inside the hollow walls, lowering correspondingly as the window rose.

I could hear their refrigerator humming. It scared me, the way the window waited so wide open.

Traffic whispered by, hushed by fog. Back in my house the TV was still warm and if I had been there, I'd have been watching the second Creature Feature. I promised I would never do this again.

I climbed through the window.

It was dark in there but my eyes were adjusting, falling on rows of Ball jars containing dried beans and grains and what might have been severed fingers. I had stumbled onto a cannibal's pantry. From the side window I could see my own bedroom window. I had watched the hippies many times from up there. I wondered if they had ever watched me.

Suddenly, with a tiny rattle, the refrigerator shut off. The silence it left in its wake roared into my ears. Too late, I discovered that its hum had been masking another sound. I heard it, faintly now.

Something was in there.

Again and again something squeaked, and as my eyes gave shape to the darkness, they detected movement. Impossible. There, in a depthless pool of darkness to the right of the refrigerator, something hairy lurched from side to side. I couldn't breathe. That creature was the source of the squeaking sounds. Was that a grinding wheel it was turning? Was it sharpening a knife? What well-marbled human hams must have dripped within that Frigidaire!

My mother had been right, those comic books were no good.

The monster was grinning at me, I saw that now. I didn't want to die yet. I still wanted to go to the moon. Everyone was going to get to go to the moon. It would be as commonplace as riding in an airplane.

My commando cap itched like crazy.

That infernal *squeaking.*

Jay had been right to stay out of there and fifty years from now he would tilt his head back and consider the reflected fire flickering on the ceiling of his study. Then he would shake his gray head only slightly, clearing the cobwebs, wondering what on earth had made him think of me, a boy who had died a horrible death so many years before. A chill would pass through him and he would pull his cardigan tighter about him, returning to his leather-bound book.

Footsteps approached from the other side of a door. The creature stopped its grinding and commenced to squeal frantically.

I was going to shit a brick.

From behind a closed door, a voice said, "Shut up, Boodle."

Boodle?

The door opened. The light was switched on. I was caught.

I had been in the dark for so long that the glare hurt my eyes like I was one of the Mole People. I was standing in the middle of someone else's kitchen, rubbing my eyes, and I couldn't move. As my vision cleared I saw, beside the refrigerator, a large wire cage. Inside the cage, a long-haired, bloated guinea pig squealed.

"There's my Boodle. There's a good Boodle," said the hippie woman, who did not even notice me as she went to the refrigerator.

I needed to scratch under my commando cap but if I moved she'd see me.

Still oblivious, she opened the refrigerator and pulled out a crescent of iceberg lettuce. I had to get out of there. She was about to give the lettuce to the guinea pig when something made her look over her shoulder. Me.

She screamed.

This proved to be what I needed to finally spur me to action. Without her scream, I might have stood there all night. I wheeled and tore toward the window, sneakers flailing. My hands slapped the sill and I vaulted outside, hitting the porch on all fours.

"Jackie?" Someone was calling me.

I dove over the railing, disappearing into the darkness.

"Jackie?" It was the hippie lady, calling after me with her Amazing Grace voice. I was wondering what it was about that voice that bothered me when I got tangled in an old Big Wheel and fell to my knees. I screamed and got up and didn't stop moving, aware of nothing else until I saw Jay's face. Only then did I realize that I had somehow made it across the yard and scrambled up the bare wall.

I found that Jay was afflicted with my former paralysis. His jaw hung open. He made no effort to move. "Hunno," he said.

We made it back to my room and lay panting in the dark as neighbors raised voices outside, doors were slammed, lights switched on. There was a long silence. How had she known my name?

Jay said, "What happened to your hat?"

The doorbell rang.

Oh Jesus, oh Jesus.

"See, I told you it was wrong," said Jay, but I wasn't listening to him. I got up and silently opened my door. I made my way down the hall and peered over the banister.

My father stood at the open front door in his plaid robe. From this high angle, all I could see on the porch beyond him was a skirt. Beneath the skirt, feet. Bare feet. The hippie lady.

She spoke quietly. So did my father.

He said, "Was anything broken. Anyone hurt?"

"Oh, no, no."

"Good, I'm glad."

She said, "I was just worried about him."

She was worried about me?

She held my commando cap out to him and the shock on seeing it was like someone had dumped a bucket of pins and needles onto my scalp. There was no denying it now. She had proof. Evidence. There would be hell to pay.

I could hear my father saying, "But Jackie's hat has one of those little balls on top of it, I think." The removal of which might have been the worst of my crimes.

She said something I couldn't hear.

"Oh, well," he said, and took the hat. Only she didn't let go of it right away. Their hands lingered there together for a moment, both holding onto my hat.

She was pretty.

Suddenly my parents' door opened and my mother, half-asleep, called, "William?"

The hippie lady let go of the hat. My father took it and her pretty feet crept away across the porch as he closed the door.

I made a break for it, scrambling on all fours down the hall and around the corner where I waited, listening.

"Are you down there?" my mother said.

"Everything's under control," he said.

"Who's there?"

98

"Our neighbor. They're gone now."

"What neighbor?"

"That hippie fellow. The one with the beard."

What?

He went on: "He said the station wagon was blocking his driveway again."

"Nonsense," my mother said.

Nonsense, indeed.

I heard him wander into the kitchen. She went back to bed.

Back in my room, with me on the floor in my sleeping bag and Jay on my bed—guests should always get the bed—I ran silently through the night's events. As Jay snored like a pig, I unwound the chronological knots, slowly revealing all I had missed at the time. So many unanswered questions. How did she know my name? Who the hell were these hippies anyway? How did they get that Volkswagen back there? Was there a tunnel of some kind? Did they ever get another TV?

But most important, why had my father lied?

In the morning, my cap was hanging on my doorknob without a word. No punishment, no hell to pay. Not yet, at least.

Eleven
Lullaby

Lying awake in bed with my glossy playmate one night in July, I heard the slack old window screen touch the glass periodically, gently, with the wind, while my father played the piano far away. I heard Macie singing one of her favorite songs: "My uncle roasted a kangaroo, wasn't that a terrible thing to do?" It was funny to hear a nearly grown girl's voice singing a children's song. The sheets lay across my chest with loving certainty. Outside, the trees held still as the fog had its way with them, licking their leaves with a dogged tongue. The foghorns blew.

I didn't know how long I'd been watching her look back over her shoulder at me, her demure hand tracing the back of her thigh, when the hallway carpet was crushed by someone's approaching feet. I flipped the pages shut, shoving her disrespectfully under the sheets, and she pressed coolly against my leg in the instant before my mother opened the door.

I had barely shaken from my head the hissing of the surf on my playmate's special warm beach in time to greet her. With pounding heart and loins I watched as my mother sat on the edge of the bed, creasing the blanket barely ten inches from the incriminating spine of the *Playboy*. I smelled the turpentine she had spilled on her shirt. She was half-asleep, exhausted from a long day of not speaking her mind.

"Why aren't you listening to the radio?" she asked, catching me at a loss. I was totally unprepared for such a simple query. I was ready for something along the lines of *Did you know that gaping at naked women in magazines while pleasuring yourself manually is a ghastly abomination?*

After a moment, I said, "There's nothing on."

"There's nothing on the boob tube either," she said. That word. Had she meant to make me flinch just then? How much did she know?

She went on: "Summer's sure going fast. We're more than half-way, aren't we?"

"Yep."

"Sixth grade, wow."

"Yep."

"You'll be twelve."

Again, "Yep."

I could hear the piano more clearly now that the door was open. She hummed along with it for a moment. My mother had a beautiful voice. She could sing as well as anyone on the radio, or on TV, but I couldn't help but be embarrassed now when she asked, "Would you like to hear a song?" I was too old for this, and she should have known it, but under the circumstances, with my damning evidence right within her reach, covered only by a layer of sheet and blanket, I thought it best not to object.

"Sure," I said, and she began:

"My lover was a logger,
there's none like him today.
If you'd pour whiskey on it
he would eat a bale of hay."

This had never been one of my father's favorite songs, whether because it was not classical or because of the subject matter, I don't know. Perhaps he felt inadequate beside the mythical logger.

101

"He never shaved his whiskers
from off his horny hide,
He'd just drive them in with a hammer
and bite them off inside."

I stared past her hair at the Wile E. Coyote–shaped water spot on the ceiling. I shimmied away from the cold magazine, which suddenly repelled me.

"My lover came to see me
upon a frosty day,
He held me in a strong embrace
that broke three vertebrae.
He kissed me when we parted,
so hard he broke my jaw,
I could not speak to tell him
he'd forgot his mackinaw."

I thought she was going to sing the whole thing. It had been a long time since she had sung me a lullaby. Now she just sang to the monkey. When I was littler she would sing to me more nights than not, songs like "Blood on the Saddle" and "Streets of Laredo." Sometimes she would read Agatha Christie books to me—mysteries like *Murder in Mesopotamia* or *The Murder of Roger Ackroyd*—to help me get to sleep in that room far away down the long hall. Now, with all the secrets I had to keep, I was grateful for that long hall, and the same voice that once warmed me, vanquishing all fear with such ease, now had something in itself that needed vanquishing. I could almost hear it; somewhere in the sound of her voice floated the reason she was singing to me. It seemed unlikely that within those fragile notes lay the capacity to save the voice from what ailed it, but the voice went on anyway, determined and sweet. The song that used to banish my tears now coaxed them from the blinking eyes of the singer.

"The weather, it tried to freeze him,
it tried its level best.
At forty degrees below zero
he buttoned up his vest."

My father's piano had long since drowned in her song, but the sudden chattering of the monkey, carried from the kitchen by the furnace register, could not be so easily ignored.

"Chee! chee! chee!"

My mother stopped singing. She cocked her head to the side. "I wonder what *he* wants?" she asked, kissing me absently, light twinkling in her undersea eyes as she rose to go. She said "Goodnight," leaving the door open as she disappeared down the hall, leaving behind the scent of lipstick and turpentine.

With one eye on the empty hallway, I moved the magazine away from me, sliding it under the bed. Lullabies were supposed to help you sleep and I felt like this one might have done some good. For once I wasn't scared, so I decided to chance it. I turned off the light.

But I was restless. A song left unfinished bothered me more than anything. With my eyes on the clock's green dial, I whispered to the pillowcase:

"It froze clear down to China,
it froze to the stars above.
At a thousand degrees below zero
it froze my logger love.
And so I lost my lover,
and to this cafe I come,
And here I wait 'til someone
stirs his coffee with his thumb."

Twelve
A Small Fugitive

I was sitting at the Hermans' kitchen table eating sugar-glazed pinwheels and snails straight from the package when suddenly that giant bumblebee appeared on the TV screen. I cursed its striped face as it beamed down at those happy children.

I didn't trust that bee. It looked like it might turn mean at any second. Suddenly emitting a farting thunder, it would catapult into the sky, hauling those adoring children to the place where the air grows thin. And they wouldn't let go, either. How could they? They loved the creature too much. As they rose, their eyebrows would gradually freeze to white caterpillars, and just before they took their final breaths, these last words would chatter from their lips:

"Bum-bum-Bumblebee, Bumblebee tuna,
I love Bumblebee, Bumblebee tu-u-na."

I watched the hated bumblebee, now made mythic by clever cameras. It rose above the polo grounds and for just a moment, there in the distance, I thought I saw a familiar boy. High in an out-of-focus eucalyptus tree, wearing a yellow T-shirt, he stood higher even than the great bumblebee itself. He could've been in that commercial, but he had better things to do.

The bee vanished and Senator Howard Baker leaned back in his squeaking chair, laughing at a joke I must have just missed, and asked

Anthony Ulasewicz, a former New York policeman who had worked for the White House, "What do you mean, a pretty good wireman?"

"Well a wireman, in uh, in police parlance, would be anyone who's familiar with applying wiretaps, any type of surveillances by electrical means, and so forth."

He talked just like a New York cop should. I thought he was probably wearing a gun under his coat.

I hollered for Jay to come see; this was important.

The last few days the hearings had been getting down and dirty—that's what Mr. Herman called it—getting right into the burglary instead of all that slush-fund business. Now, provocatively, Baker asked Ulasewicz whether he could have done a better job than the men who had gotten caught in the Watergate.

"Well, I tell you," the cop answered, "no retired man in the New York City Police Department would become involved in a thing like that, and if he had to, for whatever reason it was, he wouldn't 'a walked in wit an army. He woulda probably walked in like any decent, common-looking citizen, laid something in the right place, and that woulda been the end of it for a long time."

Jay stood next to me now, his ball under his arm.

"You see that?" I nudged him. "He said he could've done a better job than McCord and the others."

"Who's McCord?" He lifted his shirt, fanning himself.

"Man, you stink. McCord's the guy who ran the whole burglary, remember?"

"Oh."

He sat down and stuffed a snail into his mouth.

"And I tell you what," I said. "Me and you could've done a better job than either of them, at least I could've."

"Sure." Muffled by the sugar-coated snail.

"Shit," I said, the very sound of the word filling me with pride, "the bugging's the easy part."

I stopped myself just short of telling him about the Record-a-Jac.

"It's breaking in that's tricky," I said. I knew this from experience. "Shhh!"

Jay punched me in the shoulder. His father was home. From the hallway, Mr. Herman's hissing breaths grew nearer.

All summer I had tried to be like Mr. Herman. I stole the Camel straights he kept in wooden boxes, just like the ones in old movies. This drove Jay crazy, not because he was afraid his father would think that he stole them but, as usual, because it was *wrong*. He was scandalized every time I lit one. I was getting damn good at smoking them, too. All summer I had tried my hand at being laconic, like Mr. Herman. I tried hard to talk less, but I was not successful, owing to a quirk of my character that would not allow me to keep my stupid mouth shut. I was sure that I could be quiet when it counted, though. If the enemy were torturing me, for instance, I would never crack. It irritated me, the way Jay was more closemouthed than I could ever have been without even trying. It must have been in the blood.

Mr. Herman murmured, "How goes the war?" as he sidled into the room.

How could someone so large move so quietly? He shed his sheepskin and stood behind me, smoking, clamping his hand onto my shoulder.

"The cop's something, isn't he?" he said.

He must have been listening on his car radio. Whenever the subject was Watergate—and Watergate was the only subject that summer—Mr. Herman would direct his comments at me. Jay showed little aptitude for, or appreciation of, political scandal, but my inchoate fascination seemed to mesh with his father's own fervor.

Mr. Herman almost whispered, "Looks like the Plumbers are taking a beating."

That summer the word *plumber* had taken on a new meaning for us, but to those who worked in the White House, it was nothing they didn't already know. In July of 1969, four days before the first men had landed on the moon, a presidential staff member was heading up the stairs from the basement of the Executive Office Building, across the street from the White House, when he saw a new sign on the door to room 16. It was blue, shaped like a shield. It said "Plumbers."

Curious, the staff member opened the door without knocking and found a young, crew-cutted man drumming his fingers on an empty desk. The staff member asked what the sign was all about, and the crew-cutted man giggled.

"I'm a plumber," he said. "I fix leaks. Like it?"

The crew-cutted man was David Young. He and Howard Hunt, Gordon Liddy, and Bud Krogh had been known collectively as the Plumbers. It wasn't long before they weren't just stopping information leaks from the White House to the press; soon their activities included the kind of operation that had gone awry at the Watergate. Those in the know knew about them from the start, but the Plumbers had managed to conceal their presence from the rest of us until that summer. Now, in the light of public knowledge, the harmless moniker they had chosen for themselves had assumed an aspect at once sinister and ridiculous.

Jay scraped his chair back and got up, a half-eaten pinwheel careening from his mouth. He went outside without a word and shortly we heard his ball resume its thumping against the garage door. Mr. Herman was so absorbed in Ulasewicz's damning testimony that he didn't even notice his son's departure. He lit another Camel and I ate another snail, and we both stared at the screen, two silent guys who knew the score.

The phone rang and Mr. Herman answered it.

"Yes," he hissed into the receiver. He listened for a moment, then he grinned. He handed the phone to me, grinning wider. "It's for you," he said, adding, to my horror, "It's your mother."

I took the phone, no longer cool. Cool guys didn't have mothers. She was in a high state, all right.

"The little monster got away," she wailed into the phone, not really meaning it. I knew instantly who she meant, and I told her that I'd be right home. The monkey had escaped, and I was the only one who could get him back.

I found her and Macie out in the yard, craning their necks to look up at the eucalyptus and liquid ambar trees that rose from the old people's home. My mother held the monkey's red dish. Inside the dish, meal worms slalomed between his favorite green grapes. She told me that the monkey had gotten out of his cage and that one of the dogs—here, she lashed her eyes at Pie, who curled up in fear and crawled under the collapsing chaise longue—had chased him out through the dog door and over the fence.

Macie wasn't about to say anything to contradict the story. She knew better. She sat down on the chaise, and it creaked, and she reached underneath it to pat Pie's head, soothing him.

I looked around the yard and pieced together a more plausible explanation. I saw the mystery book open on the chaise cushion with its mother-sized impression, and the grape skins beside that. As far as I knew, the monkey was the only one around there who skinned his grapes. I rubbed one of them between my thumb and forefinger. Still wet. I looked at my mother, who turned away, avoiding my eyes.

That was all I needed to know to reconstruct the scene: It had been a nice afternoon; the backyard was sunny and warm for once, so my mother had dragged the chaise out of the garage, fetched the monkey, opened *The Murder of Roger Ackroyd,* and stretched out in the sun. Before long she had fallen asleep with a mystery and a monkey resting on her chest. The monkey had waited until he saw his chance. As soon as she'd fallen asleep, he made his move. I looked at the unjustly accused Pie, and he blinked, confirming my hypothesis with his brown eyes. Mystery solved. Living with my mother afforded Macie and me the opportunity to discover the truth for ourselves.

This was where my special talents came in handy. When it came to climbing, I was the one you wanted to call. "Have you tried the marshmallows yet?" I asked her, rolling up my sleeves.

"Not yet. Do you think that's such a good idea?"

"Yep." I watched as she squinted at the high branches. I understood her reluctance. Marshmallows were traditionally the last resort, and if he refused them, we would have no further recourse. Marshmallows represented the pinnacle of monkey pleasure.

"Where was the last place you saw him?"

"Straight ahead there, about ten o'clock high." She and I were fluent in fighter pilot lingo. "That was about ten minutes ago."

I studied the place she indicated for a moment, fixing it in my mind, and then I started climbing the wall.

"Watch out for the nuns," said Macie, who had managed to coax Pie a short distance out from under the chaise. He now rested his head mournfully between her red sneakers. She had a point about the nuns. Those Little Sisters of the Poor, the ones who looked after the old people, did not welcome trespassers.

I reached the top of the wall and stepped over the barbed wire. "Careful," my mother said, sucking air in through clenched teeth. "Watch that wire." It made her nervous, but what could she do?

"Watch out for the nuns, Jackie," Macie said once more for good measure, her hair hanging over her eyes as her hand frittered with Pie's ears. She was the last thing I saw before I dropped out of sight behind the wall.

I oriented myself, finding my objective, the memorized silhouette of that certain tree, and started walking.

I could hear him up there, chattering. The eucalyptus leaves were crisp underfoot, their dryness the result of three consecutive warm days, and they made a lot more noise than I would have liked. I was accustomed to sneaking around in the nighttime, when everything was moist and silent. The whole place smelled like a cough drop.

Through the trees, I could make out the outline of the old people's home. No one was moving there, no one was outside, and so I proceeded. I turned, scanning the leafy canopy above me, and when the sun broke through, its brightness burned my eyes. I rubbed them hard, seeing stars. I stopped and listened. Traffic wrapped in leaves. A dog barking on through another afternoon. The crash of dishes from the old people's cafeteria. And beyond all that, almost out of earshot, an exotic cry, unlike any other heard in the city, except at the zoo.

"*Chee chee chee!*"

He had moved to another tree, farther from our house, and was crying out louder, exulting with each acre he put between him and his confined past. I could see by the way he moved that he had discovered that the eucalyptus trees were filled with life, with insects, pods, and trickling menthol sap, with delicacies of the Australian sort, with worms that, to his miniature keen ears, probably cried out when you bit into them. They must have been far more satisfying than the lousy mealworms we gave him. I saw in his eyes that he feared nothing under the blue sky as he spread his arms and leapt to embrace the next branch, its peeling bark spreading seductively for him to work his fingers into, discovering lives that were his for the taking.

My mission was going to be difficult. Clearly, he didn't want to return, didn't want to have anything more to do with me or the rest of my family. Something had happened to him. Ravaged and intoxicated, belly swollen, he moved erratically, his muzzle dripping with the tastes and torments of freedom, a tiny libertine aloft. Monkeys are not known for their self-control, and this particular one had now flown far beyond any and all barriers of decency. He had departed our family's civilization, a peculiar world that had never understood him anyway. He celebrated this now, drizzling protein-heavy dung from his superior height, leaving his first mark on this newfound, borderless country. It splattered behind me, and I realized that I had overshot the mark.

Doubling back, my feet moving faster, I was very close. The marshmallows swung inside the plastic bag I had looped through my belt and the tiny choke chain in my pocket jingled hopefully. I ran faster. If one of the old people were to have looked out right then, he or she would have seen an eleven-year-old boy darting to and fro between the trees in the manner of a hallucinating savage.

There he was, nestled in the high crotch of a slender young tree, drifting with the wind, dreaming monkey dreams. He didn't even know I was there. Perfect.

Silently, I began my ascent. Suddenly he stopped moving. He stared off toward the Great Highway and his mouth gaped open.

I think he must have always thought that our house had been the only one in the midst of a mighty forest. But by the look on his face I understood that now he knew different. His hand opened, hope shattered, and he released a fuzzy bouquet of caterpillars, allowing them to patter to the ground below. I knew that he had realized there was no point in running anymore. As far as he could see were nothing but houses. Houses just like ours. White ones, pink ones, gray ones mounted the hills relentlessly. His future was carpeted with them. As far as he knew he was the last survivor of a noble, vanquished race. From high in the tree, he gazed down at San Francisco, and I saw a tear flow from his black eye.

"Monkey," I said.

There was no need for him to turn to see who it was. He knew.

"Monkey, look what I've got for you."

He was not at all surprised to feel my weight on his branch. It was with resignation that he welcomed me and my familiar ears, ears that he had bitten into in countless moments of rage. He even welcomed the cheap gooey pods that I offered as the chain slipped over his head.

"Jackie? Did you find him yet?" My mother was yelling far too loud. She was going to attract attention.

The monkey didn't even try to bite me as I carried him down from the tree. He just clung to my shirt, munching absently on the marshmallows. It was always funny to see the way they got stuck all over his face. My mother always had to wipe his muzzle for him. I guess monkeys just weren't meant to eat marshmallows.

The nuns were waiting for us at the base of the tree. There were two of them, and they wore big habits and things that looked like capes, as if they were superheroes. "Come down from there," one of them said, but I was already down. Black and white amidst the green, they stood atop their hidden legs and stared down at me. The first nun started to say something else but then stopped, staring.

People are usually pretty surprised to see the monkey, but for some reason this nun was really freaked out. So was the other one. Maybe they thought I had a rat or something. Maybe, living their sheltered life there in the convent, the Little Sisters of the Poor had never even seen a picture of a monkey. I wasn't sure if they had books in there. I doubted they had TV.

As these two brides of Christ continued to stare I began to wonder what was the matter with them and then I felt the monkey moving in my arms. I looked down. He was pleasuring himself, rapidly. I was used to this, so I guess I was as startled as the monkey was when one of them yelped.

I wanted to tell them that we went to church every Sunday, but then one of them took her companion's hand and they began to back away.

I said, "He does that when he's nervous."

In August, Walter Peel had a sleep-over and we all played strip poker down in his basement. Because there were no girls present, we were missing the whole point of the game and quickly grew bored, but sometime before dawn the party was salvaged when Walter reasoned that, since we were already mostly naked, we might as well streak.

We snuck out through the garage so as not to wake Walter's mother.

It was cold and foggy and the city was as silent as I'd ever heard it. We ran through the Haight Ashbury at four-thirty in the morning, eight naked prepubescent boys singing "Brown Sugar" together as their bare feet slapped the sidewalks. By choosing this hour to do it, we were missing the entire point of streaking, just as we had missed the point of strip poker. The point of streaking, as I later came to understand it, was not just to run naked, but to be *seen* running naked. Still, it was fun. The buildings flew past so fast they were invisible, but the eddies of blue and ivory fog sheared by my speed and the ten white toes flashing out before me were as sharp to my eyes as glass. That and Walter Peel's butt, which I kept a close eye on because I didn't know my way around his neighborhood while he, presumably, did. I was smiling.

When Walter stopped running it was such a surprise that I piled right into his back, and some guy named Jim piled into mine.

Catching our breath, we all watched as Walter looked up at the street sign. He scratched his head. I noticed that he was squinting, wrinkling his nose, and it was then that I realized that Walter was not wearing his glasses. The gray buildings all came into sharp focus then. My heart clutched itself beneath my cold skin. He was lost. We were all lost.

Walter, who over the course of the evening had drunk a great deal of his father's liquor and was in addition probably due for his hyperactivity medication, began to scream, kicking a *Chronicle* vending machine with his bare foot. He was, by that point, no longer any use to the rest of us.

I looked around at the other boys. Uniform expressions of shock were frozen on their faces as it all began to sink in. Houses towered over us. Walter's outraged screams slowly dwindled down to whimpers and the rest of us began to look at each other querulously, naked, keeping our eyes above the belt as the sun threatened to rise.

Jay was not with us, of course. He was inside, asleep in his pajamas in his duck hunter sleeping bag, the only one of us who was not cold and naked and lost because, of course, he felt that streaking was *wrong*.

We considered our options. Should we split up and scout the four compass points? Settle in and wait for help? Unable to decide, we covered ourselves with our hands as best we could and shuffled along the sidewalk, going nowhere in particular, afraid to hold still.

Just then a *Chronicle* delivery truck rattled around the corner and before we knew it a massive black woman wearing a Giants cap had dismounted from it and was opening the newspaper rack. She had already used her special key to open it and was lifting a stack of today's papers from the back of her truck when she saw us.

Walter stopped his moaning and looked up at her, the last to know. The street lamps shut themselves off. Dawn had come to the city.

We were all horrified to see that, instead of averting her eyes, she looked us brazenly up and down. And she grinned. An awful grin.

Our teeth chattered, but no one spoke. It was cold, the sun was coming up, and cars were beginning to rumble over the streets. Someone rudely honked their horn at us. One of us would have to ask directions of her, but who? We were now coming to understand the true nature of streaking, and we didn't like what we learned.

With one eye on us all the while, the woman finished loading papers into the machine, sliding a display copy into place so that we could read the headline: NIXON WON'T GIVE UP TAPES. Still, she made no move to depart. She just stood there, staring disdainfully down at each of us in turn, at each of our cold-shriveled members.

"Excuse me," Walter said, finally screwing up the courage to ask directions.

She tilted her gaze toward him. He took a step forward. She waited for him to state his case. For a moment it seemed like she was truly interested in what this naked eleven-year-old boy had to say. I even thought I saw sympathy in her eyes.

Then she laughed. A horrible laugh. A roaring, scornful laugh that turned Walter red from the neck up. She was climbing the steps of her van, still laughing, when I became aware of some strange music.

It came from the distance and it melded with her laughter. It grew louder, it was classical music, and it accompanied her departure, rising as she rattled off into the fog like a character in some comic opera.

The tune was unmistakeable—to me, at least—it was Beethoven's "Emperor Concerto." Now everyone heard it and we all looked up and down the street, peering into the fog, searching for its source. Suddenly, a car emerged from the fog. It moved along the far side of the street, blaring Beethoven from its radio, drawing toward us like a hearse.

It was my father's convertible.

It was impossible, but I was not surprised. This is what you get, I thought, he is omnipotent, after all. Paralyzed with shame, I resolved never to streak again.

I saw that my father was not wearing a tie or a hat and his short hair was free in the wind. The top was down. What was he doing with the top down at four-thirty in the morning? What was he doing out at all? There was no escaping him.

He hummed along with Beethoven, joy ringing in every note, taking both hands off the steering wheel to conduct the end of the first movement. On his face was a strange, unfamiliar smile. He was like some other person sailing his own foggy sea.

"Hey, Costello, isn't that your father?" said Gary.

I could not speak. I could not move. All I could do was await my father's judgment. I stood there on the sidewalk, naked, and hoped he would not notice us.

When he did, his jaw dropped open, but he didn't stop smiling. A bunch of naked boys, so what? Those days, in the Haight, nothing surprised you. Then he saw me, and his smile disappeared.

He zipped the convertible across the opposing lane, pulled up to the curb, hit the brakes. He turned off the ignition and regarded me. I could not for the life of me figure out what he was doing here. The Haight was enemy territory for him.

There was a silence.

"Is this what they call streaking?" he asked.

Some of us nodded our heads.

"I saw it on the Academy Awards," he said, and his smile, strangely, returned.

What was he up to? Where was the reprimand?

More silence. I noticed that he wasn't looking at me, wasn't meeting my eyes. I knew why. I knew what he was doing out here at four-thirty in the morning.

"Well, don't let me interrupt you," he said. "I'll let you get on your way."

I knew why he was being so cool.

He started the engine. Finally, one of us spoke. It was Walter, who had got us into this mess in the first place. Shivering, both hands coddling his groin, he asked, "Mr. Costello, do you know how to get to Cole Street?"

My father laughed. He actually laughed.

"Cole Street's five or six blocks that way," he said, pointing west. Then, for the first time, he looked at me.

He said, "I woke up and I had the idea that I'd forgot to lock up the office," though I hadn't asked for an explanation. He looked deep into my eyes, trying to fish out a smile. When he was unsuccessful, he looked away.

He was scared of me, and I didn't like it.

I wished we were alone, he and I, and that he would tell me the truth. This was some kind of a standoff and when it came right down to it both of us were naked. Each of us held our own secret hostage.

"It's five or six blocks that way," he repeated, nervous, pointing, starting up the convertible. Without looking back, he put her into gear, gave us one last wholesome wave of his hand, and pulled away.

You never knew what Walter Peel would do next. When he saw my father's bumper sticker, he made the finger and yelled, "*Fuck Nixon!*"

116

I felt bad for my father. That bumper sticker just seemed to bring out the worst in people.

This was not like looking down from my tree and seeing him at confession. It was not like hearing his Resistance fighter on the phone. I was out in the open. He could see me. For the first time he knew that I knew. Now he would have to do something. Or I would.

The convertible's right-turn indicator pulsed twice, softened by the fog, and then, just like that, my father was gone. I had never seen him so happy.

Thirteen
A Misspent Youth

The following night at dinner I ate my chicken in silence, knowing that my father was watching me. I couldn't tell if he was trying to figure out what to do with me or with himself. I got the feeling that he was tired, that he hoped our secrets would somehow go away, but while I may have just turned twelve, even I knew there was only one way to get rid of a secret.

Suddenly he started to tell a story, the kind of story I knew immediately was meant to leave me with a moral lesson, one whose purpose only he and I understood.

He told the story of Eddie, a man who worked in an office building in New York City years earlier, when my father had been young. Macie smiled and listened while my mother watched, bewildered; he was talking more than he usually did in a week. She knew nothing about the streaking incident, and for our own different reasons, neither my father nor I was going to bring it up.

Every day, the story went, this Eddie would greet my father as he entered the lobby of the conservatory of music he had been privileged for a time to attend. Though Eddie was known officially as the elevator operator, and wore the uniform of that office, he was never observed actually operating that conveyance. He was what my father called—diplomatically, in deference to Macie—"a little simple."

He told us that Eddie had had a semicircular dent in his skull, just below his hairline.

Eddie had been employed in that building for over twenty years before my father arrived, and had not always sported that dent in his head, just as he had not always had the intellect of a child. He was, in fact, originally hired to operate the elevator and had done so until one summer morning when he'd heard the sound of breaking glass out in front of the building.

Stepping outside, Eddie found that someone had shattered a liquor bottle on the sidewalk. He went to get a broom. At that moment, up on the eleventh floor, a secretary was saying to her boss what he could not have realized were meant to be her last words.

My father paused and took a sip here, the scent of his highball enhancing the setting; I smelled the tang of rye drifting up into poor Eddie's nostrils as he stood on the hot sidewalk and swept up the glass. This had been in July, and the glass had glinted up into Eddie's eyes so brightly that when something, some hunch, made him tip his hat back and look up into the sky, he saw spots. He heard a flapping sound above him, he blinked to clear the spots, but there was not enough time. The flapping was, of course, the sound of the secretary's flower-printed skirt being lifted over her head by the wind, a falling bouquet of lethal violets.

"He never knew what hit him," said my father.

I liked this story.

Eddie was released from the hospital, a gauze turban on his head, but it soon became apparent that he had sustained injuries beyond the cosmetic. Fortunately, the building's owners took pity on Eddie, a man who no longer knew how to read, and could, in fact, barely speak, but who still remembered how to sweep. Magnanimously, they decided that his pay would remain the same and that he would still be called the elevator operator, though he was no longer to be entrusted with the duties implicit in that title. The secretary survived with two broken legs, left Manhattan, and never attempted suicide again.

Back on the job, Eddie, in an eerie display of the extent to which

119

his memory had been erased, swept the sidewalk directly in front of the building's revolving doors each and every morning.

Once my father learned the details of the man's preposterous misfortune, the sight of Eddie and his broom never failed to make him cringe. He stopped staring at the dent in Eddie's head once he realized that the mark matched precisely the half-moon shape of the business end of a woman's high heel. It was just too much to bear, looking at it, once you knew.

"That's the story," said my father, staring into his glass of shimmering White Horses."

My mother belched.

Now that she had his attention, she said, "That's awful, William. What's the point of telling a story like that?"

"No point," he said, listening to the far-off cry of Mario Lanza on the hi-fi, "that's the point."

We were all looking at our chicken now.

"Jack," said my father.

Here it came.

"We have no control over some things that happen to us, so we must not be too quick to judge."

I pretended like I had no idea what he was talking about. Macie stood up and tried to clear the table. I had just been chastised through allegory, but I was not really sure what it had to do with me. My father's eyes began to wander. He didn't even notice when Macie took his plate away.

Perhaps he had been trying to tell me that in the same way Eddie would never have met up with the flying secretary if someone hadn't broken a bottle, I would never have seen my father the night before, in a place he shouldn't have been, looking happier than I'd ever seen him, had not Walter Peel forgotten to wear his glasses.

What I liked most about Eddie's story were the parts that my father left out, details I had been able to piece together over the years. Eddie provided me with a pair of eyes with which to view my father's past. Through those eyes, I saw the young pianist's hopeful arrival and inevitable departure from New York. Eddie had seen him daily, saw his young face with its yet-to-be-broken nose, saw him every day including the last one, the day when the Hungarian broke the news to him.

My father actually cried, there in the Hungarian's office. The Hungarian had been his idol and so had been the only man from whom he would have believed this news. He cried as the maestro crushed him from spine to soul, forever recharting his course with the simple malediction: "You are not good enough," and with that malediction took all hope from him.

Shortly thereafter, Eddie, my defective eyes and ears on the scene, watched my father walk through the revolving lobby door, duffel bag in hand, heading for the train station and the long trip back to the West. As he left, I imagined him casting his mind back through the war, through high school and elementary school, all those grades that had passed over him like the fog. Music had taken his childhood.

I pictured him leaving the conservatory. On the way out, at the sight of Eddie, he might have thought, It could be worse. Then he would have said good-bye to Eddie, and Eddie would have said good-bye to him, and moments later, having forgotten my father, would have returned to sweeping his same blank stretch of sidewalk. I wondered if Macie had been hit by a flying secretary, too.

Fourteen
Mission: Impossible

Just as summer was ending, Jay's mother discovered our hideout up in the crawl space. The strange thing was that we didn't even care, for the joy we had derived from keeping that secret was already lost, as was our delight in devouring each day the summer offered us. We had started arguing, we had lost our purpose, we had suffered a toxic glut of fun, so it was just as well that summer was coming to an end, because if someone can't even use a summer right, he might as well be back in school.

The crossing guard nodded at me and I nodded back as the doors of the 55 Sacramento flapped closed behind me. What do crossing guards do in June, July, and August?

Inside, in the hall, Dave Monk vibrated beside his locker, clutching a whole bundle of fresh new pencils to twiddle. When I chunked him on the upper arm, he droned, "Danger, Will Robinson!" in a voice that was a bit lower than I remembered. *Lost in Space* again. Dave was in a rut. Aside from his new, deep voice, which sounded funny coming from his stunted body, it was amazing how like himself he looked, how like the Dave I remembered from the last day of the fifth grade. How much like themselves all the others looked, as well, as if summer, in all its infinite power, really changed nothing.

Along with Dave and Walter and the rest were some new ones, some real doozies, like the new girl named Judy who already had boobs and sucked all day on individual serving-size packets of mustard stolen from the cafeteria, so that by the end of each class the floor surrounding her desk resembled the forest floor below an owl's roost, littered with the husks of tiny yellow animals. And the new boy named Chesney, with the unfortunate yet undeniable skeletal structure of an ape, which was exactly what he found himself being called before the first period was done. But aside from these new members, the sixth grade gradually revealed itself to be remarkably similar to the fifth, and two weeks after my twelfth birthday I stayed up even later than usual. My parents were having a party.

In my pocket was the Record-a-Jac.

I was in their bedroom, lying on a bed piled so high with coats that it resembled a wool and polyester yurt. From downstairs, boisterous piano chords rose and Pie returned again and again to the coats to read more news of the city. It was October, and cold, and Spiro Agnew had finally resigned.

The Record-a-Jac's companion in crime, the reel-to-reel tape recorder, waited under the bed.

Your mission, should you choose to accept it.

The trilling flutes from that great show filled my head like madness, and my chest and toes tingled. I had never attempted surveillance on this large a scale, involving scores of civilians, meaning people outside of the family.

I was preparing to cross some sort of line.

Whenever someone picked up the phone down in the kitchen, the phone beside me gave a little jingle of acknowledgment, and that little jingle, however anticipated, made me jump.

Time to hook it up. The procedure was second nature to me by now, and within seconds the reels were spinning.

Pie was the kind of ally everyone should have. He leaned against the inside of the closed bedroom door, ears and nose monitoring all activity outside of it, and if any danger approached, his tail would fan the air, alerting me. Right now he was still; all was safe. The tape rolled on.

Emboldened, with a half-dozen stolen conversations already under my belt, I actually lifted the phone to my ear while I was recording. The conversations had grown more and more interesting, and cryptic, as the night grew old and the singing louder. Once they intersected our house, the mysteries of other lives were mysteries no more.

"I'm drinking Virgin Marys," said the caller.

"The hell you are."

Behind the caller, our refrigerator slammed shut. Someone was singing "Edelweiss."

Another man called for a cab, shouting, "Hey, what's the address here?" his loud cigarette voice squalling like a needle dragged across a record.

"Just don't forget your pill," said someone's worried wife. I wondered why she hadn't come to the party. She should have been there, administering her husband's medication.

Pie was growing restless, as if he might have needed to go outside. It was time for me to pack it in anyway because soon some of them would be coming up for their coats. The phone rang and was quickly answered down in the kitchen. Though something told me not to do it, I couldn't stop myself. Just one more.

"I know what's in the eighteen and a half minutes." A woman, her voice musical and not unfamiliar, like a voice I might have heard in some song. I leaned closer to the phone because she was speaking so quietly.

"What're you talking about?" my father asked her, furtive as a spy.

Pie glanced over at me, worried.

"You know, Nixon. The part he erased."

"You called me here to tell me that?"

"I hear music. You're having a party?" She was not in a phone booth this time. She was in a room somewhere. That voice of hers was driving me crazy, but I didn't know why.

"There's no proof that he himself erased it, you know." My father was firm.

"I miss you."

"I wish I could see you tonight."

"You can."

"No, I can't."

The reels turned.

"I can't stand it," said my father. "I've got to do something."

"What are you going to do?"

"Something, I don't know. Something. She's going to have to go."

Co-conspirators, that's what they were, planning to send my mother away.

The reels spun on and Pie raised his nose, reading the cold wind from them, reading the way these words affected me. Something had changed, he could smell it. He skinned his ears back and thumped his tail. He came to me and licked my face and I pressed my face against his warm shoulder. I drew myself away from the room as their voices whispered on, preserved forever, I suppose, on that tape.

"I love you," he said.

Neither Pie nor I noticed the door opening until it was too late.

"Jackie," Macie said, "Jackie, do you want an oh dear?" That was how hors d'oeuvre sounded when it came out of her mouth.

The voices on the phone stopped their plotting then, stopped dead in their tracks, listening, surrounded by the sound of the empty phone line, which the recorder dutifully recorded, not knowing any better.

Macie held out to me what appeared to be a tiny pizza, complete with impossibly tiny mushrooms. How did they do that? Her mouth was busy chewing one of her own. The traitorous Pie went straight to her, neck craning, collar jingling noisily, drawing a bead on the pygmy pizza.

I tried to get to the phone but it was too late.

Pie barked. They heard him.

Quickly, with unasked questions poisoning their silence, the co-conspirators hung up; dual clicks clunking onto the tape.

I found myself just sitting there, unable to sort it out, watching Macie chomp her hors d'oeuvre until finally the voice of some faraway recording in the employ of the phone company screeched, "Please hang up the phone." Only then did I remove the shim and nestle the handset back into its cradle, unhooking the cursed Record-a-Jac, turning off the recorder and hiding it under my shirt.

"What's that, Jackie?" She had finished her pizza. She was a teenager who had forgotten to wear her bra and now she had red sauce all over her shirt. She tried to grab the Record-a-Jac. "What's that thing?"

I crammed it into my pocket, saying, "I was fixing the phone."

"You fixed it?"

"Yep. Broken ringer."

This seemed to make sense to her. To Macie, the telephone was a riddle. She couldn't dial and she wouldn't answer it when it rang. If you put the receiver in her hand, she would hold it away from her ear as if it might have electrocuted her. She was suspicious of the science. Macie did not believe in the telephone, so it was no great stretch for her to believe that her twelve-year-old brother could repair one. She may not have had faith in science, but she did have faith in me.

She handed me my pizza and I passed it on to Pie, who clapped his jaws shut around it.

"Don't you like pizza?" Macie asked, surprised, possibly insulted.

"Sure, I like it."

"Why didn't you eat it, then?"

"I just didn't feel like it."

She considered this. "Why don't you like pizza, Jackie?"

She continued this line of questioning as we walked down the hall, she with her worries, me with mine, Pie preceding us with his festive flag of a tail.

126

I saw that Macie was not going to leave me alone so I veered away from her and into the bathroom, gently closing the door in her face, locking it quick. She kept on talking, her voice murmuring through the door as I stashed the tape recorder in the cupboard under the sink. I'd retrieve it later. I ran the cold water for a moment, washing imaginary hands.

They were up to no good, my father and that Resistance fighter.

I opened the door and found myself telling Macie to drop it, that that was enough about pizza for now.

"Are you mad at me?" she asked.

I stopped dead in my tracks. An error had been made. "No, I'm not mad at you."

Too late. Her chin was already starting to wobble. I should never have told her to drop it. When it came to disrupting Macie's equilibrium, *drop it* was only slightly less destructive than *shut up.*

Maybe I could distract her. "Isn't it about time for you to brush your teeth and get ready for bed?"

Nothing doing. Time for the waterworks. Her face pinched up, her eyes disappeared into her cheeks and the tears began to flow. She gasped, looking just like the Creature from the Black Lagoon when he's stuck out of the water.

"I'm sorry, Jackie," she gurgled, "I didn't mean to make you mad."

"I'm not mad."

"I'm sorry I talked too much." Her forehead looked like crushed red velvet and I tried to smooth it with my hand.

Pie sat down, knowing this was going to take a while.

"You didn't talk too much," I said.

"I'm sorry."

I was held hostage by her tears. "Let's get you some Kleenex," I said.

Downstairs, someone—not my father, judging by the tempo—was playing the piano. Moon River and me. I was thinking about what I'd just heard on the phone, and that blasted song was really getting to me. I felt my own chin start to wobble but I stopped it dead. As was often the case, Macie's sadness had left no room for mine.

Lately, she was getting like this a couple of times a week and there was not a thing you could do about it; you just had to ride it out, which was what I did now, exchanging sodden Kleenexes for fresh ones.

"Do you remember when you were a baby?" she asked.

"Yep."

"Remember how I used to get into your crib with you?"

"Yep."

"You used to hug me, even though you were just a baby."

The sobs were coming more slowly now. She was winding down. I saw an opening. "Do you want another pizza?" I asked.

She responded with a questioning sniffle, looking down at me with eyes whose tears were no longer entirely genuine.

"If you can stop crying, we can go downstairs and get some more."

"You're not mad at me anymore?"

"I never was in the first place." A fine point completely lost on her; in fact, I may only have confused her. I may have incited another onslaught of tears. I had to amend it, and quickly. "No, I'm not mad anymore," I said, and she actually smiled a little. It looked like we were out of the woods.

As the three of us descended, feeling the music vibrate through our bare feet, the party came into view, people's heads bobbing and moving like blind puppies in a box.

Macie was able to move through the crowd untouched because no one knew what to say to a teenager with the mind of a five-year-old.

I saw my father in the living room. "Hey, Carl, how'd you like to buy a monkey?" he said, but at the sight of Macie he fumbled the delivery of this, his favorite joke. The smile slipped from his face. It was at times like these that his patience with Macie was worn thinnest. He sensed the stares of his peers and they hurt him, while in truth, hardly anyone noticed Macie. In truth, he was the only one who minded her strangeness. He put his hand on her shoulder to guide her toward the kitchen, to hide her from view, glancing at my mother to include her in the shame he felt.

"I can't stand it," he had said.

Suddenly I was lifted off the floor by Mr. Marks, who I hadn't seen coming, which seemed impossible as he was close to seven feet tall. His massive hands hooked me under the armpits and raised me, feet swinging, until my head brushed the ceiling.

"Careful, George!" someone yelled as Mr. Marks's mouth opened below me wide as a killer whale's, asking, in a voice so low it sounded like a record player playing at its slowest speed, "How you doing, old horse?" I liked that; I wished more people had called me old horse. I recognized Mr. Marks' voice now; he was the guy I had taped just minutes ago telling his wife he was drinking Virgin Marys. He had obviously been lying. He peered closely at me and said, "You look tired, old horse. Don't they let you sleep around here?"

"Nope," I said.

Several revelers looked up at me with shiny faces and laughed. At this point in the evening, anything was funny to them. "Make him dance!" someone yelled. The air up near the ceiling was smoky and hot. Even though I was still pretty small, twelve was too old to be carried around like this.

Mr. Marks looked up at me, opened his gold-filled mouth and said, "Don't tell your father, but I think your mother voted for McGovern."

Ever since the Watergate hearings, people had felt the need to unburden themselves on the subject of politics. I was usually interested, but right now politics were the furthest thing from my mind.

"I've got to do something," my father had said.

Mr. Marks moved us closer to the hi-fi, which was blaring "Moon River." That song, with its chorus of accordions or harmonicas or whatever they were, seemed to have been chosen as the anthem for the night's celebration. He lowered me now, gliding me down like the LEM into Tranquillity Base, setting me atop the old cherry-wood hi-fi cabinet—"Two drifters, off to see the world"—causing the record to skip a groove—"My huckleberry friend." He swayed high above me, laughing like a fiend, and for no good reason called me a black-hearted devil when just a minute before I had been old horse.

I felt my face getting hot. If he only knew that I had just been taping him talking to his wife, he would know how right he was. I *was* a devil, and my heart was certainly black. Suddenly he was gone, stomping away through the crowd, bellowing for a drink.

Black-hearted devil. I would remember that one.

Three women fit themselves easily into the space Mr. Marks vacated and leaned against the hi-fi, chatting like I wasn't even there. If I held still, I could go unnoticed. I could observe.

Beside me, a tin ashtray with the Hoover Dam painted on the bottom attracted cigarette butts, a jasmine blossom luring moths. Strains of "Moon River" purred beneath me as I took an occasional sip of whatever abandoned drink washed up on my cherry-wood shore.

"There's such a lot of world to see."

They seemed to be having a lot of fun, so much so that they even laughed at bad jokes. When some guy tried to stand on his head and fell over, they applauded. I'd never seen kids do that. Kids were more critical. These adults had a talent for pleasure. If this scene were representative, being old was a lot of fun. I sipped the dregs of someone's cocktail, quietly anticipating my tenure as an adult: one long state of ecstatic jubilation.

Through the shifting forest of limbs I saw my father, back from banishing Macie. He stood beside his piano, left knee flexed and resting on the bench, right foot planted on the floor, a glass in his hand and a smile on his face.

What was it that he couldn't stand?

He saw me watching him and gave me the kind of look fathers

are supposed to give their kids when they have company. Then something happened. His look changed. His blue eyes, his black hair shining with Wild Root, his laugh were all carried to me across the crowd with the charmed clarity of blood speaking to blood, asking me: Were you listening? Did you hear it?

My own eyes and silent breath answered him against my will. Unable to lie, they said: Yes, I heard you.

"I've got to do something."

I found, oddly, that I admired him for it, for having had that conversation, for doing whatever went along with it, for having a secret. For being more than meets the eye. And then a shade composed of flowers was drawn between my father and me, a familiar dress accompanied by the smell of perfume and turpentine, and I looked up at my mother's coral red lips.

"I love you."

That's what he'd said to the Resistance fighter. I had never before heard anyone say those words in the yellow house.

"She's going to have to go."

I was tired. I wished I could just surrender. The secret had grown too large for me, too large for the yellow house. The secret turned within me the same way it had turned around the tape recorder's spools, like a lifeless planet orbiting a cold, useless sun. Moon River, and me.

Fifteen
Be Prepared

On TV, a man in a dark suit carried a steel box across a sunny Washington sidewalk. Walter Cronkite said the box contained the President's tapes. I knew all about the tapes; we had all known since midsummer, when Butterfield spilled the beans. By fall we had grown impatient, though. We wanted to know what was actually on them, and at long last, on October 23, it looked as though we might find out.

We were in the kitchen. "You know that will give you worms." My mother was talking about the uncooked cookie dough that Macie and me were scraping from a pink plastic bowl.

She was as unconcerned with the secret of the tapes as she was with the secrets in her own yellow house. She could not see the conspiracy gathering around her.

The TV brought us closer to the box of tapes with its mimicking shadow grazing the sidewalk below. The camera moved closer, as if that might have told us more about its mysterious contents. I crunched a stray chocolate chip. I had to know what was in that box.

"What are you *doing?*" I asked Macie, my voice betraying annoyance, not at her but at the mysteries of adults, and of power.

"Looking for the worms."

"You can't see them," said my mother, "but they're there."

"They are microscopic now, Macie," I said, "but once they get inside of you they grow and grow." This was one of the myths of our peculiar tribe, handed down from my mother.

Macie peered into the bowl, soft thoughts forming behind her bangs. Walter Cronkite muttered on behind the ion-charged screen, behind the sincere frames of his glasses, telling us what he knew about the President's tapes.

It seemed that all of the previous White House taping systems had been operated manually, by a remote switch. Lyndon Johnson had used a foot pedal located under the carpet beneath his desk to start his tape system. By 1971, advances in audio technology had allowed the Nixon administration to opt for a voice-activated setup. This meant that the recorders turned themselves on whenever someone within range of the microphones began speaking, shutting off only when silence intervened. I crunched another chip. The things I could have done with a machine like that. There was only one wrinkle in this approach: It wasn't just voices that caused the President's system to activate itself. According to Walter Cronkite, *any* sound could have set the reels turning.

"This is our President?" my mother said.

Maybe Mr. Marks was on to something. Maybe she *had* voted for McGovern.

"He wanted to preserve it for prosperity," I said.

"Posterity." She slammed the oven door shut. "Oh brother, think of all the tape he must have used up. They can't be any good to anyone."

She had a point. Picture the tape machines springing to life at the opening and closing of every door. The tapes must have presented a disagreeable task for whoever had to transcribe them; imagine having to listen to hour after hour of worthless human noises. Papers rustling. The clearing of a throat. A heavy sigh in an empty room. Dull human noises stacked heartlessly one upon the next, the accumulative behavior of powerful persons left to their own devices.

My own tapes were safely hidden in the wall behind my bed, upstairs. Since the night of the party, when I stumbled upon that dark conspiracy, I had been thinking about burning them.

I was wearing my uniform tonight. That fall, in what might have been a direct result of the streaking incident, my father had decided that I would join the Boy Scouts.

If Jay and the other guys had seen me in my uniform, they would have all shit a brick. It was not even remotely as cool as the one worn by G.I. Joe, who I had lately taken to hurling out of Macie's second-story window with a precisely measured length of twine around his neck, waiting for it to catch him just before he hit the ground, snapping him up at the last minute so that his boot heels dragged on the sidewalk, the shoes of a dead man. I might have been getting too old for this kind of thing, I didn't know.

On one shoulder of the uniform shirt, my mother had carefully sewn the numbers 429, for my troop, and on the other, a round red and black insignia heralded what appeared at first glance to be a rat, but upon closer examination—much to Macie's unsolicited delight—proved to be a beaver.

The beaver represented the patrol to which I had been assigned. Lacking the clout necessary to be a Falcon, or even a Bear, I had been assigned to the Beavers, a patrol that was severely understaffed at the time of my swearing-in, owing mainly to the heartbreaking condition of the Beaver Patrol Leader, whose name was Doyle. Doyle, with his unhealthy celery green skin, black shoes so bright they looked wet, and crisply ironed uniform perpetually clouded with his awful farts. Farts so appalling that no one could stand to sit anywhere near him.

Now, I loved farts as much as the next guy, the sound of them, at least, the multitudinous sounds: high, low, long and short; corduroy farts, blue jeans farts, bathtub farts, farts in which the trained ear could detect a rising toward the last note, seeming in fact to query the listener, plaintively; others that made bold statements of fact, barking with unquestionable authority and righteousness, giving no quarter, expecting no leniency. No one fart was the same as the next. They were as diverse as snowflakes. I imagined I would still laugh at them when I was as old as my grandfather, who, it should be noted, still laughed at his farts, when he could hear them. Farts had the power to make me laugh without control; my heart threatening to shake loose, my laughter turning to wheezes. I believed that they were about the funniest thing a body could do and that squelching them was a crime against our species. I figured, if you couldn't laugh at farts, what good was living? But there were limits to everything, and too much of a good thing was no good at all, and Doyle just went too far.

I finished my dinner fast as Walter Cronkite waded, dumbfounded, through that night's hostile swamp of Watergate news. Lately the whole thing seemed to have become too much even for him. Like me, he knew much more than he wanted to. Sitting there in my uniform, knowing what I knew, I sensed the responsibilities that uniforms implied. I looked at my mother, and my sister. I was their guard. I stood between them and the Resistance fighter, between them and the co-conspirators.

All I wanted was to stay there forever. But my mother, who had no sense of the danger, of the trouble she was in, told me to get going. I was running late, she said. So, my belly stuffed full of food, belching anxiously, I headed out the front door and into the foggy twilight.

In the distant sky, some hot dog pilot broke the sound barrier and the yellow house shuddered. The street lights were just coming on and the advancing fog bank was as red as something that has been dragged through a pool of blood. My troop's anthem rang, unbidden, through the space between my ears—*We are thine, old four-twenty-nine*— stirring me, and if I overlooked the fact that my uniform featured short pants, I felt that I might have been mistaken for someone who was in the army, home on leave. Thusly deluded, I forged onward, covering ten streetlit blocks without even noticing them, culling through olive-tinted dreams of war, of *The Great Escape*—whose tangible, head-butting frustration had made me cry in the light of the TV late one night.

I took a deep breath of damp asphalt, a smell I loved, and while crossing Baker Street, starting the climb, saw someone standing on the corner at the top of the hill, holding a large canvas bag. A dark female shape against a white garage door, entirely dark except for two glittering eyes. There was no bus stop on that corner, so what was she waiting for?

I crossed to the other side of the street and slowed my pace. My furtiveness had nothing to do with fear of being mugged, or shot by the Zodiac, or anything like that, but rather with not wanting to be seen by anyone while wearing short pants.

I watched her out of the corner of my eye without turning my head. I saw that her hair was parted directly down the middle. As I got closer, the fog slipped away and I could see her clothes and the color of her hair. And her eyes, which had seemed at first to be the brightest part of her, yet I now saw were the darkest. Black, in fact. Instinctively, I ducked my head. It was her, my black-eyed neighbor.

Fate had ensured, for no good reason other than my mortification, that I would pass beneath a bright street light at the exact second I was at the closest possible point to her, near enough even for her to have made out that blasted red beaver on my shoulder. A car swooped past and I swore that from there I could smell that dark herb smell of hers, delivered from across the street by the vehicle's swirling wake. It smelled like too-sweet smoke, spicy and warm.

She was waving to me.

Impossible. She had probably just been brushing her hair from her eyes. I turned my head just a little bit toward her and right then caught the sole of my right shoe on the sidewalk and flubbed my step, almost falling over.

She waved again. What was this all about? I was sure her mother must have told her how I'd broken into their kitchen. Did the girl want to chew me out for it? Did she want her Magnavox back or did she just want to make fun of my uniform? No, she was *smiling*. Was it possible that she really just wanted to talk to me? I may have still been walking but inside I was paralyzed by my own suspicious mind. What did she want?

Think.

All of a sudden, from the base of the hill, eerie music approached. She and I both looked in that direction to where a car lumbered onto the base of the hill, gears droning down in response to the grade. It was a four-door, bronze and twinkling with moisture, and the eerie music was coming from its silvery windows. *Tubular Bells.*

As the car rose toward us, she waved again. But it was not a wave, exactly. Looking straight at her while pretending to watch the car, I could see that she was hitchhiking. Had been all along. Thumb rising from small fist with a so subtle arch from its base to its tip, arching back on itself, back at her black eyes, saying more than just, "Give me a ride," saying also, "Come here, come to me." And this car carrying its own ominous chimes slowed down and glided to a stop beside her like a curious sea creature.

How old was she, anyway, thirteen? Not much older than me.

The passenger door opened and the melody spilled out unhindered, as if the lid had been lifted on a satanic music box. Without a word to the invisible occupants; without, in fact, even looking at them, my neighbor got inside and closed the door.

The car rolled back a yard as the driver released the brake, and then the engine caught, hauling its bronze burden up to the stop sign where it briefly waited before rounding the corner and as it slid from view I figured it was just as well she had caught a ride. What would we have talked about, the Beaver Patrol? How I wasn't really a dork and they had forced me to wear this get-up? How I was the only thing standing between my mother and an insidious but as-yet-undefined conspiracy? Would she have understood?

"Tubular Bells" merged at last with all the other sounds of the neighborhood but it stayed behind with me, lodged inside of me along with that infernal tuna song.

I continued on my way, discovering hot sweat on the back of my neck when I lifted my neckerchief, allowing my skin to cool in the fog, releasing the nervous effluvia caused by the uncertain fate that she always seemed to promise. I wondered about her, and about her mother, who had somehow known my name. What else did they know about me? I assumed that the bronze car was taking her home now and that she would get there before I even reached my troop meeting, that she would already be in bed by the time I returned to the yellow house and that while I lay awake she would have fallen fast asleep less than thirty feet away from me, my strange, brave neighbor.

Sixteen
Public Opinion

Would you like to borrow my comb?" my father asked as I sat down to my mush. My hair must have been out of whack.

"That's okay," I said. He had already gotten it out of his pocket, though.

"Here you go." It was an Ace, unbreakable.

"No, thanks."

"Don't you want your hair to look good for school?"

"I don't care."

"You don't *care*. Well, that's just fine," he said, but it wasn't really. Macie was getting nervous.

The other night, she and I had heard them arguing down the hall. They got louder and louder as we sat quietly watching *The Six Million Dollar Man* on Movie of the Week. At the beginning, when Steve Austin was about to get into that disfiguring accident again, the one that turns him into a superhero, Macie repeated the words along with him. "She's breaking up! She's breaking up!" she shouted, a sixteen-year-old holding onto the tips of her crossed red Keds, rocking back and forth. "She's breaking up! She's breaking up!" They say it's going to be a series next year.

When my parents still hadn't come out in time for *Columbo,* we knew for sure that everything was not right.

My father waved the comb under my nose. I smelled the Wild-root on it.

"Forget the damned comb," my mother said, "and eat your breakfast."

Now the comb began to quiver just beneath my nose. His eyes switched from me to Barbara Walters, who was talking about the twenty-two bills of impeachment, then back to me. Barbara said that word again. Watergate. It made my father flinch.

"Isn't there something else on?" he pleaded, not really expecting an answer.

A graph appeared on the screen.

"A Harris poll indicates that public opinion seems to be turning against the President," said Barbara Walters.

"How come no one ever polls me?" my father asked.

Barbara went on: "And forty-two percent believe the President is being less than truthful."

"Have those forty-two percent met him?" my father asked. "Shook hands with him?"

Out of the corner of my eye, I saw the monkey creep over to the furnace register, where the dogs lay sleeping. I could tell he was up to no good.

"It's because of those phone calls," I said before I realized what I was doing.

My father looked at me sharply. "What phone calls?" he asked, his voice too loud. "What are you talking about?"

"Nothing," I said.

I was paralyzed. Why had I said that? It happened sometimes; if I thought about something often enough, eventually it just came out. I couldn't help it.

"What do you mean, phone calls?" he asked again, transferring his annoyance with Barbara Walters to me, momentarily blinded to the personal by the political until he came to his senses and remembered that I had heard his conversation with her, that I had seen him driving through the Haight at sunrise. He looked away from me. He knew that I knew. Damn that Record-a-Jac.

"The monkey's doing it again," I said, hoping to divert his attention to the commotion that had started over by the furnace register, but then my mother sat down across from me and said, "I never heard about any phone calls, Jackie."

I shrugged, speechless.

My father recovered. "He means the tapes, I think." He attempted a smile, prompting me: "Isn't that what you meant?"

"Yep," I said, "the tapes."

As White House press secretary Ron Ziegler bravely fought off questions, my father's eyes pleaded with me not to say anymore. It was getting harder and harder to keep secrets these days.

There was a growl. The monkey was well under way now, doing it to the littlest dog. My father, disgusted, suddenly scraped his chair and left the room, his napkin drifting to the floor.

Shifting to one side so I could observe the commotion, I found myself wondering this: The monkey was weak under that old dog's spell. Was my father weak, too? The monkey probably didn't like doing it any more than the dog did; something in him knew that they were never meant to couple, but he was powerless, goaded by a glandular message carried on the incongruous shoulders of a spaniel-poodle mix. I pondered inescapable nature and the tragic myopia of love. I wondered what my father had in store for us.

Seventeen
Wild Kingdom

One Saturday morning we all piled into Mrs. Palmer's car and drove to a faraway beach. Gary the self-fellating contortionist's birthday had finally arrived.

It was a cold one, with wind piping across the sea so hard it filled the air with the product of a thousand high waves, shearing water off their stooped green and blue backs and sweeping it inland, whole serpents of water soaring over the beach and over the long grass as the waves stayed behind to slam onto the steep shore. Seagulls pivoted above, dodging in for a closer look then skittering away from the violent surface as if it might have just reached up and grabbed them by their spindly legs. The sea was not likely to feed any of them today and the smarter ones headed inland in search of trash.

All along the beach lay the creatures we had come to see. Formless and brown, scattered for miles, they looked like large rocks, until they started to move. The sea elephants. Somehow sea elephants sounded a lot better than elephant seals and was really more appropriate when you considered their size. So sea elephants it would be.

Massive, stupid, and rubbery, they gyrated up the slopes of dunes, tipped over the crests, then plummeted downward, giant sledding slugs. And the *racket:* The several mad winds at work there carried their grunts and barks all up and down the beach. Standing among the sea elephants, I felt like a visitor to some strange, disorganized circus, a circus whose enormous, ornery performers were all on strike.

It was an unlikely setting for anyone's twelfth birthday, but when you considered Gary's curious abilities, perhaps not inappropriate. Though Jay and I both shared an uneasiness with Gary, having seen what we had seen, we had both shown up anyway, bearing gifts—Hot Wheels, Brain Games—victims of our mothers' telephone conspiracy. Aside from our small band, there were no other people on the beach.

"Stay away from the god-damned sea elephants!"

Mrs. Palmer was trying to establish some kind of order, spreading a sad little half-assed picnic down among the grassy hummocks that bolstered the parking lot from the advancing sand. It was a lost cause. As I watched, zipping up my jacket, she tried to smooth out an old bed sheet upon which Sylvester and Tweety cavorted, Sylvester's black-and-white body faded to gray, Tweety's yellow torso reduced to a noxious ocher, the two of them gloomily chasing each other across a dingy field. The corners of her mouth downturned, Mrs. Palmer cursed the bedsheet, cursed the wind and the sand, growing older even as I watched, her face lopsided, misshapen by and convinced of the inevitability of despair. I felt sorry for her, but I didn't help her. No, it was time to harass the goddamned sea elephants.

The idea may have sounded like innocent fun when Mrs. Palmer first came up with it, but the result was less than benign. Nine hyperglandular sixth-grade boys and three superior, precocious sixth-grade girls turned loose on an unsuspecting community of *Miroungi angustirostris* who had gathered at this isolated locale for the sole purpose of doing it was perhaps not the most auspicious of birthday scenarios. And, though all of us carried the unspoken assumption—promulgated and enforced by picture books and Sunday night nature shows—that all animals to which we were allowed access must be benevolent and neighborly, otherwise they would be behind bars, there was, in reality, grave potential for disaster here.

The male sea elephants weighed upwards of a ton, had suggestively bloated probosci, inflated for the occasion nearly to the point of bursting. Their bloodstreams were infused with monstrous quantities of testosterone that had lain dormant as the melancholy beasts roamed the polar current, dining on lackluster krill, frustrated, praying salty prayers, living only for this moment. But now, on this of all days, on the very beach that had been selected by their ancestors thousands of sea elephant years ago, the poor beasts heard the sound, carried through the top layer of sand, of a dozen pairs of sneakers. Hearing it, they raised their heavy, sex-clouded heads just as a crowd of savages surged over the top of a dune, bearing down on them, screaming like nothing ever heard in the briny deep.

Oblivious and red-cheeked, we descended, a platoon of sadistic half-grown land dwellers, bipeds who viewed both land and sea as a carnival spread out for nothing other than the satisfaction of our own greedy impulses. We screamed, shoving one another down onto the sand without a thought, growling like bears, whistling like pimps, our hearts unfettered by law, our urban minds confused by all of this open space and wind, not really knowing what to do with it but ready to start anyway. Fortified with sticky handfuls of birthday cake and Kool-Aid swill, we would have fun at the sea elephants' expense.

As usual, just like the time we streaked, it was the pagan Walter Peel who led us all into evil.

There was a spark in that boy's eyes, an unholy gleam that could not have been accounted for solely by his diagnosed hyperactivity nor by the medication he took for it. Walter had this mole in the middle of his left cheek, just like Ginger on *Gilligan's Island*. We followed him—we boys, at least—as he raced down a steep dune, flared cords flapping, a large, lethal driftwood sword held aloft. We tumbled painlessly down the dunes and charged into the wind. Twisting and flailing through the sky, I waited for the steep slope to come up and get me, my body meeting the sand with an organ-loosening shudder before rolling, twirling, my skull threatening to fling itself happily loose of my neck. Then Jay and I picked ourselves up, laughing and coughing, sand blown into our eyes, sand fine as lunar dust trapped in his eyelashes. Sand in our underwear. The giant sound of sand sifting from our ears.

The birthday boy and the rest of us gathered around one of the sea elephant bulls, unconsciously dancing around him as around a woolly mammoth of old, shaking our corduroy buttocks, gaudy windbreakers filling spinnaker-like with wind, making raspberries, shouting insults.

The bull humped one way then the other, feinting. His flesh spread out on the beach. He was massive, the seagoing equivalent of a Caterpillar tractor, a Sherman tank shrouded in bristly rubber. I saw scars on his body from fish nets, sharks, who knew what? Giant squids, maybe. Good lord, someone had even carved their initials into its left rear flank. How had they done it? *W.A.*, the carving said, the letters chiseled into his skin like it had been a picnic table, or something.

Who carved their initials into sea elephants? Heartless sailors? Could the letters have been some kind of brand left by Eskimos who, in lieu of cattle, raised the creatures for their tangy blubber and sturdy hides? If so, how did they do it? They must have been strong, those men. I envisioned superhuman cowboys paddling kayaks the size of tugboats beneath the midnight sun, crossing dark mercury waters that would freeze an ordinary man's heart within three seconds of immersion. Far afield, out on their icy range, they would work in pairs; the first man—whose name was Rudy, I felt sure of it—holding the critters down while the second man, Tom, made the mark of their particular ranch, the venerable *W.A.* And at night, or what passed for night up there, they would skewer strands of blubber sliced from one of the dogies and sear them over a fire laid in the center of a drifting sheet of ice, watching out over the sea elephant herd, alert to strays, their beards sheathed in blue ice, their ears attuned to the ominous cries of polar bears.

I stopped speculating when Walter started slamming away at the bull with his driftwood sword and, with a howl, jumped atop the beast. The rest of us scattered as the bull took off.

As Walter rode away like a spastic jockey, I wondered if we would ever see him again. Then he spilled off onto the sand, the bull crashed into the sea, and we looked for another animal to torment.

You would have thought the sea elephants would turn out to be the high point of the day, but things were actually just beginning to get strange. For me, at least.

Gary's older sister—the one who he may or may not have done it with—was along that day. She was fourteen. She'd spent most of the time helping her mother and being an all-around good sport. She was wearing white jeans that had laces, like the ones on shoes, running up the back, sneaking up and out of sight beneath the bottom edge of her sweater. It was an eye-catching thing. Her name was Shelly.

Though we had all pretended to ignore her all day, Shelly had come to command the imaginations of more than a few of us. Feigning aloofness is a strain on twelve-year-old boys—it goes against the grain, somehow coming more easily to girls—and the strain this pose placed on us had to find manifestation somewhere. It would not be appropriate when it did.

Down in a nest of sand, surrounded by dunes, five of us boys were lying on our stomachs, mulling over the day's events. We were there because we had opted out of a touch football game, which would never go anywhere anyway because they were using a Nerf football in fifty-god-damned-mile-an-hour wind. We could hear shouts from the game every so often, girls' voices mostly, carried to us over the dunes. It sounded pretty lame.

We lolled about, smoking weed, sheltered from the wind there and even able to feel a little bit of warmth from the sun, which was trying to come out. God knew why he was invited, but Dave Monk was there, among us and yet not. Dave occupied his usual station on the periphery, a few yards removed from the group, out in left field.

Not stoned, he slumped over, legs crossed in the lotus position, his jacket zipper jingling softly as he wiggled his foot, twiddling the pencils he brought.

Walter told that joke we'd all heard. It went like this: "Why did Nixon see *Deep Throat* five times?"

"Why?" someone asked, just to shut him up.

"Because he couldn't get it down Pat!"

We'd heard it a hundred times even before those reporters started using "Deep Throat" as a nickname for that stool pigeon who spilled all the beans on Watergate. I read about it in *Playboy*; no one knew who he was, and it was driving everyone crazy. I bet the President would have liked to get his hands on him. I knew my father would. I wondered if those reporters told the Deep Throat joke, too. Maybe. I hoped the President hadn't heard it; Pat too. That would've been terrible. Lately, everyone was up in arms about the remaining tapes he still refused to turn over. They were looking for what they called a "smoking gun." Everyone was out to get him. I felt sorry for him. I figured someone had to root for him.

Me and Jay were sprawled side by side, as usual. Lying on my belly, I pulled sand in toward my face then blew it away from me, watching the specks of silica, quartz, and black mica whirl around like popping popcorn, excavating twin craters the way Pie did when he rested his velvety muzzle in the dust.

There it was again, a boner. Unbidden and inflexible, it pressed into the sand beneath me, a root pushing into dark soil.

Since Gary was not there, the conversation naturally turned to his sister, Shelly. Walter—the natural, if not entirely sound—leader, gave voice to the question that we had all been asking ourselves: *Did the laces on her pants actually work?* Well, between the warm sun on my back, the distant sounds of the sea elephants' epic couplings, and the squeals of football-playing girls, the thought of those laces coming untied was driving me crazy. I pictured them fraying, slowly and surely, to a point at which they at last *must* break, unraveling like the rope that holds an Allied spy suspended over the chasm beneath the Guns of Navarone. It was all too much for me.

My boner had actually gotten painful. I was participating less and less in the conversation, less than Dave Monk even, who turned out to actually have an interesting point of view on the subject. He speculated that the laces were just cosmetic, placed there to provoke precisely the sort of response we were all presently enduring, and that behind the laces was actually a zipper, the sheer canniness of which was even more exciting than the laces alone. Although I would never have admitted it to Dave, it occurred to me that there might be something to that. Behind the laces, *a zipper*. And behind the zipper . . . what? As I pictured it, the inside of Shelly's pants looked something like the series of doors and bars and shutters and gates that Maxwell Smart had to pass through at the beginning of his stupid show. I raised my head to suggest this, but there was a frog in my throat and sand on my tongue and no one could understand a word I said.

"What?" said Walter hatefully.

They were all staring at me, I could feel it. I thought I might have smoked too much pot. My boner stubbornly excavated the sand beneath me. My presence of mind had melted away. I waited in fear of discovery.

In my mind's eye, Shelly had slid onto a green park bench beside my tan catamaran-riding girl. Together, they soaked up the sun. If I were to have rested my head in her lap, and if I were to have looked up at her, her hair would have blocked the sun so I wouldn't have had to squint, and we could have had a conversation. I suddenly found myself wondering if it was too late to join the touch football game. I couldn't even stand up, though, what with that bump in my pants and my pants covered with sand, throwing my dick into relief like a fossil found in the deserts of Utah, the sand gently brushed away by Shelly, the beautiful paleontologist. There would be no escape from this kind of thinking. I was trapped; I couldn't stand up, not with these guys around. They would never have let me forget it.

All this time, Walter had been idly constructing, out of wet sand, a crude likeness of a naked woman. This project had begun to look kind of attractive to me. From where I lay, with my head low on the sand, her breasts towered above me like the great pyramids at the necropolis at Saqqarah, only rounder.

"No, man. They're not big enough," said Matt Ricci, digging deep down into the sand. "You've got to use the really wet stuff, so they'll hold together." He pulled out a paw laden with wet sand and carefully patted it into place. Walter quickly caught on, reaming his hand down even deeper and coming out with a messy dripping mass, which he roughly slapped into place. He lacked Matt's artistic precision.

"Now she's all off-kilter." Jay was growing interested. You could tell he wanted to join in, but he was shy. For the moment, he just watched, quietly biting his nails, a really annoying habit he had recently acquired.

Walter and Matt continued, simultaneously lovers and creators, twelve-year-olds assembling their seductress with care and respect.

No one questioned my lack of participation because they all understood that I was too high.

"Give her a headband." I said once, because I had in mind my playmate, the one with the catamaran. She often wore an orange bandanna, like an Apache, "I think she'd look cool with a headband."

All four of them were working on her now, even Dave Monk, who was handling the toes with great care. They applied themselves in a kind of organized daydream, all of them in agreement as to their goal. They were working against the clock, for the sun was coming out and she was drying. Her improbably steep slopes were eroding, releasing tiny avalanches—now from a hip, now from a breast—landslides that made you want to cry, the way they diminished her. Wind and sun and cruel gravity all conspired to take her from us, yet they toiled on, worshipping her even as they created her.

There was a general slowing of efforts as it became clear that she

149

was as beautiful as could be. Still, there was something missing. No one could quite put his finger on it. No one except Walter, of course. Without a word, he ran off over a dune, toward the sea, moments later tumbling back, trailing a streamer of seaweed in the wind. We all realized its purpose as he carefully shredded it, dividing it then applying it, creating wanton locks above and salty pubic fleece below. Then he leaned back, legs bent at the knees, reaching back and holding his ankles contemplatively. She was finished.

We all sat back and admired her.

Sea elephants trumpeted and seagulls strafed us, their shadows slipping over the uneven sand, rippling black spirits. The sun warmed us even as it destroyed her. The sun had heated the ground between the sand woman and me and miniature mirages had begun to bend the light, inflating pockets of air that softened and ovalized her, ennobling her even further. Sunlight ricocheted off Dave Monk's jacket zipper for a moment and it looked to me as if she was stretching out, arching her back so that blue sky slashed through the space beneath her and the cool sand. Sand slipped from her stomach as she stretched upward. I had bad cotton mouth.

"Come on, baby," Matt suddenly said to her.

"You're high," said Walter, who still felt a kind of proprietary relationship to her, having been the one who had both started and finished her, after all. I'd never thought he could be so respectful.

Even Walter could not stem the rising tide of our affection, though. Soon Matt was joined in his wooing of her by Jay, who was displaying a shockingly randy side today.

"You're a fox, man," he confided to her.

Before long they were all bantering on at her, competing for her attentions, all except Walter and me. He was jealous, I was stoned and paranoid.

From where I lay, I made the sand lady at about six and a half feet tall; if she had been capable of standing, that is, standing like some kind of Saharan, sexual Frosty the Snowman with a twinkle in her sandy eye.

I had to get a closer look at her.

Suddenly, Gary Palmer appeared at the top of the highest dune, pretending to be shot, clutching his chest and hurling himself down the dune like a sack of potatoes. Everyone ran over and dived on top of him, pummeling him. Everyone except me.

Now was my chance.

I made a tentative move toward her, crawling infantry-style, like G.I. Joe. I looked around and, finding that no one had noticed, continued, making my way toward her legs, which I now saw were demurely, partly spread. Her toes were perfectly symmetrical and anatomically correct—Dave Monk's handiwork.

I was close enough to touch her when suddenly, just as I was reaching out, I heard footsteps. I withdrew my hand. They were coming back.

Walter filled Gary in on the situation. "Jack's really stoned," he said.

Sometimes I wondered if Walter even inhaled, the weed had such a miniscule effect on him. Glancing at me, Gary nodded knowingly, then, seeing her, laughed as if he were watching the Road Runner. This was not what we'd expected, we who had been so swayed by her charms. We were hurt and so, in retribution, Matt said, "Look, man, it's your sister."

"Yeah," said Dave Monk. "Suck my dick, baby."

Dave was full of surprises today.

He had said quite enough for Gary, who could take that kind of crap from Matt or any normal guy but not from that little pud, Monk. I never thought I'd ever see someone really do this, until then: Gary Palmer actually kicked sand in Dave Monk's face.

We all watched as Dave dove out of the way, his parka slipping off his shoulders, revealing its simulated sheepskin interior. Gary kicked him in the back then and a half-dozen bright yellow pencils tumbled from Dave's pockets, scattering like *I Ching* sticks across the sand.

Gary turned to the rest of us then, challenging us, while behind him Dave carefully gathered up his pencils, selected his favorite Ticonderoga and tenderly brushed the sand off of it, absently nibbling the eraser and looking across at the sand woman, allowing himself only one small smile before resuming his twiddling, his buzzing, all of the mysterious interior computations upon which the stability of his world relied.

He may have vanquished Dave Monk, but Gary still had the rest of us to contend with.

"Oh, Shelly, you're such a slut." Matt cooed to the sand woman, looking right at Gary as he did this. In a way, he was acting in defense of Dave.

Things had taken an unexpected turn. I was vulnerable, sprawled right at the center of the conflict. Even though my prone position protected my vitals and my inflated love, I really should have cleared out. Instead, I moved closer. I didn't think she looked a bit like Shelly, but she looked pretty good just the same. I thought I saw a beret on her head, gamely aslant like the one my father's Resistance fighter wore.

I was coming unhinged.

Matt and Walter were kneeling in front of me, past her towering breasts, perched at her right and left shoulders, a cartoon angel and a cartoon devil. Behind them, up on the dunes, gaudy torn wrapping papers and Chinette plates smeared with frosting were borne aloft, fluttering like so much cheerless confetti into the gray sky in celebration of my doom.

Matt said, "Look, it looks like Jack's going to do it to her."

"Go for it," said Dave, spitting sand out.

"Look how high he is." Walter's tone urged caution, but, like all the other voices, sounded as if it was coming from very far away, from far away Tranquillity Base or the adjacent Ocean of Storms, where Apollo 12 had landed. I was losing contact. Houston, we've got a problem.

"Do it, Jack!" Matt yelled.

He was beside himself to the point where he had begun grabbing fistfuls of sand and hurling them into the air like some kind of murderous chimpanzee, hitting himself in the face with sand, chanting, "Do it! Do it!"

Gary, who moments earlier had been busy acting really pissed off in defense of the sister he may or may not have done it with, was now just staring at me, watching nervously as I pulled myself up to my knees.

I don't know what came over me, but it came just the same, and before I knew it, right in front of God and everyone, I had hurled myself atop the magnificent woman of the pyramids.

I felt great.

I sank into her and joined with something I couldn't see. I could hear it in the sighing of the sand, though. The sand sighed and I was as free as anyone, as free as the sea elephants, as Carol Doda, or Snoopy. As free as the monkey, at least.

"Do it!"

Somewhere people were cheering, somewhere far from me. Maybe it was the seagulls, crying, "Do it! Do it!"

Blissful, I felt her cool, wet sand against me while the seagulls shrieked, hanging over my back, and somewhere to the west the girls sang "Happy birthday to you" one more time, unabashed by the sea elephants' orgasmic clamor.

I felt so good I had to tell someone, so I whispered in her ear. I told that sand woman my secret, his secret. I told her the only words of romance I knew, words I had heard only once in the yellow house and had on tape to prove it.

"I love you," I said.

Someone was yelling at me. An afterimage of the group's com-

munal shock—a frozen gallery of sickened, scandalized faces—
flashed behind my eyelids. I burrowed further into the sand woman,
my lust as impolitic as the monkey's, destroying her even as I loved
her, for she was unable to support my weight and crumbled beneath me.

And then it was over. I leaned back on my haunches, grinning
stupidly at them even after I realized that they were not grinning
back at me, that they had not been yelling "Do it! Do it!" after all but
instead had been calling me every name in the book.

"Queerbait!" Gary shouted. *Gary,* the extravagantly aberrant
onanist, of all people.

"You sick turd" was all that Matt Ricci had to say. Moments ago
he'd been tossing sand and egging me on, but now he stared at me as
at a flaming paper bag full of dog shit.

"I love you!" they all chanted. "I love you!"

I hadn't realized how loud I'd said that.

Through it all I was aware that the coming days and nights had
been changed by me in ways I couldn't yet imagine, changed by the
sea elephants, changed by Gary's sister and by those words heard on
the phone back in October, words now turned against me.

"I love you! I *love* you!"

It was Walter, who had instigated the sand woman's creation,
who responded most harshly.

"You retard," he said. "Didn't know it ran in the family."

I think he had been waiting a long time for a chance to say that.

Jay was by far the most disgusted, though. Since the end of summer, he had been avoiding me. I saw now that this was the last straw
for him. Ever since I bungled the break-in at the hippies' house, I had
been on probation. Now I had been cut loose for good. None of the
guys he played ball with would ever have done something this ridiculous. I wondered if tomorrow he'd tell them all about this jerk he
knew who humped a pile of sand. I thought I might have been too

old to be doing things like this. Just by being weird, I had lost my best friend.

Unlike the others, Jay didn't say a word. He just turned and walked away beneath the sky, which was clearing now, wiped clean and silver like the freshly shaken screen of an Etch-A-Sketch, with all that remained of the previous picture the silent, graphite-inscribing point, waiting to draw who knew what other evil across the sky.

Sometimes you don't know how far is too far until you are already there, and then it's usually too late. I thought: From now on I will try to be good.

Eighteen
Sweet Music

That Christmas would have been just the same as the previous Christmas if it hadn't been for the past month and a half, during which time news of the episode among the dunes spread throughout the sixth grade, girls and boys both. I had become an outcast.

I found myself more and more often in the company of Dave Monk, Chesney the Ape, and their ilk, and less and less in the company of Walter and Matt and even Jay. I had a lot more time to myself. At lunch I usually ended up sitting with someone I used to tease, someone like the Ape or Judy the mustard girl who, strangely, never put mustard on any of her food, not even hot dogs, preferring it as a between-meals snack, I guess. Even though she was weird, I stole looks at her boobs; she knew it, but didn't seem to mind.

One day I was walking to lunch and Walter and Matt started cooing, "I love you" at me. Then a whole bunch of kids I didn't even know joined in. I may not have known them but they knew me—I was the guy who screwed the sand lady. I kept walking and they followed me, the whole bunch of them taunting me. I had heard those blasted words only once in the yellow house and now I never wanted to hear them again.

"I love you!"

Even the Ape was doing it. Three months ago I'd been howling "Hoo hoo hoo!" at him along with everyone else and now here he was

pursing his primate lips at me and chanting, "I love you, I love you."
I almost laughed.

Then I saw Jay.

He was doing it right along with them. My uptight friend, the
one who wouldn't do so many cool things because they were "wrong."

"I love you!"

Jay had finally made the team. All his hard work, his repeated
kicking of that ball, had paid off. Also, he was no longer so fat. He had
emerged from what was merely a persistent sheath of baby fat, legs
magically straightened, an athlete whose abilities took him places
where I could not follow and brought him new best friends, like Walter and Gary, of all people, since they were on the team too. He never
would've hung out with them the year before.

Now he punched Walter on the arm, looked at me and called, "I
love you! I *love* you!"

Damn those words. It had gotten to the point where I would have
rather been home with Macie, eating lunch in the yard when the
noon siren went off.

I'd decided not to go out for the swim team this year. So, since
my after-school time was now spent mostly alone, I was forced to invent some new pastimes. For instance, when Pie had a cough after
Thanksgiving I spent the better part of an afternoon pretending to
cure him by a laying on of hands. As I was touching him, my eyes
closed, picturing Jesus and the loaves, it occurred to me: So this is how
it happens. This is how you go beyond the pale.

Twelve and a half years old and it was now official. I had become
a weirdo, a pud. Just like Dave Monk, just like the crossing guard, just
like my sister.

Another of my pastimes was pretending that I was like Macie. A
certain mood would come over me and before I knew it I would find
myself shuffling down the stairs in that peculiar, swan-like way she
had, fluttering my hands—which became in those moments as un-
reliable as hers—my imagination so effective that I actually forgot

whole parts of my past. I even forgot how to turn on the TV, how to change the channel. I messed up my hair and stared into space. It was fun. This was something the other guys had done for years; how many times have you seen a kid pretend he's a moron? But until then, I had never done it. How could I? In the yellow house the consequences of using the word *retarded* were worse even than those you could expect if you said "Vietnam" or "Watergate," worse by a mile. We weren't even allowed to watch Jerry Lewis movies when they came on TV.

If I really had been like Macie, I'd have had good reason to feel sorry for myself, wouldn't I? Except I probably wouldn't have been able to feel sorry for myself, because my mind wouldn't have worked that way. I knew this because Macie never felt sorry for herself. People like her don't even know they have a problem, so they don't even have the luxury of self-pity, which may be one of the precious few perquisites available to someone in that condition. What kind of a life is that? To have all the justification in the world to feel sorry for yourself but to not even know it? A blind man has all the time in the world to feel sorry for himself because he sure as hell knows he's blind. Deaf man, same thing. But members of Macie's special clan usually don't even know there's something wrong with then and, in this respect, they float separate from the rest of us. They float unafraid, cursed, alone, content.

When I acted like Macie, I imagined myself getting all kinds of slack, and the burdens placed on my presumably normal mind were lifted for a time. At least, that was how it worked until one day when I was out in the yard, idly unraveling a length of laundry line for what reason I did not—in fact, could not—know, simply because I was, at that moment, effectively retarded. At least, I *was* retarded until a shadow swept over me as ominously and suddenly as ink from an octopus and I felt the awesome *clunk* of a flattened hand, enlivened by a wedding band, cracking the back of my skull. I was a normal boy again, just like that. My mother had cured me. She looked down at me, one of her flowered dresses drifting, filled with the kind of anger that made her whole body tremble and her face turn the color of rhubarb. I guessed she was just not up to the idea of having two Macies around the house, even if one of them was just pretending.

Sometimes I wondered if my mother knew what was going on, what people thought of me at school. What if she were to find out what I had done that day at the beach?

Now I was just like my father, with my own secret.

On Christmas day no one member of my family knew what mischief any of the others might have wrought, or if they did they weren't saying, so I was able to pass among them with my sin unknown, as forgiven as the next guy, and I got no fewer presents than anyone else. All was calm, all was bright.

My father was watching me. "What's Jay's family doing for Christmas?" he asked.

"I don't know."

"Haven't seen him around for a while."

"Well," I said.

He could tell something was wrong. Ever since Gary's birthday party I'd been in a state. "You know," he said, "I find it always helps to look people in the eye, Jack. I learned that from Richard Nixon. When I met him."

"Oh."

"Shake their hands. That's the way to make friends."

"Yep."

"Atta boy."

He looked at me and raised an eyebrow. He started to say something else but stopped himself. He was afraid to ask me what was wrong. It might have had something to do with him, with the Resistance fighter, and he did not want to hear about that, so instead of asking he roughed up my hair, smiled, and backed away.

We gathered around the piano, leaning against it, feeling its vibrations in our chests, praising the savior in ancient song, invisible, fond arms wrapped around one another in lieu of the actual ones we were far too sheepish to employ. In between songs my father roughed up my hair. I could have done this every day.

When there were no carols left unsung, he played Schubert, even though my grandfather hadn't asked him to and had in fact fallen asleep with his chin on his chest after singing one chorus of "I love to go swimmin' with women, and women love swimmin' with me."

I found Pie under the piano and decided to join him. No one could see us down there. We lay beneath the sleek black engine of music among the faded yellow Schirmer Books, Bach, Bartok, Beethoven, all of them smelling of my father's breath, his Wildroot.

The smell of dog paws.

Pie's black chest with its white blaze rose and fell beneath my cheek as above me my father struck the right combination of wires with a legion of hard, soft felt hammers. The tune was "Traumerei," a real tearjerker. The music filled my ears to the exclusion of all else, falling from above me, from my father. When I opened my eyes, I could look across the carpet and watch his huge foot lightly work the damper pedal. No one else could see that.

I had lately started wishing that time would just speed up and let me out of the sixth grade so that I could be with different people, people who didn't know what I had done. Still, there was the conspiracy to consider. "I've got to do something," he'd said to his Resistance fighter. "She's going to have to go." A dark outcome was promised. For that reason, I didn't want time to pass any faster than it had to. Right then, I didn't want my father's tune to end. I wanted it to slow down. Like the way a notepad grows shorter as each sheet is torn off or the melancholy way you feel when you're making a model and you fit the last piece into place, things that reminded me of the passing of time made me sad, made me think ahead to when they would be gone. Like the music he played right then, each note sadder than the next simply because it was that much closer, by a quarter, a half, or a whole note, to the end of the piece.

Nineteen
Political Differences

One night before dinner I heard Macie singing "My Uncle Roasted a Kangaroo" in the basement, so I headed down there to find out what she was up to, running the knuckle of my middle finger across the vertical slats of paneling as I descended the creaky stairs, varying the speed, making it sound like the revving engine of a motorcycle. It was really loud, since the wall was hollow. It made me think about the secret cache in my bedroom wall, about the tape I'd made of the Resistance fighter. It made me think about the sand woman. Now that I had my own secret, I figured that everyone must have one. I couldn't stand it. I wondered what was inside all the other walls. I wanted to get a crowbar and crack them all open, starting with this one. I'd pry the paneling from the lath and the lath from the studs and find out once and for all what was really inside that yellow house. A house holds so much more than you can see.

Macie had cleared the paintings away from my Magnavox. She was dusting it off, singing as she dusted. She loved to clean. There were colors under her fingernails, evidence of recent crayoning. It made me mad, the way Macie colored. She couldn't stay within the lines. I had seen her color Archie and Jughead completely black, black from head to toe.

She was really getting tall. We all had to remind her to wear her bra these days. She'd been acting funny lately. She got angry a lot and broke things on purpose. Sometimes she'd just sit somewhere, staring, sunken into what my mother called a blue funk. Other times she just couldn't stop laughing. I had to admit it was a little scary. She'd slap her thigh hard and double up, her laughter silent as her face turned red. She'd have trouble breathing. Squeaks came from her throat as she got the hiccups. "That's enough!" my mother would say, but that just made Macie laugh harder. No one else was laughing anymore.

She was acting extra good tonight, the way she did when she wanted something. She said, "Isn't it time to do the news, Jackie?"

So that was it. The reason the dust had grown so thick on the Magnavox was that I'd pretty much stopped putting on those little TV shows for her. I'd moved on to other things, things Macie knew nothing about.

"No," I told her.

"Why not?"

"I don't feel like it."

"Why not?"

"Because."

"Are you sleepy? You look sleepy."

"No."

She was watching me out of the corner of her eye as she gingerly smoothed her rag around the channel changer. Her hand moved so lightly, she could have worked in a china shop if she were a normal sixteen-year-old.

"Remember how when you were a baby and you fell asleep, I used to get in your crib with you?"

"Yep."

What was it with her and that crib?

"What did you have for lunch?" she asked, buying time in which to come up with a new tactic.

"SpaghettiOs."

"Me too."

"You could do Watergate," she said, coyly returning to her real desire. She knew all my weaknesses and exploited them without pause.

"All right. Okay."

I gave in just to avoid those awful tears of hers.

I climbed inside the TV and looked out at an audience of my mother's portraits. The only living face belonged to Macie, who assumed the lotus position, settling in between an Orthodox priest and a tow-headed brat, pulling her red Ked up through the space behind her right knee. She raised her chin slightly, her head trembling from side to side to the rhythm of her gentle palsy. She watched me closely. She was a tough audience. She expected the world from me; how did she ever get the idea that I could deliver it?

I cleared my throat and did Walter Cronkite for her. "Good evening," I said, "the federal grand jury today announced the indictment of former United States Attorney General John Mitchell, White House Chief of Staff H. R. 'Bob' Haldeman, John Ehrlichman, and"—I couldn't remember the rest of them—"and others in the Watergate case."

My heart was not in it. Macie sensed this right off the bat.

"That's not right, Jackie," she said smugly.

"Call me Jack. How would you know, anyway? Are you an expert?" I don't know why I was so angry at her.

"You're not doing it right."

"*You* do it, then," I said, climbing out of the TV.

"All right," she said with brave uncertainty, "I will."

And she did, climbing inside the Magnavox, squeezing her sixteen-year-old self into a space it had no business occupying. She was way too big for it, but she wanted to do it—needed to do it, apparently—as much for my sake as for hers. She was guided now by an impulse identical to the one that forced her to continually remember how she used to climb into my crib with me, the same impulse that instructed her to hold tightly to her stuffed red cat and wait for the return of the girl who gave it to her. Macie wanted me to stay here forever, to be the same age forever, just like her. Somehow, by climbing into the TV, like climbing into my crib, she ensured that I would never leave, unlike all the little girls she'd grown up with.

"Ten thousand soldiers died in Pol Pot today," she began lustily, "and there was an earthquake in Russia."

I furrowed my brow, concentrating, listening carefully as if my life depended on it.

"At Cape Carnival"—she always called it that—"the astronauts had a birthday party in the Skylab, and everyone got presents." The first part was actually true. "But the presents all floated away," she said.

If I had known she had this talent for extemporaneous speaking, I would have encouraged it earlier. I had no idea.

She went on. "And . . ."

She stopped. Something was wrong. All of a sudden she was at a loss for words. She must have seen the interest in my eyes, sensed my engagement, and it must have scared her away. Macie was like that. She was losing her confidence, batting her eyelids.

Footsteps—two human, sixteen canine—clattered down the basement stairs and we were joined by my mother, Pie, and the other three dogs. Also the monkey, who rode my mother's right shoulder, clinging like a charioteer to her apron strap.

"The mouth is wrong," she said, all business, staring at some painting to my right, "completely wrong." I followed her gaze and found that in the process of getting the Magnavox out, Macie had uncovered the old, unfinished portrait of my father. This was what my mother now scrutinized. "He never smiles like that," she said.

Meanwhile, Pie wagged his way over to the TV, stuck his head in through the screen, and licked Macie's face.

My mother's eyes narrowed and so did the monkey's as they both studied my father's unfinished portrait. "What are you two doing?" she asked, holding up her thumb just like Van Gogh while the monkey, her haughty apprentice, sneered down at me.

"Macie is doing the news," I said, "because I didn't want to do it."

At last she turned toward the TV, wagging her head from side to side, denying what she saw there. "What have you done to your sister?" My mother always was dramatic.

"Nothing. The news." I pointed at the TV. "Do some more, Macie."

"Mr. Zodiac killed seventeen ladies last night," Macie blurted. She was getting back into the swing of it.

"Jackie, what have you been telling her?" my mother asked, ice acrackle in her voice.

"Call him Jack," said Macie helpfully.

The monkey jerked his proud little chin toward the street windows. His black eyes shimmered. Someone was coming.

"I don't understand. What is she doing inside the TV?"

"I already told you, she was doing the news," I said, then something sour inside of me added, "until you so rudely interrupted."

My father always said that, but from the look on my mother's face it was not an appropriate turn of phrase for the likes of me. Not now, at least. I don't know what got into me. I was overcome with a kind of swaggering desire to break something, anything. My body felt like nothing more complicated than a clenched fist.

My mother and the monkey both turned their incendiary eyes on me, actually looking at me for the first time since they'd entered the room, and now that I had their attention, I wanted to be rid of it, to deflect it away from me.

"Do Watergate for us, Macie," I said. "Do the President."

"Over at the White House," Macie began, her almost grown-up voice such a dead ringer for some newscaster—Barbara Walters, maybe—that my mother couldn't help but see the humor in it. She smiled, granting me momentary amnesty.

Macie sensed approval and drew inspiration from it, saying, "Mister Nixon . . . Mister Nixon gonna be peached."

"Ha!" laughed my mother, laughing like Barry Fitzgerald, slapping her thigh. "Ha!"

Macie laughed too, and she would've slapped her thigh if she hadn't been crammed like a sardine into the TV cabinet. "I made a funny," she said as her eyes closed in manic glee and tears rolled down her cheeks. Her face shined from the TV, not looking much at all like Walter Cronkite.

"That's right, you made a funny." My mother was just as hysterical as Macie.

I felt the need to distance myself from these two lunatics. I especially wanted to distance myself from Macie. Even though I had become a weirdo, I wasn't like her, and I wanted her to know it.

"*Im*peached," I said, surprising everyone, including myself. "It's impeached, you retard."

I'd been waiting a long time to say that.

I looked at my mother. Now I'd done it. For a moment, some delusional part of me actually thought that nobody heard what I said, that no one noticed the harm I'd done. It was my cowardly mind's way of deceiving itself with hope. Hope can be a rogue, a con artist, and he always knows when to flee; I could feel the last of him draining away even now as my mother's eyebrows began to rise. I don't know what got into me.

Her eyes grew steadily bluer and narrowed down to dangerous slits as she decided what to do about me. Macie finally realized that something was wrong and laughter left her with a loud hiccup. The furnace rumbled to life, swelling the ducts with warm wind.

I spoke first, filling the catacomb air with my stupid words. "I didn't mean it," I said, adding feebly, "she didn't hear it anyway."

My mother glided toward me undeterred, anger rising off her like a mirage, a molten corona distorting the portraits as she passed before them, enraged, kaleidoscopic, slipping toward me through the hot air while her dusky familiar clung to her shoulder, holding on for dear life; his eyes, like mine, focused on her angry hand.

167

"Don't you ever call her that."

"I'm *sorry.*"

Even the monkey was scared now. He could feel her rage trembling through the grape-sticky pads of his feet. He turned toward her cheek, hoping for some sign from her, and found nothing but danger. Still, his little fist clenched her apron strap, the black fingernails as dull as raisins. He would ride it out, as he always did.

"You of all people should know better than to call her that."

Me of all people?

I felt blame being attached to something else, something far from this room and long ago.

Macie watched the scene unfold from inside the TV, a reversal of perspective which suddenly struck me as more than a little weird. It was as if by some occult means Hogan or McHale or Gentle Ben were suddenly watching us instead of us watching them; reruns unleashed on a world that had the arrogance to think itself real. It was upon us, the audience, that the mandate of entertainment had now fallen. I pictured Captain Kirk leaning back in his magnificent swivel chair, deep inside the Magnavox, laughing at us as if he was watching Edith and Meathead, laughing at our tawdry little scene even though it would almost certainly end in tragedy. What did he care?

At times like these it really seemed as if my mother might just kill me, just put her hands around my throat and choke the life from me. And I was certain that she would have been right to do it. No judge in the land would've found her guilty, I thought. I had turned like a snake on my sweet, defenseless sister. I could only wait as she closed in.

And then, salvation. In the form of giant footsteps, pounding right over our heads. Giant hands opened the front door the way they always did and my father's giant voice bellowed the exact same thing it bellowed every weeknight, a phrase that ordinarily jangled my nerves but now floated down to me like sunlight, like the purest measure yet composed.

"I'm ho-ome!"

The door slammed shut and the dogs rushed upstairs to adore him and lick his hands and read news of the street from the cuffs of his gray pants. "Where is everybody?" he hollered for what must have been the ten-thousandth time, and my mother's wrath was switched as crisply as a train from one track to another, one minute hell-bent for me, the next rocking slowly into the station, where my father waited on the platform, checking his watch, unsuspecting.

"Come see what your daughter's doing!" she yelled, her perpetual irritation with him taking precedence over the rage I had provoked.

"What are you doing down there?" He was balking. His voice betrayed worry. He suspected a trap of some kind. If she was in the basement, he wondered, then what about dinner? He couldn't think straight until he'd eaten dinner. And he was tired, and it was a long way down those stairs.

"Just come down and see!" She rolled her eyes at us and the dogs.

Macie was uneasy. She didn't know where all this was headed. There were too many people down here, too many thoughts. The basement air was too thin. It could not support all of us and all of our conflicting points of view. She started to climb out of the TV, a plaintive little smile below her downturned eyes, but my mother stopped her. "Stay there, honey." There was mischief in her voice as she said, "Tell Daddy about Mr. Nixon."

I knew then that she must have really voted for McGovern.

Macie frowned. She was not so sure about all this. She knew that my father loved the President and that he didn't like it when the rest of us made fun of him. My mother reassured her. "He'd love to hear it," she said slyly, and Macie looked up at her, trusting her.

My father's long legs preceded him through the door. Jangled by fatigue and hunger, diverted from his rightful spot at the kitchen table to the basement, of all places, he entered the room one half second before completing the requisite arrangement of his face, the application of the traditional broad grin and the wiping away of the soot of despair he allowed no one but his steamy predawn mirror to see. For me, it was an instructive moment: to watch the tardy smile spread, to watch the eyes as they filled with a sparkle that was remarkably convincing. He would need to be alone tonight, after dinner, with the piano.

"What's everybody up to?" he said, laughing in anticipation of whatever folly we'd wrought this time while he'd been out there working. He looked at his unfinished portrait and grew still. He shook his head. Then he turned and surveyed the room. He said, "Where did that thing come from?" when he saw the TV, and it occurred to me that he may not have even been down there for a year, perhaps more. He was too busy to go poking around his own basement. He frowned at the TV. "I don't know," he groaned to my mother, "do you really think it's safe to have something like that around the house?"

Well, *we* were all sure that it was safe, that he was just overreacting, but there was no stopping him now. He was getting himself into a high state.

"Where on earth did it come from?" he moaned.

Didn't he remember seeing it on the sidewalk the day after the election? No, how could he? That had been the same day his convertible had been defiled, a black episode that overshadowed all else. He shook his head slowly. "Someone could cut themselves on it."

I saw that we were at an impasse, that a battle might be in the offing.

"William, stop being so silly." My mother knew very well that all he needed was dinner. "What's the matter with you?"

He started to respond, but something stopped him. I'd seen this before. This is what happened: Suddenly he seemed to grow pale, his face the color of dead leaves. He looked down at the three of us, perhaps thinking, They can't be real. They must be sculptures in some subterranean gallery he stumbled across by mistake on the way home from work. He must retrace his steps; where did he go wrong?

While the hot exhaust of the dogs lapped against his ankles, patient breaths of jackals, he kept a close eye on the humans in the room. The three of us stared up at him, surrounded by dozens of portraits of what appeared to be fairies and pirates, priests and coarse children. The room was subsumed in a fog of linseed oil, turpentine, and dust. The furnace duct rumbled above his head. Damnation, that was what this must be.

He smelled the yellow house's sinking foundation, its aged concrete decaying right beneath the soles of his shoes. He heard the sound of voices. He blinked. This is how his family must have looked to him: The sixteen-year-old one with the subnormal intelligence and no bra had been somehow packed into a wretched cast-off television set while the younger one, the male, sat cross-legged on the floor like the god-damned Maharishi. And that one, the adult, the one with the filthy imp perched like some weird parrot upon her shoulder, looking like some cracked Long John Silver, that one was his *wife*. No, he didn't belong here. It was a mistake.

His eyes looked cloudy to me, the way a dog's eyes will when you shine a flashlight at them and they change like stoplights; it could be anybody's dog caught in the beam then, so veiled is the personality. His face must have looked like this when he said to his Resistance fighter, "I can't stand it. I've got to do something."

Macie chose this moment to repeat her funny for his benefit. "Mister Nixon gonna get peached," she said brightly, and what was left of his hellish smile now completely evaporated.

"*Im*peached," he said without a trace of humor, a stern tutor. "Impeached. And he is not going to be." His nostril flared in disgust at Macie.

Well, he may not have been in a good mood, but he was back with us, at least, back from wherever it was he used to go. That was the important thing. Poor Macie, though. That was twice she'd been brutally corrected for the same mistake and she didn't even know what the word meant, much less how to pronounce it. She had only been trying to please him, to make him laugh, but she'd ended up prodding at the abscess that had been growing on his patriotism ever since the first Watergate indictments were made. Since then, my father had been finding himself ever more isolated in his support of the President. He was starting to feel like the only sane man left in San Francisco, wondering, Can no one see?

He walked over to the TV and stared darkly into it, staring down at Macie as if she were that pest Dan Rather. By now she was pretty scared. A kind of grin I'd never seen before appeared on his face as he reached down and changed the channel.

Macie began to cry.

I felt the need to do something. "Jay's dad thinks they might impeach him," I said.

"I don't think so," he said, turning to go, the twist of his lazy about-face scraping the floor so loudly my scalp tingled.

He wouldn't get away that easily.

"They know what's in the eighteen and a half minutes," I said, disastrously quoting my secret recording, the one with him on it, and her. What was I doing?

He stopped and looked down at me. I looked him right in the eye, sure to my bones that I was about to witness that sudden look of guilt Columbo coaxed forth every Sunday night.

"What are you talking about?" he said. That was the same thing he'd said to his Resistance fighter. Did something flash in his eyes?

Yes, I had him cornered.

"You know," I almost stuttered, "the eighteen minutes the President erased from the tapes."

"There's no proof that he erased them, you know."

That was *exactly* what he'd said to her.

He went on: "And who are 'they?' Who is it who claims to know what's in the eighteen and a half minutes?"

"Some people."

He flinched. He knew what I was talking about. What had I

done? The cat was really out of the bag now. I would have to move out. God damn the Record-a-Jac. God damn it to hell.

Suddenly he grew indignant. "He's still a citizen, you know. He is innocent until proven guilty, just like the rest of us."

You would think, under the circumstances, faced with the threat of exposure, that he would have dropped the subject, but he had such a stake in the outcome of Watergate and that stake was rooted so deeply in the wellspring of his pride that he would sacrifice family harmony for it. Even at his personal peril, he would not abandon the President who had so firmly shaken his hand years ago.

"Do you have anything to add?" he asked.

I felt the way you do when you get too high, when the headrush comes and it is much stronger than you intended and the only thought you have is a vain wish that you were not high at all. I wished I hadn't started this. Outside, the foghorns blew. Inside, all was still. The dogs were wary.

"Well, I think I know what was on the tape, anyway," I said.

His black eyebrow lifted. "Oh you do, do you? And you think that the presence of the erasure is enough for an indictment?" The eyebrow again.

"Yep," I said, even though he had lost me. He was a pretty smart guy.

As we talked, his smile began to slip a little. By now he must have understood that we were talking about two things at once, he and I. It was like we were not even there with my mother, with Macie. Our secret removed us from the room.

I found myself borrowing a figure of speech from *Columbo.* "Maybe if he came clean now," I said, "maybe if he promised to knock off what he was doing before things got worse, do you think people would forgive him?"

My mother chuckled. The prospect of Richard Nixon apologizing on national TV, promising never to do it again, amused her. When she saw my father considering the question seriously, though, she stopped chuckling and looked more closely at him. She knew that it was not like him to give such weight to childish ideas. Was she finally aware of our secret transaction? She blinked, and her eyes were starting to shine.

My father looked back at me for just a moment and then looked away. He patted Pie's head softly and said, "Maybe so, maybe so."

My mother exhaled.

I couldn't really expect more than that.

"So, how soon's dinner?" he asked absently, turning and walking up the stairs, and at that moment I heard the strangest sound I'd ever heard in the yellow house. It started low, a deep roar, and then it grew louder. The house seemed to rumble.

Hearing it, my father came back down the stairs slowly, fear of the unknown in his eyes. My mother's face turned sick white and the roaring grew louder as all three of us turned toward the Magnavox.

The TV cabinet was rocking back and forth, banging on the concrete floor like a washing machine with a crooked load. It looked like it might rattle apart. The roar was so loud it felt like it was inside me. It roared in my chest, like my own sobbing.

It was Macie, thrashing around in there.

Her eyes were white, rolled back; her cheeks shuddered. Her mouth was open wide to allow passage of that titanic roar.

My parents were frozen in place, but I knew what to do. It was a good thing, after all, my joining the Boy Scouts. Thanks to the Scouts, I'd seen this kind of thing before, in a movie they'd showed us. Macie was having a seizure.

"Your wallet," I said to my father. "Can I have your wallet?"

His eyes glued to the TV set, he pulled out his billfold and I took it. A wallet is the best thing to put in their mouths, to keep them from biting off their tongues. Terrified, the monkey abandoned my mother and headed for high ground, leaving her to clutch at her mouth with both hands, covering it as if the roar were hers and she were trying to stop it. Her eyes were too terrible to look at.

The roar was now a moan and there was a choking, liquid gasp as well. I had to move fast because Macie couldn't breathe.

She was big, but I managed to pull her from the TV and out onto the floor. She was flopping like a fish. Her eyes rolled back in her head; foam came from her mouth.

I'd heard her choking once before, heard her gagging, but I couldn't remember when.

Time stopped.

I was surprised how calm I was. Just like I'd learned in the Boy Scout movie, I pried her mouth open, reached inside, and looped her tongue back to where it belonged. Before I could pull my hand out, though, and get the wallet into place, she clamped down hard on my first and second fingers, her jaw a bear trap.

This had not been in the movie. It felt like she was biting through to the bone.

I didn't scream, though. In fact, I couldn't feel any pain at all. I lay on top of her, holding her down as best I could, for she was a lot bigger than me. I felt her body shudder beneath mine and I raised her head up so she wouldn't crack it open on the concrete. I'd always known Macie was strong, but this strength was something else again, and it was all directed at herself. The smell of strange chemicals rose from her as her steel muscles crushed and pulled at her bones, trying to snap them. I wished I could stop her, but it was all going on inside of her, out of my reach. Where had I heard that choking before?

My mother was beside me now.

She pried Macie's jaw open and I pulled my fingers free. My mother was helping now and Macie's roar was subsiding. Now I could feel the pain in my fingers. I heard dog licenses jangling, worried. The monkey chirped softly. My father's feet shifted on the floor. The furnace ticked, and slowly, like blue fluttering wings, Macie's irises flitted back into view. She couldn't see us yet, though; she was somewhere else. Her muscles began to relax, her breathing slowed, and then she yawned.

"I fell asleep," she said.

Before I knew it they had called Dr. Root and whisked her off to the hospital, leaving me to stay home, and to wonder.

The things my mother didn't say to my father, the things he did not say to her, the things I could not say to either of them, Macie heard them all. She stored them up, quietly, while asking what we had for lunch, but tonight she couldn't hold any more and all those things no one said came vibrating forth from her, from inside my sister, where my family dwelled.

A fter returning from the hospital, Macie slept for eighteen hours, and all they would tell me was that her brain was changing.

"It's called a seizure," my mother said. "Dr. Root says this kind of thing is normal for Macie. Her brain is not like ours, you know."

As if this was news to me.

The following afternoon, when Macie woke up, she didn't remember a thing.

"I fell asleep, Jackie," she said, clutching her diamond-eyed cat. She yawned, and her mouth was so small and polite it was hard to imagine the terrifying roar that had come from it the night before. "What happened to your fingers, Jackie?" she asked, poking at my Band-Aids, and I told her a lie.

In the middle of the night I was awakened by the sound of my father turning off the hall light. I saw the plaid of his unraveling bathrobe as he stood in the dark and stared out the window. He was listening to the neighbor lady sing "Amazing Grace," the only song she ever sang. When the song ended, I heard him drift off and away, a large silent man whose shoulder grazed the wall, disturbing a class picture hanging there. Then he disappeared around the corner. I listened as each floorboard recognized his weight and greeted him with a polite creak as he roamed through his house, his family—all but one—dreaming around him. I sat up and stayed awake until the fog came in and the *Chronicle* hit the front porch. My father had his secret, and I kept it for him. I listened, and heard him return to his bed, allowing him at last to sleep, and all of a sudden I wanted to remove all the secrets from the yellow house, from inside these mysterious old walls, before they were discovered. My father was a Nixon man. What did that make me?

Twenty
The Smoking Gun

The next day the hippies' old VW microbus was gone. I awoke to find its grimy steward, the man of the house, standing alone in the oily spot where it had been, gazing at the narrow space between our houses through which it must have somehow squeezed, scratching his head in wonderment. In the ensuing weeks, we no longer heard "Amazing Grace," and I concluded that it must have been the hippie lady, the one who sang that song, who had hijacked the object of his daily ministrations. After all that work, that's the thanks he got. Now it was just him and the ghost girl over there.

One evening in early July there was a special report on TV about impeaching the President. It looked like they were really going to do it after all. I was glad my father was working late so he wouldn't have to hear it. I couldn't believe it. It was the night before the fourth of July and the President was saying that he would not on his life resign, then the report ended and that blasted bumblebee launched itself across the screen, just to torment me, to remind me for the umpteenth time of that missed opportunity. Why didn't they stop showing it? Fortunately, we bought only Starkist.

My mother was in a high state. She put Macie to bed early, went down to the kitchen, and picked up the phone.

And I got out the Record-a-Jac one last time.

I had promised myself I would never use it again, but I couldn't help it, I needed to know. I had to find out what was going on. My mother and father had been not talking about something for too long. Things had a dangerous feel to them. There was something about my mother's angry muttering, something in the way the fog was darkening the yellow house that night. I was edging nearer and nearer to the truth, I could feel it.

I had to rewind the tape all the way because it was at the end of the spool. I planned to tape over all the old conversations. I didn't want to hear them again anyway.

I switched on the tape.

I didn't dare pick up the receiver at a time like this, that would have been foolhardy. I waited, listening to their faraway voices, understanding a word here, a word there until I heard them hang up.

I went back to my room, crawled under my desk, and listened. The recording was so bad I had to turn the volume up all the way.

"Did you talk to them?" said my mother.

"I did."

Behind my father, someone was typing. The whole evening looked dark out of the corners of my eyes.

I had to strain to hear them over all the hissing and popping. I could hear enough to tell that they sounded different. Their voices were deeper somehow. I'd never heard anything like it. "My life . . ." he kept saying, "that monkey." Was it the monkey that drove him to join the Resistance? Was it the monkey who had to go?

"She needs supervision all the time now," said my mother. "Now this."

"Now this," he said.

"Think of Jackie."

"Yes."

They went on and on about Macie and how much trouble she

was now that she was older. To hear them tell it, everything was her fault. Macie this, Macie that. What were they getting at? I could barely hear them, their voices were so faraway and tinny. That tape was like a photograph of a ghost, where you know it is there because of the shadow it casts. The shadow it casts is the truth.

Gradually, they were agreeing on something. A plan had been forming for some time. This was it, the conspiracy. I had gotten it all wrong. It wasn't my mother who had to go. It was Macie. They had decided to send her away. She was going to live somewhere else. It was like a school, this place, but far away, in another city.

The tape spun on.

"I'll call them now."

"You will?"

"Yes."

"All right."

"Thank you."

"All right, good-bye."

They hung up. After a moment my mother picked up the phone again and dialed ten times, calling some place outside our area. I held my breath so I could hear better.

"Nash Institute."

"Mrs. Block, please."

"Just a moment."

My mother took a deep breath and waited. We both waited. I could hardly stand it.

"This is Marta Block."

"Hi, this is Mrs. Costello, Macie's mother."

"How are you?"

"Fine. We've made a decision."

"Yes."

"If the space is still open."

"Of course it is."

180

"Then we'd like to go ahead and . . ."

"Good for you. I'm so glad." I heard Mrs. Block rustling paper. "Now, Macie is not a Down's, is she?"

"A what?"

Mrs. Block was sipping something, probably coffee.

"Down's syndrome. Obviously she isn't, then. Her condition is not genetic?"

"Um, that's right."

"A birth accident?"

"No."

"I see, then . . ."

"She used to sleep in the same crib as her brother—"

"There's no need to tell me everything."

"He pushed the covers over her face, they got into her mouth."

"So, asphyxia. At what age?"

"She was three and a half."

"It's very common, you know." Mrs. Block gulped her coffee.

"No, I didn't know that."

"It is. It really is."

"I guess I knew that. He was just crazy about her. He couldn't get close enough. Her face was blue—"

"We see a lot of it. Accidents in early childhood are a major cause. No one's to blame."

"No point bringing it up." My mother was breathing hard.

"Yes. Now, Macie is sixteen, is that right?"

"Nothing we can do about it now."

"That's right. Is Macie sixteen?"

"Yes."

"Her intellectual age?"

"Dr. Root says she's as smart as a five-year-old."

Mrs. Block asked more questions and filled out her form, but I'd heard enough. I turned off the tape.

My heart was beating, I could feel it. Macie was always talking about how when I was a baby she used to climb into my crib with me. How it had been her crib first. She was always telling me how in my sleep I would hug her.

One morning I awoke and she did not.

You're a good boy . . . when you're asleep.

I saw nothing but plaid as I pictured my father flying out of the darkness in his robe, which would not have been tattered then. I heard the rain falling on the garbage cans.

Her face was blue.

I used to think there had been a limited amount of intelligence to be distributed in my family and that Macie had gotten short-changed. In a way, I was right, and I was the one who had short-changed her. On that night years ago when I hugged her, pushing the blanket into her mouth, I ensured that she would never grow up, that she would always be a child. Always asking if I remembered that crib. I had good reason to fear sleep. My heart was beating, I could feel it.

There was a sound, a bump, and then the floor creaked. Someone was there, in my room.

I switched off the tape and jumped out from under the desk, bonking my head on the drawer. My door was open. Macie stood beside it. She looked around the room, her head trembling from side to side the way it always did. She looked down at me.

"Are you mad at me, Jackie?" she said.

"No."

How much had she heard?

"I'm being a good girl, aren't I?"

"Yep."

She turned and walked away down the hall.

"Good night, Macie."

No answer.

"Macie, good night."

She disappeared into her room.

Curiosity killed the cat. I didn't know why I'd sent for the Record-a-Jac in the first place, I just knew I had to have it. From now on, as I tried to stay awake each night, I would know who to blame. It wasn't my father the Record-a-Jac revealed to me after all.

Twenty-one
The Creeper

The next day I found that I couldn't look Macie in the eye. I kept thinking about one of the Agatha Christie books my mother used to read to me at bedtime, the one where the guy who's telling the story is really the killer.

After dinner Macie sat beside me, tall and quiet, still not feeling well, and we watched *Hogan's Heroes*. It was the Fourth of July and Pie was hiding under my bed because he couldn't stand the sound of firecrackers. My parents still hadn't come out of their bedroom and it was getting late. We were going to miss the fireworks.

Pie was having a lot of bad dreams, which he did whenever he was worried about something. Well, he had a lot to worry about. With those ears of his, he didn't miss a thing. He whined and twitched his paws and I had to get down there on the floor and put my arms around him.

I'd already finished the LEM, which the Apollo 13 guys never got to land on the moon, since they'd had to abort mission. On 11, the command module floated alone for so long that when at last it spotted the LEM and approached it for docking, the LEM looked just like a face, with two window eyes and a titanium mouth, moving nearer and nearer, at last joining the command module in a kiss. I could almost hear the words, "I love you."

Everybody watched Apollo 11, even the Pope, who had his own

private telescope. Even soldiers in Vietnam watched. "Hot dog!" Walter Cronkite kept saying, "Hot diggity dog!" It was just not the same since they'd stopped sending them up. I, for one, wanted to know why President Nixon canceled Apollo 18, 19, and 20. It seemed like they'd just started to get the hang of it. It just made no sense, especially when I remembered how excited he'd gotten about that first landing. Back then, I got the feeling he wished he could've been up there with them, up on the moon. He probably could've been, too; when you're President, you can do anything.

Because the Fourth of July was coming, there were a lot of black-market firecrackers around. Walter Peel had been stuffing them up pigeons' asses, blowing them up all over town. Down at the park I traded some lumbo I'd stolen from Jay's mom for a dozen packs, and had been detonating my models all week.

I heard my father's voice rumbling through the wall, angry. I watched *Hogan's Heroes* and crossed my fingers, hoping—for Hogan's sake, and mine—that the blond Resistance fighter with the black beret would put in an appearance, but it looked like we'd have to wait till next week because now it was time for *Hollywood Squares*. I peered sideways at Macie. She watched TV the way she usually did, with her mouth hanging open and her legs crossed in the yoga position. Every so often she would rock back and forth. Her hands shook. The contestant was trying to figure out if Paul Lynde was telling the truth. There were already two Xs and one O on the board. I pointed to one of the Xs. "Can you read that, Macie?"

"Read what?"

"The letter. What is it?"

"Oh yeah, the letter."

"What is it?"

"What?"

"What is this letter?"

"I don't know."

"Well, take a look at it," I said, but it was too late. The X had moved out of sight. I pointed to the O. "There," I said, moving up close to the screen, tapping it. "What's *that* letter?"

"Um." She was getting nervous, rocking back and forth. I tried to go slowly.

"Try again. That letter is what?"

"What?"

"Is that an O?"

"Yes?"

"Right. And this?" We were going too slowly; the Xs and Os were gone and now they were showing an ad for Breck shampoo. "Let's try something else," I said, and got down the World War II book I loved so much. Now Macie was really nervous. I knew how much she hated to be taught anything, but I couldn't stop myself. I had to try.

"See that, Macie? That word is *General.*"

"General."

"Very good. What's that word?"

"I don't know."

"Sure you do. It's *France,* right?"

"I like TV."

"Plenty of time for TV. We're reading now." Her chin was starting to wobble. I pointed to another word. I was getting myself into a high state. "What does this word say?"

"France?"

"No, that word is battle. Let's try another. What's that word?"

"I don't know."

"Sure you do."

"I can't do it, Jackie."

"There's nothing wrong with you, Macie," I said. "You can read as well as I can." Even she knew this was absurd. She looked at me as if I was crazy.

"Look," I said, "that's an *a,* that's an *n,* that's a *d.* What's that spell?"

"Jackie."

"Come on, what is it?" By now I had one hand on the back of her neck, forcing her to look at the book. "Read it, Macie," I said, and she started to cry.

I couldn't help thinking about Eddie the simple elevator operator, the one with the high-heel print on his head. Now I knew why my father had told me that story. I was Macie's own flying secretary.

I turned to a picture of a bunch of British soldiers piled into a ditch, a favorite of mine. I said, "These are soldiers, Macie, see? Now see the word? *Soldier.*" She was whimpering, but I couldn't stop. "See this word? It's *mortar*. These soldiers were killed by mortar fire."

Though I still gripped her neck, she wasn't looking at the book anymore. *Hollywood Squares* was back on and her eyes were drawn to it. She didn't hear what I was saying. She had no idea how important this was to me, or why it should be. I looked in her eyes. They held no blame because they did not know. She had no idea why the crib interested her so. I looked at her and thought: Dead men tell no tales. She stopped crying and rocked back and forth when the audience laughed. "Kumquat," said the host, and bells rang. Macie clapped. There was nothing I could do. She was retarded and that was that.

I didn't realize my father had come in at first. "Put your shoes on, Jack," he said. "We're going to watch the fireworks."

I had forgotten all about the Fourth of July.

My father and I took the convertible over to the beach at the edge of the army base. Usually we all went together, but it was just me and him that year.

I'll tell you one thing, those fireworks didn't look at all like the ones at the beginning of *The Wonderful World of Disney*. In fact, we couldn't really see them at all. We watched the fog light up over the bay; wet red, white and blue flashes spreading like watercolors, accompanied by the far-off sounds of explosions, muffled by cotton-thick fog. Back home, Pie was probably under my bed, curled up in a ball like a baby.

The concussions were so loud I could feel the air moving, yet I still hadn't seen a single explosion. The fog was just too heavy. We stood in the dunes at the edge of the army base and watched the fog light up, our hands in our pockets, standing a little apart from everyone else because that's the kind of guys we were, my father and me.

All around us kids were drinking. I smelled pot in the air and shook my head in commiseration with my father at what had become of the youth of today. The wind flapped his pants around his skinny legs and his pocketed long fingers stood out in relief, pushed through the khaki like ancient bones discovered in Africa. He wore the kind of gigantic basketball sneakers they used to wear in the fifties and his feet stuck out to the sides at embarrassing angles and atop it all, atop his maroon windbreaker, was his hood. A maroon hood, it was, the kind that rolls into the collar of your jacket. Most people had the sense to leave them there, but not my father. No, he was actually wearing it, the drawstring pulled tight under his chin like a skullcap, like Quasimodo's. I sure wished he would dress like other guys.

You could tell that the fireworks were almost over, not because you could see it, but because the sounds of the explosions were growing louder, more bunched together, climactic.

I looked up at my father and said, "It's my fault Macie is the way she is, isn't it?"

I waited. It took me a second to realize that he hadn't heard me; the fireworks were too loud. I started to repeat myself but then he said something at the same time. I could see his lips move but all I heard were explosions. Then there was a lull in the fireworks.

". . . done things differently," my father was saying.

"What?"

"If I could start over, I would do some things differently."

Suddenly a scrap of fog, blown no doubt by a patriotic sort of wind, moved aside just long enough for a single fiery chrysanthemum to bloom over the bay and at that moment we saw two men lying in the sand right there in front of us. They must have been there all along, concealed until then by the darkness. We both saw what they were doing at the same time and both pretended we had not seen. My father stopped talking immediately, expressing his revulsion with a clearing of his throat and a sigh. "The evening is ruined," his sigh said. "It's time to go." So we left behind the sight of two men lying there in the dunes, squeezed in each other's arms. They had bearded cheeks, skeletal as Halloween corpses until the tongue of one distended the cheek of the other, a sight revealed to us at the pink crescendo of a befogged fireworks show. There were things happening around my father, in San Francisco, that he had never seen when he was a boy, things that they never would have allowed back then. This was not the city he grew up in.

He'd said he would do things differently. So would I. There were some things you couldn't do differently, though, things you couldn't take back, like my grandfather's deck chair, like Eddie's flying secretary, like Macie.

I thought about what had happened in the crib. I could go to confession. That would do no good, though. I habitually lied at confession, telling all kinds of stories, thinking my own sins were too boring for Father Tracy. He'd never take me seriously now. And my father had enough secrets. I decided then and there that I would never tell a soul, and stopped crying.

My father and I did not look at each other as we walked back to his car. We were each occupied with our own transgression, and it was not until he gently turned the steering wheel and guided the car out of the Presidio and onto Lombard Street that my father was able to say, "Well, that sure was something."

"Yep. Are you going to keep your hood on?" Enough is enough, I thought.

"Don't want to catch cold," he said cheerfully, then something occurred to him and he turned his whole trunk suddenly toward me. As he did, his windbreaker whooshed loudly, nervously. *Whoosh.* He had to do this since his hood would not allow him to turn his head. He looked at me with his high-strung eyes, his face registering fear and concern all out of proportion with what he was about to say. I knew exactly what it was, too. He said, "Shouldn't you be wearing yours?"

"What?"

"Your hood."

I shouldn't have stuck my neck out; I should have just let him go on wearing the stupid thing.

"Doesn't that jacket have a hood?" he asked.

"But we're almost home."

"Put your hood on, Jack."

"I don't need it. I'm warm enough."

"Don't contradict me."

"Come on, man."

"I'm stopping the car."

"It's not even cold."

He stopped the car, whisking its humble shape directly into a bus zone.

"Put your hood on."

I pretended I didn't hear him. I kind of appreciated what he was doing, though, in a way. It helped take my mind off things.

He screwed his face up as if he'd smelled something bad. I didn't know what came over him sometimes. I didn't know what came over me.

"Why are you being so difficult?" He was jerking around so much now that his windbreaker was deafening, swishing and whooshing with his every gesture. "Why don't you just put it on?"

I was in a tight spot. How could you explain that wearing a hood makes you look like an idiot to a man who proudly wears one himself?

A bus as big as the *Lusitania* glided alongside us, nearly smashing the side-view mirror, its air brakes farting into our ears.

"We're in a bus zone," I pointed out with more than a little plea-sure, but my father didn't hear me. He was reaching out with his clumsy fingers, trying to extract my hood from the back of my jacket, finding the zipper, tugging on it. He probed the space like a tumor-hungry surgeon, then stopped. He froze.

"Where is it?"

"I took it out."

"Well, why would you do that?"

"I didn't need it."

Only morons wear hoods, that's why.

He withdrew to his side of the car, eyes front. "What did you do with it?"

"I don't remember." I'd thrown it away.

"I see."

He went to start up the car and an evil sound came from the en-gine as it tried to tell him it was already running. He winced. Not a little wince, mind you, no benign jerk of surprise, not for him. No, this wince traveled the length of his body, from tip to awkward toe, a veritable shudder of terror.

"Isn't that our little neighbor?"

"What?"

I hadn't heard him because I'd been anticipating another salvo in the battle of the hood.

"Right there. That's her, isn't it?"

Oh, blast.

Most of the time, my father didn't notice things around him. This was because he was so busy thinking. Sometimes he surprised me, though. It was her, all right.

There she was, my black-eyed, nameless neighbor.

Little did she know she would soon come face to face with an angry, nervous man with what appeared to be a skullcap on his head, accompanied by the shy fruit of his loins. Oh well, it would certainly be in keeping with our other embarrassing encounters. On our first meeting, she'd been mad at me because I was taking her old Magnavox. Then, of course, there was the time when she'd been hitchhiking, and had seen me in my Boy Scout shorts.

"She shouldn't be out here alone at night. Do you think she needs a ride?"

"I think she's waiting for the bus."

"She's not in the bus stop."

This was true; *we* were in the bus stop. She was across the street, holding out her thumb.

"She's hitchhiking," he said, shaking his maroon head, releasing the brake. "Do you know what happens to hitchhikers these days? We've got to help her."

"She's fine, she's fine!"

Swish, his windbreaker screamed as he turned his entire torso around in the seat in order to look over his shoulder before pulling out. It was horrible.

When I heard the left flasher clicking I couldn't help it, I had to look back over my shoulder too. We were all instinctive backseat drivers in my family. We had to be: So often the driver was in some kind of a state. I believed that cars themselves could cause discord. It had something to do with the way you had to sit so close to each other, with only one of you controlling the fate of all.

All clear, he pulled out, angrily snorting.

I sneaked a peak to the front. Suddenly a car cut us off and pulled up in front of our neighbor. It was a van, an Econoline with a twisted old grill protruding like an overbite. My father didn't notice it, though; he was busy preparing to make a U-turn.

Our neighbor lowered her thumb as the van pulled in front of her like a shade, blocking her from view. Overhead, bus wires crackled in the fog. I was always surprised that they didn't just burst into flame all the time, all over the city.

The convertible leaned into the U-turn and we came to a stop just behind the van. Mandalas hung in each of the Econoline's two back windows, gods' eyes whose blacklight colors had long ago been drained by sun and smoke.

Our neighbor turned toward us. She'd seen us. There was no way of knowing if the driver of the van had, though, no way of knowing what lurked behind those god's eyes. Our neighbor's black eyes glittered in our headlights and she shielded them with the suede fringe that hung from her coat sleeve.

"Open your window," my father told me, and I wound it down just a little. This was not good enough for him. He leaned across me, the windbreaker roaring in my ears, and wound it all the way down himself, saying, "We can't let her go with those hippies." Why was he so concerned with our neighbor? I hadn't realized he'd even known she existed.

He stuck his head out the window and cleared his throat. "Excuse me!" he hollered, turning this, the politest of phrases, into an assault.

She looked from the van to us then back again, as if deciding who would take her to her mysterious destination. If I had had a car, I thought I would pick her up.

"Excuse me!"

She said something to the van, but I couldn't hear what it was. She reached out and there was a jarring screech as she slid the side door open. Pot and cigarette smoke billowed from inside the Econoline, breath from a dragon.

Our neighbor started to get into the van.

"Oh Lord," said my father, opening his door. "Stay here, Jackie. Lock the buttons."

How could someone who acted like him survive as long as he had in San Francisco?

I stared down at my new shoes to save my life as he pried his legs from under the steering wheel and got out, shutting the huge door behind him.

I pretended it was not happening. I opened up the glove compartment. I could have discovered something in there if I'd really applied myself, but instead I closed it up. I liked to think I'd learned my lesson when it came to secrets.

Wires snapped as an electric bus bumped by, its hum rising as it got up to speed. I locked the doors as the light changed and the bus passed through the intersection, the stoplight turning the rear bumper of the van from green to yellow and then to red. There was a bumper sticker there. It said "mcgovern '72," the letters all in lower case; it was the sticker with the little white dove on it. There was something familiar about that van, about those two ghastly gods' eyes, but I couldn't think what it was.

My father leaned close to the girl. I couldn't understand why he was so interested in talking to her; he never spoke to strangers. I was surprised when he put his hand on her shoulder. I couldn't make out the words of their conversation but the overall tenor was friendly enough. My father, my hooded, gangly father, was talking to the ghost girl. It was turning into quite a Fourth of July.

Their voices were joined by another. Suddenly the conversation was no longer friendly. The new voice bleated like a sheep, conveying thoughts low and unsound from the dark innards of the van.

My father turned to face the van and I could hear him clear as day as he said, "It's no problem; we're neighbors, you see."

He was as polite as if he'd been asking for a dance. No one could have possibly misunderstood that voice, nor taken offense. The driver of the Econoline did, though; at the rear of the van, the brake lights were quietly extinguished, not because the van was leaving, but because the driver was getting out.

He moved like a drunken rat, this man, simultaneously furtive and awkward.

"Get out of there," I said quietly. This was the kind of guy who would hold you down and do things to you, I knew it. He was wearing knee-high rubber boots, as if to facilitate wading through the blood of his victims. He wore jeans with a little Union Jack on the seat pocket. On his head, a dented gray cowboy hat. He wore no shirt on his back even though it was pretty cold. Though he held no cigarette, smoke came from his mouth and nose; he must have taken a hit just before he'd stepped out onto the street.

There was something familiar about this guy.

Maybe he was the Zodiac. That would have been just our luck. He could very well have been; they still hadn't caught him. The Zodiac's unpredictability was his power. He might have been anywhere at any time.

Get out of there.

The windows were fogging up. I could barely see. I wiped the windshield. Incredibly, my father was holding out his hand for the hippie to shake, as if he'd just beaten him at chess and wanted to say, "Gosh, thanks for the game." I didn't think he understood that just because you shook hands with a guy, it didn't mean he wouldn't harm you. Shaking hands was not some magic inoculation against aggression. It occurred to me that if everyone were like my father, though, it would have been. My father, who always rooted for the underdog. My father, who always played fair.

I couldn't bear to watch.

The hippie moved closer. He was a good head taller than my father. Though I couldn't see his face, I could tell that he had not shaken my father's hand; they didn't do that where he came from. He swayed in his boots, doped to the gills. He reached out and laid a hand on the girl's fringed shoulder. Things were shaping up pretty badly.

I wiped the windshield again just in time to see the hippie lurch forward, place his hands on my father's chest, and shove.

My father was dumbfounded. *Who does this fellow think he is?* He blinked, as amazed as he was outraged, not really knowing what to do.

It was all I could do to stop myself from jumping out of the car and going to his aid. My father was not very athletic.

The hippie was wasting no time moving in on the girl, grabbing her arm like a zombie. She needed my help.

I slid the button up and unlocked my door, but in the time it took to open it the whole thing was over.

My father shoved the hippie back.

He extended his arm—shakily at first; he was a thinking man, after all, and this kind of thing was new to him. Then, with growing confidence, he executed a maneuver so simple, so intrinsic to one's dignity, that only the most beleaguered or enslaved of men could not have performed it. He stood there, bright and hooded and maroon, rising above the sidewalk, and shoved the man with one huge hand, not hard, almost lazily, as if it wasn't worth his time.

It was nothing like what you saw on TV or in the movies; usually those guys just punched each other silly. Not my father. He merely conveyed to the aggressor his belief in the *correctness* of his position. I'd never seen anything like it.

Neither had the hippie; he didn't know what hit him. He completely lost his balance.

My father's shove was not unlike the shove that President Nixon dealt to poor Ron Ziegler when they were walking across the White House lawn toward that big green helicopter. I'd never before seen the President do anything more physical than shake hands and wave. He must have forgotten himself. I figured he was irritated with all the questions the reporters were asking him and he just took it out on Ron, right there on TV. The pressure must have been getting to him.

My father's shove, like the President's, was not so much an act of aggression as an expression of disdain, purest contempt made flesh. But unlike the President, who through his televised shove seemed almost to shrink before our eyes, my father, being just a man, seemed to gain size with his shove, growing larger, towering above the street, above the hippie. His nostrils flared as he reclaimed the sidewalk for himself, for our neighbor, for all good citizens.

He turned toward me now, his right shoulder rotating like a gentle rudder, and the girl followed him as he left the hippie still flailing away, reaching into the fog for balance. It was amazing.

As the hippie steadied himself and turned to watch them go, he faced me for the first time. His cowboy hat fell off, wobbling into the gutter, revealing a bald, defeated Mr. Clean head gleaming in the streetlight. It was not the Zodiac, after all. It was Mr. Herman.

Mr. Herman, father of my erstwhile best friend, my Camel-smoking, Nixon-hating, punching-bag-hitting idol. Mr. Herman, former assistant deputy district attorney, painter of idyllic blond people. He'd lost a good deal of weight since I'd last seen him; that must have been why I didn't recognize him right away. Also, you don't expect to find someone you know out prowling the streets, inebriated and half naked, trying to pick up adolescent girls. To think how happy he had made me once when he called the President a bastard. I felt my face turn red, remembering those cool sayings of his that I had repeated verbatim while smoking his Camel nons, and it was because of shame that I slumped low in the seat.

Our neighbor opened the door on my side and my father opened his, saying, "Slide over, Jackie."

I did, straddling the transmission hump, and my neighbor swung herself in beside me. My father fired the ignition and music blared from the radio: Souza marches for the Fourth.

It all happened so fast that I didn't even have time to take offense at being called Jackie in front of our neighbor. As my father dropped it into gear, his hand still shaking with rage, I felt for the first time ever the full force of homo sapiens and all the dangers implied therein buzzing from him, the size of his hands more than a little startling there, spinning the wheel, conducting us swiftly away from the scene of the crime, leaving Mr. Herman behind, awash in the fading strains of "The Stars and Stripes Forever" from our radio.

My father's face was pale, but he radiated the righteousness not of the underdog but of the victor, for once. I sat there between him and our neighbor, whose exotic legs were all too visible to my wide eyes, and I did not say a word.

He turned and looked over my head at her, saying, "I won't take you downtown. I'll take you home, though."

"That's all right. It's too late anyway."

I sensed the last wisps of anger evaporating off her. Maybe their conversation out there hadn't been so friendly, after all.

My father said, "It's Lee, right?"

"Right."

"Lee, this is Jack, my son. Jack, this is Lee."

Thank goodness—I'd thought it was going to be Jackie for the rest of the night.

"I can't believe you two have never met each other before," he said. "We're next-door neighbors, after all."

How did *he* know her name?

He looked us over. "You're almost the same age, aren't you?"

Almost. Thirteen, soon. I waited, tense, but she made no mention of the Magnavox, or of my breaking into her house. This was a good sign. She wanted to put it behind us. Who knows? I thought. She wasn't that much older than me.

On that night when I broke into their house, how had her mother known my name?

"Boy," my father said, "here we are, meeting in the middle of the night on the other side of town."

What had gotten him so chatty? He went on: "It sure is a small world, isn't it?"

I'll say. I didn't think it was necessary for him to know just how small, to know who just who had accosted him back there. The vein on his neck still pulsed with rage.

I turned to look at our neighbor and realized that, what with her blond hair and those oversized eyes, she looked more than a little like the pixie creatures in Mr. Herman's awful paintings. I didn't want to think about what might have happened if she had gotten into that van of his.

With a dusting of fog on them, her eyelashes were drawn together into little triangular bunches. They looked like stars, like the points on the crown of the Statue of Liberty, a row of brambles guarding her fertile black eyes. They were that way when I first saw her, on the night of the Magnavox. That had been a wet night, too. I loved the way she had not grown into her lips yet, the way her mouth was so wide and wet, and when she spoke I was transported. How could she be there, so close to me, and be speaking, too? How could someone who smelled so good have the gift of speech as well? My heart hurt. She was wearing clogs with splintered wooden soles. This was all too much, just too much.

For a moment I imagined that if my father hadn't been there I would have had more to say, and I would have said it well. Then his elbow, perhaps not inadvertently, bumped me in the ear as he made a left turn and I thanked heaven that he was there after all. If he hadn't been, I would have spun yarns about how I was a football star who had climbed many mountains in the off season, about how I was on the fast track at NASA, being groomed for the first Mars mission. I'd done this before with girls; they seemed to bring it out of me. I thanked heaven my father was there to stop me from making a fool out of myself.

He may in fact have been helping me make a friend, and not a moment too soon. Thank goodness he wasn't calling me Jackie in front of her. With him calling me Jack, the sky was the limit; he and I could have just been a couple of guys out for a spin. It was in that spirit of nonchalant liberty that I turned to her and said, "Did you get a new TV?"

"What?" There was nothing in her eyes, no recognition. What

had I done? At last, she opened her tremendous mouth and said, "Oh, that was a long time ago."

Our first meeting obviously hadn't meant much to her.

Looking ahead through the windshield, suavely pretending to recognize someone I knew at a bus stop, I ventured, "I thought you said TV was the instrument of the Devil."

Risky.

"Oh." She laughed, which was nice. "What a memory you have. My father gets these ideas sometimes . . . my mother got a new one, but she took it with her."

I remembered back to the night when someone finally managed to start that ramshackle VW bus and how in the morning it was gone, presumably carrying with it the hippie lady who I now understood to be the girl's mother, leaving behind the featureless man who must have been her father, though I saw no resemblance. Everyone was leaving.

I turned to sneak a look at her but she caught me. She said, "You have dark circles under your eyes."

My father said, "Oh, I'm fine."

She crinkled her forehead and looked from me to him, then back again. I started to explain, but my father interrupted. "How old are you, Lee?"

Yes, how old *was* she?

"Fourteen."

"You know, you really shouldn't be out alone this late."

"Why not?"

No, no, no, I thought. Just go along with him.

"You shouldn't hitchhike, either."

"I like hitchhiking. You meet all kinds of people."

Her shoulder shrugged frivolously against my own. I could smell the leather of her jacket and her beneath it. She sure had a lot to learn; didn't she have parents?

All my father could muster was an offended, loose-lipped exhalation of breath. What had gotten into him tonight? There was no telling what he'd do next.

"I know your mother wouldn't be very happy about this if she was here," he said. "Do you ever hear from her?"

"Sometimes."

How did he even know she'd moved out? He hardly noticed what went on in *our* house.

"Where is it she's living now, Colorado?"

"Right, Colorado."

I remembered the night I watched the hippie woman secretly clean the *fuck* from my father's Nixon bumper sticker. And that voice on the phone.

"Colorado," he said, "that's a long way away."

That voice, the Resistance fighter's voice.

"Her only heat is from a wood stove. I might go visit her at Christmas."

"Oh really?"

I remembered the times my father stood at the hall window in the middle of the night, listening to that woman sing. I remembered her handing him my commando cap, their hands touching for too long. That voice of hers, how could I have missed the voice?

"Well, here we are," said my father as we pulled up to our two houses.

Lee opened her door.

"Thanks for the ride," she said, as if we hadn't just saved her life, as if this kind of thing happened to her every day. I liked her. I liked knowing her name.

"You're welcome," said my father, just as confoundingly unwilling to acknowledge tonight's events as she.

"Good night," I said, bold and casual, opting not to use her name, not yet; that would take some practice.

Then she ran away, clogs banging up her magenta steps.

I turned to my father. He had still not gotten over the indignity visited upon him by Mr. Herman, that hallucinating son of television and democracy. His hands were shaking. He was trying to untie the string that held his hood in place and it was driving him nuts.

Sometimes people surprise you. You never expect your father to surprise you, though. To look at him, struggling with that goofy maroon hood, you'd never have known that tonight he had bested a drug-addled Democrat and rescued the daughter of the French commando woman to whom he had once, on the phone, secretly pledged his love. I felt suddenly angry at the men who had constructed the Record-a-Jac. It was clearly an inferior device. The fidelity was poor. How else to explain my inability to identify her voice? I would have to write them a letter.

How had it started? How had they kept it a secret, more or less, while living next door to each other? If I had loved the hippie lady, I would've had to tell everyone. I looked at him in his hood. What had she seen in him? It was amazing. To look at him, you'd never know how accustomed this unassuming man really was to living close to danger.

Vive la Résistance!

It was pulled too tight, the hood. He couldn't get it undone. His spidery fingers were not getting anywhere. Thank goodness Lee was gone.

Watching him, I started to feel kind of funny. I offered to help him. He let me, dropping his hands into his lap, sighing and staring into the rearview mirror, at the yellow house lit red by his brake lights, and I worked the knot out using my fingernails, and together we got that hood off him.

He looked at me. I saw what it was the hippie lady had liked about him.

"Go on up to bed, Jack," he said. "I've got to talk to your mother."

So he had decided. He would not let the secret grow any larger. He would give the whole thing away.

I got out of the car because I didn't want to be there when he backed it into the garage. I walked up the steps, quietly ordering and embellishing tonight's events so that by the time I reached the top step, my father hadn't just shoved Mr. Herman, he'd *choked* him— yes, the way Rondo Hatton, the Creeper, would—and slammed his head on the sidewalk. He'd had to; the guy had a gun, after all.

The porch light came on and in the moment before my mother opened the door, before the story was ready, before Mr. Herman had become the Zodiac and my father the Creeper, I heard my father slamming the car door.

There was that funny feeling again. Respect, that's what it must have been. Tonight my father had earned my respect, and no matter what he might have done in the past, he would always have it. And love, he would have that, too.

My mother opened the door, looking like all was well for the moment, saying, "Welcome home."

There was so much to tell her, so much not to tell her, but I would leave that to him.

Twenty-two
My Mother's Paintings

I dreamt that Macie and I were sitting in the back row of the Star of the Sea. There was no one else there. The marble was cold, the church was dark, and in the distance I could hear doors slamming, footsteps pounding. You could barely smell the incense from the last mass. From deep inside the confessional, someone shouted, "I voted for McGovern!" Macie was wearing her big checked wool coat and she was crying, so I gave her some wine from one of the big jugs they keep in the sacristy, which I just happened to have with me. As she drank it, I realized why we were there. We both had a secret, the same secret. Macie didn't really understand the secret, and that was why she cried. Suddenly the smell of incense got stronger, blooming, and the door crashed open behind us and there was my mother, wearing her night-gown, standing over my bed, tiny eyes glowing from the dark place on her shoulder where the monkey crouched. I was not in the Star of the Sea. I was in my bed. I wasn't dreaming anymore.

"Get up," she said, "I need your help with something."

I didn't feel safe, like I had escaped something, like I usually did when I woke up. My chest felt hollow. The air felt gritty and com-plicated. It was the middle of the night and I could still smell the in-cense from my dream as I tried to find my slippers with sleepy feet and before I knew what was happening I was rushing down the stairs in my pajamas, Macie on my left, my mother on my right.

"Where's Daddy?" Macie asked, out of breath from hurrying.

"Gone," my mother said.

Gone?

My mother was crying. I'd never seen her do that. It scared the hell out of me. She was in a state, all right.

She led us down into the basement. There, under the hanging light, she was nothing but a shadow pierced by the silver gleam of tears. There was something horrific about her face then, like the face of an axe murderer caught in an introspective moment.

"What's for breakfast?" said Macie.

"Shut up," said my mother.

I'd never heard her say that before. I wondered if there would ever be another breakfast.

"I'm cold," said Macie.

"Oh, you'll be warm soon enough," said my mother, ominously.

I had never seen the monkey's eyes so large.

I didn't know what she had in store for us, but by now I'd figured out what was the matter. Last night, when we came home from the fireworks, my father must have told her his secret. I wondered if he'd told her everything, told her who his French Resistance fighter really was. I wondered when he was coming back home.

I could hear Macie's tiny whistling breaths. She was still not feeling too well because of what they were calling a period. "I'm tired," she said, but the look my mother gave her stopped her from saying any more. How much had she heard last night? What did she know?

My mother looked around the basement at all her paintings. Then she clapped her hands. "Take that one and that one upstairs," she said, pointing to the Greek Orthodox priest and the raja beside him. I didn't think she'd gotten any sleep at all, and by the looks of his bloodshot eyes, neither had the monkey. I wondered just what was going on. Was someone going to buy those paintings at last? Now, that would have been something. I didn't say a word, though. I knew when to shut up.

Since I had picked up the priest, Macie let me go first, out of respect. I held him up high so as not to bump him on the steps. Macie followed me, carrying the raja on his jeweled elephant. If those paintings were being sold, the raja was the one I would miss the most.

When we reached the top of the stairs my mother yelled, "Put them in the living room!" I carried the priest in there and leaned him against the wall. Macie concentrated hard on not breaking anything and I pointed to a spot where she could set the raja. Neither of us spoke. The only sounds came from Macie's corduroys as she walked. *Zish zish.* Now that we were alone, she grabbed my sleeve and whispered, "Where's Daddy?"

I started to make something up for her, but I didn't want to. I didn't want to lie. I said, "I don't know."

"You always know, Jackie," she said. The way she looked at me was terrible.

Downstairs, my mother banged into something hard. "Come get some more!" she yelled.

By the time we made our way back down to the basement I'd figured out what was missing: the dogs. Sensing danger, they'd made themselves scarce. They were upstairs, under their favorite beds. Who could blame them? Something strange was afoot and if I could have hid under a bed that's just what I would have done too.

After a while my mother set the monkey aside and helped us, hefting some of the larger pictures, whistling while she worked, whistling as if she hadn't been crying, as if she hadn't spent the whole night wide awake. My mother was a mystery.

At some point, I noticed that she'd stopped being so choosy about which paintings were to go upstairs. She grabbed any and all of them, scenes of antiquity and adventure, of the old West, the holy land, of beer gardens on the Rhine. She had a plan, but she wasn't letting on about it. She liked to surprise you, my mother. I recognized the tune she was whistling: "My Lover Was a Logger."

Once, when I reached the top of the stairs, I stopped and looked back to check on Macie and all I saw was Sacajawea careening up toward me, floating, supported not by moccasins but by two bright red Keds that rose and fell with exaggerated care beneath her.

"Let's not forget this one!" my mother yelled, grabbing the unfinished portrait of my father and running up the stairs with it.

We had moved about twenty paintings when she started looking for the matches.

Now, I could've made the whole thing a lot easier if I'd just gone up and gotten one of the matchbooks from my collection—there were a hundred and twelve the last time I'd counted—but I didn't say a thing. I just watched as she searched. I didn't want to encourage an enterprise that had begun to look more than a little sinister.

She found them at last, a mildewy box of Strike-Anywheres, and the final detail of her dark scheme unfolded. She opened the box and said what I was afraid she'd say.

"Put the paintings in the fireplace."

Macie started laughing. A fire in summer!

I was more circumspect. This would not be a fire in the conventional sense; it had nothing to do with heating the house, nor with the Fourth of July. I wanted to cry, but I couldn't remember how to get started.

Macie slapped her thigh and after a while her laughter turned to hiccups, the way it often did. She gasped. This was all too much for her. I thought she was going to spaz out. The span between her hiccups began to grow shorter and each one was louder than the last. I patted her on the back, but it didn't seem to help.

My mother fixed one unsympathetic eye on each of us and said, "Get with the program, for God's sake."

Well, that should've just about done it. After a line like that, I knew that Macie would probably burst into tears any second, tears or worse. I braced myself. To my surprise, though, she stood up straight, took a deep breath, and wiped her eyes. My mother and I watched, amazed, as Macie pulled herself together, picking up the first painting, carrying it toward the hearth. She led us now into derangement.

It seemed that Macie's very alienness had made her the perfect citizen of this strange new country of ours.

She paused once, hiccuping.

"Just throw it in!" My mother was pacing.

"I'm *trying,*" said Macie, but she was taking too long and my mother snatched Sacajawea from her and threw the painting in herself.

"I've just about had it with you, Macie," she said.

My mother struck a match and, without even the tiniest hesitation, tossed it in.

"Happy Fourth of July!" belched Macie, even though that had been yesterday. I watched her closely, fearing a return of that horrifying roar with which she'd launched the seizure.

It was still dark outside. Something in me felt like closing all the shades so none of the neighbors would see what we were doing in there.

My mother took the poker and rammed it through the picture of the raja, through the cloudless sky just to the right of his turban, which I was very sorry to see. Macie hugged herself, saying, "I'm being a good girl," as my mother pushed her fingers into the hole in the canvas and forced open that blue sky. Before long an oily flame ran up the elephant's trunk like a fuse, igniting the entire surface of the painting with turquoise, spangling heat. Once it got started, the fire worked fast, blistering the paint, boiling the oil, burning the landscapes and the people.

The rest was easy. We just piled the pictures in one after another and soon the living room was so warm my mother told me to open some windows. She was too busy to do it herself. Sweat shone on her forehead. Her ponytail stuck to the back of her neck. She stopped tending the fire only once, only long enough to take off her sweater, then she was back at it, feeding the fire, gazing down heartlessly as cities burned. Acres upon acres of forests burned. The poor flesh of nudes turned black and peeled off like the bark of madrona trees. Eyes popped and all the while the high notes of escaping gas sang discordant evil, accompanying my mother as she sang, "It froze clear down to China, it froze to the stars above. At a thousand degrees below zero it froze my logger love."

I felt like I was dreaming.

"Where's Daddy?" asked Macie.

It was still a bad question and still received no answer, unless you wanted to call my mother's tossing of a showgirl onto the blaze an answer. The fire hurt my eyes as I watched it sear the showgirl's feather boa, her carnivorous smile. When she ran out of the smaller ones and found that the Orthodox priest, a four-footer, would not fit, my mother leaned it against the couch at an angle and slammed her sandal down on it, snapping its stretcher bars like so much kindling, saying, "If it's not worth doing right, it's not worth doing at all. Isn't that what your father always says?" I looked for my father's portrait. She hadn't gotten to it yet.

Macie was brave, carrying paintings like a good girl, showing no sign of roaring. My father had said the flying secretary never attempted suicide again. After what she did to Eddie, I didn't see how she could live at all. I knew how I felt, but there was no point bringing it up. What was done was done.

The living room had gotten hazy. The chimney was just not up to the task. Smoke rose and filled the spaces in between the rafters, pooling there like upside down black ponds. The smell of all the colors of my mother's erratic palette had gotten too strong. Smoke burned our eyes, swirled around our heads, and rose up the staircase, carrying with it all the flowers and rivers and mountains she had painted; all the still lives, the nudes who'd never hurt anyone.

Macie laughed out loud when a stream of flame burst from the hearth like an animal, curving upwards, scorching the paint right off the mantelpiece, setting the naked wood afire. At this point things had gotten officially out of hand.

"Open all the windows!" shouted my mother, sounding strangely gleeful, as if here at last was a problem that presented itself to her face-to-face, a dilemma she could grab ahold of. "Open all the doors!"

I opened the front window and purple smoke plumed past, stinging my eyes and joining with the fog, offering no clue as to the debauch that burned at its source. Everyone in the neighborhood was asleep at this hour so no one noticed the desperate signal rising from our yellow house.

"Maybe we should call the fire department," I said.

My mother looked at me hard.

"Have you lost your mind?" she said, running from the room, leaving for good for all Macie and I knew.

We watched the mantel burn.

"We sure as hell don't need the fire department!" my mother yelled from the kitchen, where she was banging large objects around.

The fire had now consumed the entire mantel and was starting in on the adjacent bookshelves, heading for my father's piano. Just in time, my mother returned bearing our bright red fire extinguisher. She pulled the safety ring and blasted away, putting the fire out just in time; it had been about to reach the piano. She crossed her arms and looked at me, making me feel that I had, once again, *overreacted,* that this was really not such a big deal after all.

Sirens, however, were now approaching our house.

My mother stopped in her tracks, a bank robber caught red-handed. "Oh, blast," she said.

You hear sirens every night in the city, but none of them ever sounds quite like the one that's coming for you. Macie and I went to the window and looked out. Though the fire had stopped, smoke still billowed from our house like a crowd of restless spirits, swathing the streetlights. Soon the sidewalk swarmed with concerned neighborly noise and the crashing of air brakes. A light brighter than any street light glared into our eyes, a search light. It traced the outline of the the yellow house, scanning, removing all mystery from the smoke the same way a flashlight will rob a camp fire of its dignity. It blazed into our eyes. Macie's teenaged mouth hung open. From her lower lip bloomed a little bubble, saliva inflated by fear. A hook and ladder pulled up and Macie's bubble popped, releasing a tiny cloud of smoke that swirled up into the night, falling at last, like fairy dust, into the light below.

I wondered when my father would be coming home.

There was the judge from down the street, the one who Pie used to bite. There was his wife. There were our neighbors, Lee and her father. I hoped she wouldn't hold this against me. Macie waved to them.

"Mind your own business, you god-damned hippies!" shouted my mother. My father must have told her everything. She pulled us away from the window.

My mother steeled herself. There in the searchlight, her eyes bright, her hands capable, she yelled to the firemen, "Everything's all right!"

But the firemen were not so easily convinced. One of them banged on the front door. My mother sent us upstairs and we had to watch the whole thing from Macie's window. We heard my mother's voice and the deeper voice of a fireman. Out in the street, front doors closed amid chuckles and "Good mornings." We watched the firemen rolling up their hoses, packing up their trucks, until finally they left, telling jokes, laughing. I didn't think firemen should go around laughing.

When the front door closed, Macie and I went back downstairs. The soda ash from the fire extinguisher had settled in cheerful drifts upon the couch, the hearth, the piano, making our living room a winter wonderland. My father's piano had survived.

My mother sat cross-legged on the snowy floor, looking at her remaining paintings. There was one of an awful little girl, a real dog that my mother had somehow managed to make pretty. This was quite a feat. Also there was the portrait of my father, the one she'd never finished. She held her hand up before her, extending her thumb and squinting at the portrait. She hummed the logger song and cried as the snow drifted and curled all around her.

She saw me watching her, pointed to the half-done portrait and spoke. "Do you know what your father said about this when I was painting it?"

"Nope."

"He said it was 'a nice effort.' How do you like that?"

I didn't say anything. I studied the painting. Maybe my father's blurry smile wasn't a smile after all.

She said, "What're you looking at? Don't you ever cry?"

Nope.

From the windows, there was a light that kind of poured over everything like a cool blue rain. It was the sun, coming up.

Twenty-three
Gone for Good

Macie and I acted as if everything was normal, with mush for breakfast and SpaghettiOs for lunch. Macie spent most of the day cleaning up after the fire. Wearily, bravely, her broom scratched away at the hearth, leading the way toward a clean living room, toward the restoration of order. She was getting so tall. Something was wrong with her, though. Her hands were shaking more than usual. She was too quiet. I tried to figure out how much she knew, how much she'd heard. Did she know what I'd done to her? Did she know they were planning to send her away? She wasn't telling. She just swept.

It was midafternoon and Pie and I had fallen asleep under my desk when we heard my father come home. The front door closed, then there was silence. I listened through the furnace register as he said, "The living room is burned."

"Calm down," my mother said.

"What happened to the living room?" he said. I was so glad he was home I didn't mind that he was in a high state.

"Everything's under control now," said my mother.

"What on earth have you been doing?" he said.

I heard him coming up the stairs. Pie ran to greet him and I got out from under the desk.

"What's going on here?" my father said. I watched from my doorway as he poked his head into Macie's room and said, "Where's Macie?"

I heard my mother say, "What are you talking about?"

"Hasn't anyone been keeping an eye on her?"

"She's probably watching cartoons."

But the TV was off. Macie was not watching cartoons.

"Well where is she then?" said my mother as she moved into Macie's room. My father sucked in his breath, blinked, then stood aside to let her pass. Her mood was dangerous.

I worked my way down the hall carefully, stopping when I'd gone far enough to see that Macie's room was empty. My father turned to me and asked, "Have you seen your sister?"

"Nope."

My mother turned and went down the stairs calling Macie's name over and over, a little louder each time. She was getting angry, thrashing her arms, so we followed her at a distance. Macie wasn't in the bathroom. She wasn't in the basement. My mother came to ground finally in the kitchen where, confounded, she leaned against the counter and stared at the blank TV screen. Finally, my father said it. Macie was gone.

I should've known. Macie's hearing was fantastic, like a bird's. She never missed a trick. She'd heard that tape and she'd been thinking about it ever since, working things out in her head. She was out there somewhere in San Francisco, knowing more than she should ever know.

Without a word to anyone my mother grabbed her keys and walked out the front door.

"Just a minute," my father said, tagging along behind her, watching as she got into the station wagon and pulled away from the curb. "Well, that's a good idea," he said as she roared off, "we can cover more ground if we split up."

I followed him to his convertible. Most of the time, we could pretend that everything was all right, but this time Macie just wouldn't let us.

My father and I drove slowly around the neighborhood as the sun went down behind the fog. We passed my mother once, out on Geary, but she didn't even see us. She was too busy scanning the sidewalks, her eyes glowing behind the turquoise wheel. People were still exploding their fourth of July fireworks; I heard them every so often.

The streetlights came on.

My father headed toward the sea, slowly, and after a while turned left to California and took us back the way we came. I watched the right side of the street, he the left. He was silent in the dark beside me. When we passed the Coronet theater, I checked the marquee. Sadly, I saw that they wouldn't be changing shows until September eleventh, when they would be getting *Earthquake*.

We spent perhaps two hours searching. It was hard to tell. It was not an interval you'd find on an ordinary clock. Fear can be a time machine, too. It was completely dark and the fog was thick when my father finally cleared his throat. "The police," he said, and turned the car back toward home.

But I wasn't ready to give up yet. I started thinking like Macie, something at which I had some practice. I made sure my father didn't notice me rocking back and forth and shaking. That was all he needed to see right now. I closed my eyes. The way I pictured it, things looked colorful through Macie's eyes, only a little out of focus. A cartoon seen through fog. I opened my eyes.

"School," I said. "She must've gone to school."

I could already feel the convertible turning toward Macie. It knew where to go. My father understood as only one of us could the logic behind what I had said. He understood that Macie was trying to show us she was a big girl who didn't need to be sent away, that she was a normal sixteen-year-old girl after all. Of course she had gone to school.

215

The convertible headed down the avenues toward the old pink building where she used to go. The fog came in thicker and thicker and Chinese firecrackers barked alongside us. My father hunched forward, showing his teeth as he rolled through one stop sign after another. A seagull squawked past over our heads, incongruous and white in the black sky, dizzying me with its wings. We rounded the corner and there was Macie's pink school, and Macie.

We parked on the opposite side of the street and got out. She sat on the school steps, a sixteen-year-old girl who had remembered to wear her bra, balancing a Mary Poppins lunch box on her lap. Those red shreds of firecracker paper were blowing all around her ankles, remnants of loud births. My father walked toward her, waving his wholesome wave.

"Hi, Jackie, hi, Daddy" Macie called, smiling. Her manners had always been good. "The monkey got away. Is Mommy mad?"

"What?" my father scratched his head.

"The monkey's gone," she said.

"Gone?"

"Gone for good, this time."

He couldn't help it, a smile was growing on his face. "Really?" he said.

"The windows were all open for the smoke. I was hugging him once but he went."

"Oh my," said my father.

The loss which was sure to cause my mother such despair evoked from him now a quiet delight. He tried to put the best face on it, though, for our benefit, making a mock-sad face, saying, "Poor little fellow" in that Old World way of his.

I found myself smiling a little, too. I was relieved to see that this wasn't about the tape. Macie was afraid of getting into trouble for letting the monkey escape, that was all.

"Don't forget your lunch box," said my father, taking Macie's hand in one of his.

"School's closed today," said Macie. I calmed down. She hadn't heard the tape after all. She didn't understand anything. Dead men tell no tales.

I sat in the back on the way home. Macie was up in the front seat beside my father. From behind, she looked like a grown woman. She asked, "Am I going away, Daddy?"

My father ignored the question, turned the wheel, and said, "What did you have for lunch, Macie?"

She opened her lunch box and looked inside. "Baloney sandwich," she said. "With a Twinkle and barbeque chips." Her blond hair fell into her eyes. "I didn't eat them yet, though."

I couldn't see my father's face. I had never heard him ask Macie about lunch before. The topic usually annoyed him.

"What did *you* have for lunch, Daddy?" she asked.

He thought for a minute. He didn't usually bother to answer her questions.

"Baloney, too," he said after some time.

"And a Twinkie?"

I don't think he even knew what a Twinkie was, but he answered anyway. "A Twinkie, too," he said, and then my father took his hand off the wheel to wipe his eyes.

My mother was waiting for us when we got back to the yellow house. She took Macie by the hand. I noticed that they were the same height now as they walked together up the steps and my mother said, so softly, "I've just about had it with you, Macie."

The monkey was in fact gone, and none of us had the slightest doubt where: the forested yard of the Little Sisters of the Poor, where they kept the old people. The problem was, he had a huge lead on us; it had been hours since he'd escaped and the eucalyptus trees were laden with those strange ornaments of summer, cocoons. I knew that we would never see him again, for he loved cocoons beyond measure. I pictured him, seduced by all these ripe chrysali. Madness must have overtaken him. There was no telling how far he'd gone. Now it was dark. There was no way we'd find him. I went to bed without a word to anyone.

I might have even fallen asleep.

In the middle of the night there was a strange sound in the back yard. I got to the window in time to see my mother drop out of sight over the back fence. A moment later she came back into view, creeping through the Little Sister's forest in the fog, wearing nothing but her nightgown, like one of those women who go out looking for Dracula.

I watched her move along the far side of the same gully where I'd found two roasted cats in a Safeway bag a long time ago, a plastic bag of California grapes clutched in her hand, her nightgown as white as the moon. There still seemed to be a little hope there in her blue eyes as she stomped across the leaves. Under my breath, I said, "Watch out for the *nuns!*" She was so *noisy*. She ducked her head, crouching down and sticking her hands flat out at her sides. Then she squinted: My mother, the cat burglar.

I thought I heard his screech then. *Chee chee chee!* It sounded prehistoric, ringing through the forest like something from *Mysterious Island*. Then there was silence and I was sure that that had been the last cry of his we would ever hear. He got too big a lead on us, that was all. He was gone, gone for good.

The back door opened and my father stepped out into the yard, carrying her red sweater. I jumped back a little, thinking he'd seen me, but he just stared straight ahead, walked to the fence and started climbing. I had never seen him climb anything before; I was worried for him when he reached the barbed wire. He had a hard time, but he made it, groaning a little as he dropped into the old people's home.

I couldn't see him for a moment, but my mother could. She didn't really seem surprised to see him land there in the leaves.

"Don't you want your sweater?" he called.

"Shhh!" She put a finger to her lips.

The fog carried their voices to me as clearly as if they were standing beside me. It made me wince. If I could hear them so well then everyone else could, too—even Lee, next door—but no one complained, no one said a word. The neighborhood was still.

My father joined my mother beside the gully and they spoke quietly so I could only make out some of what they said. She held up the bag of grapes. "Maybe he'll go for these," I think she said. Her bright eyes were sad, her eager face fallen.

He said, "Sure. He loves those."

My mother looked to my father for an answer, but he had none. He had tears in his eyes, that's all he had.

She said something I couldn't hear, then he said something I couldn't hear, and he touched her face.

She cleared her throat and spoke louder. "If only I'd thought to put him in his cage," she said, never for a moment questioning the astonishing behavior that had enabled him to escape in the first place. "What a dummy," she said of herself.

Her eyes were still filled with the fire from before, but my father was no longer afraid. He spoke quietly, so I couldn't hear what he said to her, but I saw him put the red sweater around her shoulders, and as they walked together back toward our house, the shapes of trees loomed out of the fog like something you're trying to remember, like a word that's on the tip of your tongue.

"Owls," my mother said, loud enough to wake the neighborhood. "The owls will get him."

They were close now and I could hear them better. He tried to tell her that there were no owls in the city, that while there may have been all kinds of owls back where she grew up, there were none in San Francisco. He didn't sound completely sure of this, though.

"He's just the right size for them," she said. "He hasn't got a chance."

I pictured him then, stolen by owls, lifted into the sky like an angel, carried through the Golden Gate, green and unrepentant till the last.

"It's probably better that way," she said, now convinced that this was how he had met his end, in tatters at the beaks of sophisticated, urban owls. "I just hope it's over quickly."

When they reached our fence, my father gave my mother a leg up, just the way a friend might, and she climbed.

They were crossing the back yard when I heard him, clear as anything, telling her that he would get her another one, another monkey. *Yes,* he meant it. *No,* he didn't know where he'd find one, but he'd get it for her. He promised to go out of his way, to do anything in the world to get another of those creatures the first of which he had so reviled, a creature he had tried repeatedly to sell to anyone and everyone he met. Everyone knew where he'd stood on the subject, but tonight, standing under the moon in the back yard, his arm around her shoulders, he promised to get her another monkey, and do you know what? I believed he would.

Twenty-four
We Leave Our Mark

"Those aren't grackles." Black-eyed Lee lectured Macie and me as she carved a peace sign into the wet concrete. "We don't have grackles in San Francisco."

For the last month or so we'd been watching a street-repair crew fixing the sidewalks in our neighborhood. They used jackhammers to tear up the old slabs then poured shiny concrete in their place, replacing the simple squares of sidewalk, those portions of the city's skin that the earth is forever trying to cast off.

The crew finally made it to the stretch in front of our house that morning, and as soon as they'd left for the day—before they'd even rounded the corner, in fact—we sprang from our hiding place, each of us intent on leaving our marks in the concrete, messages left for the grateful eyes of future generations.

"They're not grackles. They're blackbirds," Lee said with an officiousness I found unbecoming. "My bird book says that grackles are only back East."

"I don't care," I said, so she pushed herself up to her feet and ran into her house, vowing to return with the aforementioned book.

A cloud stepped between me and the sun. Another of my family's myths was about to be exploded. I didn't care, though. I would continue to believe in grackles because I chose to, because I was used to them, because I liked the way the word sounded. *Grackles.* I refused to call them blackbirds. Grackles were what my mother had always called them, what I had always called them, and grackles they would remain. I would continue, willfully ignorant, in allegiance to the customs of my family.

Lee returned, clogs aclatter, bearing *The Audubon Field Guide to North American Birds*. She found the picture, and the map of America that was shaded in the East only, and I didn't bother to argue with her because she would never have understood. The way I saw it, there *were* no grackles in San Francisco—until my mother came. She had brought them with her.

"I still don't care," I said, knowing full well that it was this kind of apathy that irked her the most.

Lee and I had very quickly established a happy repartee based almost completely on argument and disagreement; with us, everything was fair game for debate. I loved to watch her get mad. The sun gleamed off the saliva that always adorned her lower lip as she bit it. She pulled her own hair in frustration. It made me want to punch her. It made me want to put my arms around her. It was wonderful.

She may have had a point when it came to the grackles, but when it came to the peace sign, there could be no doubt that I was right.

This was a charged dispute and Macie was more than a little worried; she tried to distract us, singing songs, asking Lee what she had for lunch, and when I snapped at her, telling her to stop interrupting, she almost cried, saying, "Am I annoying you?"

"No," I said, giving her a twig. "Draw a dog, Macie. Draw Pie."

She promptly drew something resembling a lopsided fish. No one said anything, though, no one laughed. Lee never laughed at Macie, which was good.

"Listen to me," I said to Lee. "It needs a leg in the middle there, otherwise it's not a peace sign."

The symbol in question was by no means an original creation; once you started looking, it was remarkable how many peace signs you found carved into the sidewalks of San Francisco. From North

Beach to the Sunset, they were everywhere. Still, Lee acted as if she'd invented the thing. "I know what a peace sign is, Jack. My mother's only heat comes from a wood stove."

It was hard to argue with that.

"We have a furnace," said Macie.

"That's right, you've got a furnace, man. It's furnaces like yours that are polluting the air, you know. And I know you voted for Nixon."

Macie smiled nervously.

I could see that this issue meant more to Lee than it did to me, so even though she was unwittingly reproducing the symbol found on a Mercedes Benz hood ornament, I would let it pass.

Ever since I'd gotten the Record-a-Jac, ever since I'd learned of that illicit summit between a Republican and a hippie carried on right here on this street, things that I used to get worked up about no longer bothered me. Allegiances once clear to me had become unclear. Once you find out what people are up to when they don't know you're listening, it's hard to take seriously some of the things they say the rest of the time, in public. Our secret lives don't care who's a Republican, who's a Democrat. They have other concerns.

Once I'd learned what had happened in the crib, how Macie had come to be the way she was, it got hard to find fault with people. I figured if my parents could still bear to look at me, then there was nothing so terrible you couldn't forgive. Maybe if Lee had had a Record-a-Jac, she might not have expected so much from people, might not have been so hard on them.

Macie sang, "These boots were made for walking, and that's just what they'll do, one 'a these days these boots are gonna walk all over you," in her usual perfect pitch as Lee put the finishing touches on her Mercedes emblem.

The air around us vibrated as the cannons over in the army base went off, blank charges fired out at the friendly bay. That meant it was six o'clock. My father came out on the front porch and Lee, who knew the ropes when it came to parents, figured it was time for her to go home. She left us as my father came down the stairs.

He didn't say a word about the signs we had hewn into the sidewalk. I'm not sure he even saw them.

He said, "Time to get ready, Macie."

"Okay, Daddy," she said brightly, happy for him to be telling her what to do.

The night before we'd packed her things. Her clothes, all of them bearing her special smell, also her books and snow globe and crayons. She'd wanted her stuffed red cat, the one with the diamond eyes, left out for her to carry. My mother said that since her new school was so far away, Macie would only be able to come home every so often. We would still see her, my mother assured us, on the holidays, but she and I would no longer be able to go trick-or-treating on Halloween. She, my overlarge happy companion in clown suit or witch's hat. She would come home on Christmas and Thanksgiving, and on those occasions we would make up for lost time. But it would never be the same.

She was a big girl now, my mother explained, and it would be better for her to live at this school, because everyone there would be like her. I found that hard to imagine.

Macie had always been afraid that I, simply by growing up, would leave. Who would have thought that it would be she who left? I think it might have been easier to leave than to stay behind, still growing up, alone within the secret walls of the yellow house.

With Macie gone, there would be a lot fewer questions for me to answer. I would no longer have to give a full and precise accounting of my lunches, my breakfasts. Now when I walked past Macie's room, I would no longer have to pass through a cloud of spilt cologne. I would no longer have to hear that music from her scratchy close-and-play. There would be fewer things for me to check up on, like whether any doors were open that should not have been or whether anything was broken, or if any water had been left on and was even now overflowing.

I would have to find out when she would be eating her lunches from now on so that I could eat mine at the same time, the way she used to, out in the backyard, while I was off at school.

My father opened the passenger-side door. "Don't want to be late for your airplane ride," he said.

Macie had never flown in an airplane before and she was more than a little worried about it. Her little eyebrows knitted and twitched and she looked all around her at the ground, perhaps thinking that she would never touch it again.

"What did you have for lunch, Jackie?"

"A grilled cheese sandwich, same as you."

"With tomato soup?"

"Uh huh."

My mother stayed inside, painting a portrait of someone else's child. She would make this child blond, and sunny, and perfect.

Macie cried as my father led her toward the convertible. She clutched her red diamond-eyed cat and dug in her heels.

"You're just going back to school, Macie," said my father, but she wouldn't move.

Macie had always loved those TV commercials for back-to-school clothes and whenever we went to the market she would go straight to the aisle with the binders, the pencils, the dividers. "You're going to go back to school, Macie," was what we'd told her all week, but she didn't understand. Why did she need all her clothes?

"Say good-bye to your brother, Macie," my father said, tugging her arm.

"Okay. Good-bye, Jackie."

"Yep."

My father pulled her, but she wouldn't budge. Macie was strong. Sixteen and strong. She stood her ground and looked at him like he was a monster. She started to cry.

225

"Macie, don't make a scene," said my father softly, looking up at the houses around us.

I didn't care if every blasted neighbor was watching.

Macie looked down at me and said, "I'll come back next week, right Jackie?" She had these funny ideas about time, like the way Christmas was always tomorrow.

"Right, Jackie?"

My father gave me a look, both eyebrows raised. Asking me to be a monster too.

I didn't even think about it, I just did it. "Yep," I said, "next week."

She always believed me.

It was the worst kind of lie, and it worked. She gave in, letting my father guide her into the car, taking the truth with her.

As he walked around his convertible, my father gave me a look that said, "Good boy. That wasn't so hard, was it?" And that was that.

I had to look away. The truth was gone, the transformation was complete. I was a monster. I might as well have been the Zodiac.

He started the car.

I stood on the sidewalk and waved, watching the Nixon sticker receding down the street, doubled, tripled by my tears. Macie was in the air before the concrete, with that lame peace sign, with that picture of Pie, had dried. Macie, my hero, bearer of the Magnavox. My big sister, my little sister.

Later on, just like it was any old night, my father's convertible pulled into the driveway, his curb feelers scraping the curb. I watched him from the window in Macie's room.

He got out and started to close the door behind him when right then some thought flashed into his blue eyes and he stopped. He raised his huge hand and snapped his fingers, remembering, producing a sound as clear and hollow as a horse's hoof striking a cobblestone. He reached back into the convertible and pulled out a bouquet of flowers.

Like Darren on *Bewitched,* he had brought my mother flowers, a bunch of the dried ones they were selling those days. They'd never die, those flowers. You couldn't kill them because they were already dead, like Frankenstein.

He was as tall as ever, and he was silent as he walked up the stairs, his gait a little unsteady because the brick steps were crooked, worn away in an extravagantly uneven fashion.

He'd always loved music, my father, right from the start. He sang in his crib, they said. He sang throughout the waking day and sometimes in his sleep. The start of school did not diminish his ardor; he just kept on singing, right there in class—while the teacher was talking, even—until they made him stop, that is. It was exactly like the way old Dave Monk used to take off all his clothes each day for about the first three weeks of the first grade. Just as no one in the Monk household had thought it expedient for their boy to wear clothes, no one in my father's house had presumed to curb his crooning. I wonder what must have gone on in my father's mind after his teachers managed to stop his singing. I knew that for Dave Monk, living the enforced life of the clothed had not been without its drawbacks. In fact, it was soon after the teachers succeeded in keeping his pants on him that Dave's first *Lost in Space* meandering began.

I watched him ascend the last few steps.

Sometimes I pictured my father, the way he must have pictured himself back when he was fifteen or so and practicing the piano every day. He must have seen himself standing in tails, bowing from his place atop the shiny planks of a stage older than the Union itself, standing beside a piano with that habitual modest smile dimpling his young face, his right eyebrow rising in stupefaction at the admiration flowing from the many who rose ecstatically from their burgundy seats.

These stairs, this house.

The intervening years had replaced *The Lives of the Composers* on his nightstand with *How to Win Friends and Influence People* and dreams of Vienna and Carnegie Hall had seceded to a cold regime of sleepless nights spent roaming the halls of our yellow house.

Blame held him there, as it held me.

He opened the front door and stepped inside. He guessed he belonged there as much as he belonged anywhere. He would make the best of it. We would all make the best of it.

Twenty-five
The Yellow House

On Saturday, twelve blocks from our house, Jay's father paid a rare visit to his son. Cowboy hat atop his Mr. Clean head, greasy sheepskin coat smelling of camels, Mr. Herman came down from his cave in the hills and let himself into his ex-wife's flat. It was 7:00 A.M. when he tiptoed up the stairs, snuck into Jay's room and yelled, "Happy Birthday!" tossing the morning's *Chronicle* onto Jay's bed.

"NIXON RESIGNS" was the headline.

"This is the best present I could give you!" he shouted to his groggy son. It wasn't actually Jay's birthday—he'd turned thirteen two days earlier—but it would have to do. Mr. Herman looked happier than he had in years.

Over at our house, my father stood in the kitchen, staring at the TV. He was so close that its light flickered on his throat. His lips were ghastly and silent. My mother and I kept our distance.

The night before, we'd all watched the President on TV. He'd said that he would resign, even though he had just said the other day that he never would, and this morning we watched as Pierre Salinger reported from the White House, standing out there on the lawn. What was a guy with a name like Pierre doing reporting from the White House?

"We all make mistakes," said my father when the President finally appeared, standing with his family, smiling bravely.

"Yes, we sure do," said my mother, looking at him, not Richard Nixon. When my father didn't respond, she left the room.

Her words had thickened the air.

"Is it true that your mother voted for McGovern?" he asked. I figured she must have really let him have it the other night.

"She wouldn't do a thing like that," I said as I sat down beside him and he and I watched as the President gave his last speech.

"You see?" said my father, pointing at the President. "No notes. Completely extemporaneous."

All the people who worked for the President started to cry, weeping like some kind of huge family that lived in the White House. When the speech ended, my father said, without looking at me, "I shook hands with Richard Nixon."

I had heard the story a million times, but now I listened more closely than usual.

"It was when he was running for governor. He was giving a speech and I went down to Union Square on my lunch hour to hear him. I didn't really know anything about him then, but I was curious. He gave a wonderful speech, and afterward, he shook hands with people."

The TV was silent. The kitchen was silent.

On TV, the President walked out onto the White House lawn. My father's voice was low. "He shook hands with me, and when he did, he looked me right in the eye. Didn't look past me, or at the next person. Just at me."

On TV, the President said good-bye to his staff and my father almost whispered, "Then he said to me, 'Beautiful day,' and I agreed that it was."

I looked at the TV, at Richard Nixon's right hand. I pictured my father's hand held in it.

"I could tell he'd be President some day," he said. "Remember to always look people in the eyes when you shake their hands, Jack."

We watched as the President ascended the steps of his big green helicopter, and even my father knew that he had lied. Like me with the grackles, though, he would continue to believe one thing when all evidence pointed to the other. Like me, that was all he knew how to do.

Pat went inside the helicopter ahead of the President and when he turned back to us and waved from the top step, waving the way he always had, my father blinked his eyes, then wiped them, pretending there was something stuck in one of them. And then the President turned and ducked inside the helicopter, darting out of sight quickly, athletically, like a mirage.

No one said a word. No music played. There were none of the cheers that had customarily adorned each and every one of this man's departures and arrivals for as long as I could remember. Everyone stepped back and the heavy ship rose from the grass, turned, and drifted away, taking my father's eyes with it. His eyes watched as it flew over the fountain, over the trees. He watched until it had gone over the horizon and out of sight. My father, still standing motionless in the kitchen, was on that helicopter. He was a Nixon man, and I was his son.

I left him alone then, taking a last look back at him before the kitchen door swung shut. He was lowering his head into his hands. Lately everyone had been leaving, even the President. My father was staying, though; I knew that now for sure. He was not the kind of man who left.

Up in my room, I could still hear the helicopter on the TV as I crawled under my bed.

I found the chisel, pried open the baseboard, and looked into my secret hiding place. There was the reel-to-reel, the Record-a-Jac, and its wire. The tape.

I could've played the tape back, but I didn't need to. It would play forever in my mind, my mother talking to that woman on the phone, talking about Macie, her crib, and me. And I would always know who to blame.

The Record-a-Jac had worked all too well. I didn't want to even touch it. So I left it there. I closed up the wall and never opened it again. There, under my bed where no one could see me, I pretended something was stuck in my eye. I had to stay under there so long that it was dark when I finally crawled out.

It was August, and September was coming for me, and with it, the seventh grade. In two months I would turn thirteen, an age I thought they should let you skip. I thought they should just leave it out altogether, the same way they almost never put a thirteenth floor in a hotel or some other tall building. It drove me crazy when they sent up Apollo 13. What were they *thinking?* It amazed me that they could send men to the moon but didn't know any better than to use that blasted number.

I remember when Richard Nixon placed a call to two men on the moon. It was on the morning of July 20, 1969, and we all watched it on TV. They split the screen in half, so that the President was on the left and the astronauts were on the right, like in a movie. The President sat at his desk, holding the phone. The astronauts were on the right side, standing on the windless moon with the flag between them. The President talked for quite a while and when he was finished the astronauts saluted him and then, strangely, a trick of the black-and-white transmission and the untamed light of the moon made them look like ghosts. You could see right through them. They seemed to possess no more matter than do clouds.

They unveiled a plaque then, those ghosts. It had been bolted to one of the LEM's legs and its message to anyone who might happen across it is still there, at Tranquility Base, neatly engraved on stainless steel. Over the years, tiny dents will appear on it, the result of the impacts of speeding micrometeorites, but Walter Cronkite seemed to think that that would be about all the damage that would befall the plaque, and that it should remain pretty well intact, probably forever, bearing along its bottom edge the signature of Richard M. Nixon.

Things on earth are rarely so enduring. The yellow house, for instance, is not even yellow anymore. Several years ago my mother and father moved out, some new people moved in, and now it's gray with white trim. Those new people probably haven't even noticed the faulty peace sign carved into the sidewalk by Lee, but it's still there, right near the property line between the now-gray house and the beige house next door, a house that you'd never believe was once dipped in psychedelic filigree.

Our old house got a new coat of paint inside as well, and now all the musky smears of green high on the walls are gone, the smears left by the monkey as he danced along the moldings above us. Eggshell latex now covers the worn place beside the furnace grill where the dogs and I huddled each morning.

Minor repairs were made to the house, but I doubt that anyone ever found what I left hidden behind the baseboard in my bedroom. The Record-a-Jac is still there with the tapes, entombed forever in the walls of the yellow house along with a couple of empty, wizened alligator baggies still redolent of darkest hashish, a half-smoked pack of Camel straights, and a never-chewed Eye of Terror. As far as I know, they are still there to this day, but if someone were to be searching for termites or dry rot, or adding on a den, and they pulled that baseboard away, there it would all be. And if they were a naturally curious person, as I am, and they took the time to plug in the old reel-to-reel and thread up one of the tapes, and if the machine still worked after all these years, then they would hear a conversation, fuzzy, muted, some static, and that's it. It wouldn't mean a thing to them. It's all a matter of context.

The sound of the rain beating on the lids of other trash cans now comforts me in the moment before I risk everything and allow myself to sleep. And it makes me remember. I remember Sam Ervin sitting at his green felt table, his inverted-V eyebrows telegraphing to us at home his incredulity. I remember my first *Playboy* and how its eventual loss left only an empty field where once she frolicked, wearing nothing but an orange headband. I remember the sea elephants, the astronauts. The Rat Patrol.

Music. I remember my mother singing "My Lover Was a Logger" to me, sitting on the edge of my bed. The rain outside and Macie in her room down the hall, singing "My Uncle Roasted a Kangaroo" to her diamond-eyed cat, and my father taking shelter from all of this, the rowdy culture of the yellow house, in the respectful tones of his piano. My mother's paintings, my father's unfinished smile.

And Macie's crib.

I remember the day we discovered that the hippies had left a message in the back seat of my father's convertible, the same convertible that took Macie away. I remember my father sailing out of the darkness in his plaid robe, bending over me as I lay in bed and the rain settled onto the trash cans outside, saying to me, "You're a good boy . . . when you're asleep."

I remember things I can never tell.